BREAKFAST AT THE HONEY CREEK CAFÉ

BREAKFAST AT THE HONEY CREEK CAFÉ

JODI THOMAS

THORNDIKE PRESS
A part of Gale, a Cengage Company

GALE
A Cengage Company

LIBRARY OF CONGRESS CIP DATA ON FILE.
CATALOGUING IN PUBLICATION FOR THIS BOOK
IS AVAILABLE FROM THE LIBRARY OF CONGRESS

ISBN-13: 978-1-4328-7763-7 (hardcover alk. paper)

Published in 2020 by arrangement with Zebra Books, an imprint of Kensington Publishing Corp.

Printed in Mexico
Print Number: 01   Print Year: 2020

For Tom
I'll meet you at the Gate

PROLOGUE

Wednesday, May 23

MAYOR PIPER JANE MACKENZIE

The mayor of Honey Creek, Texas, walked slowly down the long hallway to her office on the fourth floor of city hall. It wasn't dawn yet and she already felt a heavy weight bearing down on her slender shoulders.

This may be her last day in public office. It may be the end of the Mackenzies occupying the mayor's seat since the building had been built over fifty years ago.

And she'd be the one at fault.

As she turned the key to the private entrance to her office, she glanced at her grandfather's picture. "Morning, Granddad." No one would hear her this early, she may as well talk to him. "I screwed up bad this time. You know how you always told me that sometimes doing nothing, saying nothing, can get you in more trouble than

7

doing or saying the wrong thing?" Piper patted her chest. "Well, that's me. I didn't lie, but I wasn't honest either."

Her granddad seemed to be smiling back just at her.

Piper touched the glass as if brushing his beard. "I wouldn't mind if you sent in the cavalry about now."

She heard the elevator door opening and rushed into her office. The last thing she wanted to do was talk to the press.

As she closed the door, she noticed a square white envelope on the floor. Someone must have shoved it under the door — the private door that few people ever noticed tucked away in the corner.

Before she could turn on the light, the phone rang. Piper dropped the envelope and moved to the window. The first hint of dawn bloomed to the east, but the town was still only shadows.

The phone rang again.

Piper didn't move. She needed time to think. Fear crawled up her spine.

Her pretend boyfriend's body was probably floating down the Brazos River by now, and somehow everyone thought she had all the answers.

Kicking off her four-inch heels, Piper seriously thought of hiding under the desk, but she was a Mackenzie and Mackenzies stand their ground.

As light moved through the windows, she picked up the mail and slit it open.

One note folded once. Two words written inside.

SAY NOTHING.

CHAPTER 1

Friday, May 25
Dawn

SAM

Samuel Randall Cassidy pulled his dusty blue Audi into the rest stop parking lot forty miles from Honey Creek, Texas. It was time to clean up and step into the parallel life he might have lived if he'd turned down another road after college.

He laughed softly to himself and wondered if the Devil was joining him in the joke of thinking Sam had finally gone mad. Five years of seminary school, then ten years in the army flying, and another five as a firefighter in the Rocky Mountains. He'd been called a student, a captain, and a smoke jumper, but now he was stepping into a new identity . . . a preacher.

He'd spent almost half his life shifting, just being one of many. Moving among the crowds, never standing out, and now he was headed toward a little town where everyone would be inspecting his every word and action.

At thirty-eight, he knew it was impossible to rewind his life and go back to a simpler time. If he could truly look into his childhood, he might discover that it wasn't as peaceful as he remembered. But he had to try. His life, his sanity depended on it. He'd been invisible so long he'd lost himself. It was time to go back to his roots and see what might have been.

He'd passed through this part of Texas several times as a kid. His father had even preached a revival a few times in the small town he was headed for.

As he walked across the deserted parking lot, a gray cloud floated over the pale sunrise. Humidity peppered with dust, he thought. The kind of dawn no one would want as the backdrop for a selfie. Not that he had anyone to send a picture to. He used his phone mostly for directions and weather reports.

Today, though, there were no directions helping him travel down the path he hadn't taken that fall after school.

Sam had been born in Texas, spent most of his youth here moving from school to

12

school, following his dad's work. But Texas wasn't home.

Nowhere had ever been. Even the small farm his parents went to between jobs wasn't home. It was just a little house his mother had inherited because no other relative wanted it. When Sam inherited the place, he'd sold it to fund his last year of school and a trip to Europe after graduation.

Sam lifted his old suitcase shoulder high to stretch his muscles, then walked into the public restroom designed to look like one in a turn-of-the-century train station — lean, steel and porcelain, empty. The place was about as welcoming as disinfectant. A line of stalls. A line of sinks. A line of tall windows.

He pulled off his T-shirt and hung it on a stall door, then opened his shaving kit and began removing his short beard.

After that, he changed into a funeral black suit that matched his hair, pulling the price tags off as he went.

He felt as if he were traveling backward through the layers of his life. He couldn't tell whether he was running toward or away from his destiny.

Fate had chosen his path, and he'd been fool enough to follow. A letter from a small

13

church in a place called Honey Creek traveled though half a dozen former addresses to reach him. Sam knew before he opened the tattered letter that the mail was meant for his father. Samuel Cassidy, Sr., had been dead more than a dozen years, but the churches he'd preached in still wrote asking him to return to fill in for a sick pastor or stay long enough for them to find another shepherd.

For once Sam didn't toss out the letter meant for his father. Instead, he decided to take the two-week calling. He might not have been in a church since his folks died, but he grew up on Sunday school crackers and funeral food leftovers.

One thing was certain. This assignment would pull him back to the past and maybe help him remember a period when the world was calm. This time he wouldn't be flying for the army or fighting forest fires. This time, he'd be reliving the life of a man he'd never understood.

Just out of high school, he'd boarded a plane to head for seminary with his parents waving proudly. He'd felt the whisper of a calling to preach, to be a man of the cloth like his father and grandfather, or maybe become a missionary in a land he'd never heard about. Sam longed to see the world and this might be his ticket.

Five years later, three months after he graduated, he'd stepped on another plane after swearing in at the army recruiting office in Dallas. No one stood waving or wishing him well that time. But the calling to serve his country had been loud after the bombing of the London Tube he'd witnessed that summer.

After a few tours in the army, he left his uniform behind and drifted. No callings spoke to him. He'd crossed the country, stopping now and then to rest. By the time he'd finally stopped wandering, his hair was over his collar and his clothes rags. Sam decided to be a chameleon moving with the seasons. With no family, no roots, he just blew with the wind.

Until he met April Raine in San Diego. Sunshine wearing a ponytail and honey brown eyes that saw him completely, she became his home, his heart. He told everyone that he loved her from the moment they met.

He took a job as a firefighter their first summer when wild fires seemed rampant in California. Before long he was boarding planes to fly everywhere he was needed. He loved the rush of excitement when he parachuted behind the fire line.

Sam was a born leader, and his skills as a pilot made him even more valuable to the team.

April had said what he did was a gift. The world needed men like him.

He flew on a moment's notice fighting wherever he was needed, but it seemed every time Sam left, he missed her more. When the mission was over, he'd go wherever she was. April had been a travel writer whose home was on wheels. When he wasn't working, he was seeing the world through her eyes.

Buttoning his clerical collar, Sam gazed into the tin mirror wondering what had happened to the man who used to laugh. The man who took gulps of life. The Sam who camped out with April beneath the stars. The wild man who'd fallen in love with a free spirit and howled at the moon just to make her laugh.

In his reflection now, he saw his father, a traveling preacher who never had his own church. But Sam saw no peace in his own dark eyes.

"Hi, Pop." Sam raised one side of his smile like his dad always did. "I'm finally going to use that divinity degree you wanted me to have."

Silence. The hint of a smile vanished.

16

Sam swore under his breath and continued his transformation. He combed his black hair back, letting the widow's peak show. April would have hated it this way. His California girl would tell him he looked "New York slick." Then she'd tease him and say preachers' sons never learn to look sexy.

He stood perfectly still for a moment as if waiting for her to dig her fingers into his hair and mess it up. "Let it curl," she'd say, laughing.

April had loved him and she never seemed to need more than what he gave. When they were together, the world was theirs. Tomorrow didn't matter as long as they had today.

But she hadn't been waiting for him the last time he'd come home from an assignment. When he finally found her RV parked at a police lot, she'd been dead two weeks and no one had told him.

"She wasn't your wife," one clerk of the station said. "You'd listed no living relatives, Cassidy. I heard you say your folks died when you were in college, so we had no one to notify."

April had died without anyone knowing she was his world, his anchor. The doctor who checked her said her heart just stopped beating. Sam had taken the words calmly,

17

but he felt his heart had stopped beating too.

He'd said he would survive, he'd heal, he'd march on, but in truth, a big piece of him died that day — the most important part. He didn't know how to be anything without her. He couldn't be a fighter in a world he didn't care to live in. He'd lost his mate and had no plans of ever allowing anyone close again.

Samuel Cassidy continued to work, but mentally he was drifting. Never staying one place long enough to get to know anyone. His only goal was to survive until the next fire came in. He was no longer on a mission to see new things, no longer counting days before he'd be home with April. All the fight, all the passion, all the peace he'd known was gone.

Then the letter came. A chance to go back in time for a while. The offer for Samuel Cassidy to fill in at a church in Honey Creek might be just what he needed. A change. A place where he could hide out from his life.

He stared at his reflection in the tin mirror. He could play the part of a preacher.

The metal door on the public restroom rattled as if a strong wind blew past.

A man in scrubs and a lab coat stormed

in carrying two plastic bags. He glanced at Sam, then disappeared into the last stall.

Sam watched as the lab jacket was tossed over the door. The guy was cussing as he bumped against the walls of the stall. Scrubs, bloody in places, were thrown over the door next. Then plastic shoes slid out from under the door as if trying to escape.

More banging against the walls.

Just as Sam was shoving his old clothes into the suitcase, the man burst out of the stall. The stranger now wore jeans and a western shirt. Worn boots had replaced the hospital shoes. He turned and collected the clothes and shoes he'd discarded, dropping them into the trash bin. Then he pulled a Stetson from a bag, crammed it down over his ginger-colored curly hair, and turned toward Sam.

For a moment they looked at each other. Sam could see now that he was a few years younger than he was, a few inches shorter, but still over six feet.

Just as the man seemed about to speak, a dozen Boy Scouts suddenly invaded the restroom. Talking, laughing, pushing one another, they formed a line in front of the five stalls.

The cowboy nodded his head once at Sam. "Guess we'd better head 'em up. . . ."

Sam grinned, realizing he'd just met a chameleon like himself. "And move 'em out."

The man headed out the door and Sam turned back to the mirror and his own journey. The mirror reflected a stranger's face now. No longer his father's and not quite his. He'd been trying to save the world in one way or the other for half his life, but no more. He'd take this trip back in time; then he'd bury all the past. His childhood, his parents' deaths, memories of April.

He was mad at God.

Not because He took April, but because God had left him behind.

Chapter 2

Colby

Colby McBride watched the man he'd seen in the restroom walking toward an Audi. He had the stride of a man who'd once marched, Colby thought. Now, the guy looked like a preacher going to a funeral, not the type who'd give a hitchhiker a ride.

There was something about him Colby couldn't peg. A priest maybe who didn't seem to fit into his clothes. Or maybe it was his skin that he didn't fit into. He was a tall man, 6'4", maybe 6'5", with black hair slicked back and eyes that missed little. The man of the cloth was drinking in every detail of his surroundings.

Colby sensed there was more to this preacher than met the eye. Colby could usually spot the ones who weren't what they seemed — a drug pusher or someone who

21

drove stolen cars out of state. Private investigator or undercover feds tracking movements on the interstate. They moved easy, almost invisible, and they watched their surroundings as if their life depended on it.

As a state trooper, Colby McBride had seen all types in the ten years he'd worked the Texas highways. If he'd been in uniform he might have pulled this guy over or maybe followed him a few miles down the road.

But then, Colby was always skeptical of strangers, and even sometimes friends. He caught himself looking for the criminal in everyone he passed. Maybe he was wrong this time, but he would swear this easygoing man in black was hiding something.

Colby laughed to himself. Get in line, he almost said aloud. Who isn't hiding something these days? People were rarely what they seemed, and today that included him.

He hadn't felt properly dressed in a decade if he wasn't wearing a badge and his service weapon. But today — no badge, no patrol car, no backup. Now was Colby's turn to pretend to be someone else. For the first time in his career he'd be investigating *off* the record.

Texas Ranger Max Mackenzie had asked Colby to go into Honey Creek without call-

22

ing too much attention to himself. Check the place out. Find out what was going on. Keep any scandal away from the Mackenzie family and especially his sister, who just happened to be the town's mayor.

And damn if the assignment wasn't so intriguing Colby had to break out of the hospital to make it to Honey Creek as fast as possible. Doing this favor for the Mackenzie family would be great for his career. He borrowed scrubs and a coat, had a friend pick him up at the back door of the hospital, and headed straight to his unofficial assignment.

The friend dropped him off at the nearest rest stop to Honey Creek, and Colby planned to hitchhike into town before noon. He'd cowboyed enough in his college days to drift into town and fit in. The friend had provided clothes, and Colby had made up a great cover story.

Max had told him over the phone to spend the day mingling with the locals. Mingle? Colby had no idea how to mingle. It wasn't in his skill set. But he'd come up with something.

Now, with no sleep and little money, Colby walked toward a line of trucks on the back lot of the rest stop. They'd probably stopped to rest until full light. Places like

23

this were quieter and sometimes safer than the big truck stops near towns.

The driver of the third rig was walking around his cattle truck. He wasn't tall, but he was wide, with a beard like a scruffy Santa Claus.

Colby kept his hat low. "Mornin'," he said. "Any chance a cowhand could catch a ride. I got a girl waiting for me in Honey Creek. My pickup broke down a few miles back and I'm not sure how long my girl will wait."

The truck driver looked him up and down.

"I got kin in Honey Creek who'll help me tow the truck in later." Colby shrugged. "It's only forty miles."

"I'm not supposed to take on passengers, but if you're stranded, I could take you a few miles. I'd enjoy the company."

Colby nodded his thanks. If he ever stopped this truck on the highway for a driving violation, he'd return the favor.

Colby had made two phone calls, in order to disappear from his real life. One to ask for a few vacation days and another to his neighbor asking him to pick up the mail.

Max had made it clear that no one was to know what Colby would be doing in Honey Creek. He even hinted that he'd owe Colby a big favor for doing this. Most of the Mackenzie family were in politics. They couldn't

24

afford any rumors.

Apparently, the mayor and little sister of Max, Piper Jane Mackenzie, had a fiancé who had disappeared. The town sheriff of Honey Creek suggested to the nearest news station that this could be foul play. It had been a back-page news note until the fiancé's car was found floating in the Brazos River just outside of town. No fiancé. No body.

Colby thought about turning off his personal phone. The only one who ever called him was his ex-girlfriend, and she just dialed now and then to remind him that she never wanted to hear from him again.

But then Max might call. He was collecting info from official sources and promised to send along anything significant.

This would be Colby's first private job. An "off the books" case. A missing person's case if he was lucky, a murder maybe, who knows. Colby hadn't fully believed it was real until Mayor Piper Mackenzie called an hour ago and said he needed to start digging fast and report in to her at dusk. She sounded as bossy as her brother.

She'd had an *all business* kind of voice, like her idea of a fun time would be guessing how many paper clips are in the jar on her desk. Maybe the fiancé just got bored and left, and she was up before dawn trying to find him.

Colby could picture her just from her voice. Flat shoes, shapeless suit with padded shoulders to make her look like a general, hair short or tied back so tight her eyes bugged out. Glasses, definitely glasses. She'd expect his work to be the best, and he planned to do just that. An assignment like this could move him up the ranks faster and a connection with a mayor, rumored to be on her way up in politics, couldn't hurt. Who knows, she might be governor in ten years and he'd be guarding her as the Texas Ranger he'd always planned to be from the day he signed on with the Texas Highway Patrol.

Problem was, her call came in before dawn while he was getting stitched up from a really bad evening at work.

Don't bleed on the mayor, Colby reminded himself as the truck driver pulled into the postcard-cute town of Honey Creek.

26

CHAPTER 3

Friday late afternoon

PIPER

Mayor Piper Jane Mackenzie sat in her cramped office on the fourth floor of city hall, looking out over the town square. She'd barely slept in three days, but by dusk she'd meet the man who would help her get to the truth.

Her nitwit *almost* fiancé was still missing. Which wasn't a crime but could mean trouble for both their families. She'd known Boone Buchanan all her life. His grandfather and her grandfather had been friends and political allies. People had teased her since she was a kid that she'd grow up and marry him. She'd be the governor's wife and he'd be the governor. Only Piper wanted to be the governor.

Boone was handsome, impulsive, fun, and popular all the way through law school, while she was plain, shy, and bookish.

But Boone also had a wild streak. Life was a game to him and he had to win. Their engagement was just a card up his sleeve that he'd played for fun or to get something he wanted. She wouldn't be surprised if he walked into town with some tall tale.

The truth and Boone had never been more than passing strangers. She'd let him win at games when they were kids, she'd listened to his rants when they were teenagers, and she'd gone with him to a few political rallies where he rarely talked to her.

Six months ago, at a big fund-raiser for her father, Boone had seemed the perfect date. He lived in Austin. He was rich and handsome. His family was powerful. He was a young partner in his uncle's law firm. Surely he'd outgrown his pranks and temper tantrums.

She talked about her work and he acted like he cared. He talked about himself and she made an effort to act like she was listening. Best of all, there were no sparks between them. She didn't have time for romance in her life and she wasn't his type.

Boone liked the press he got with a mayor on his arm. After their first fund-raiser, he offered to accompany her again, getting friendly when there was a camera around.

Last month someone, probably Boone, leaked a rumor that he and Piper were engaged. Maybe he wanted a little more attention.

She should have shot the rumor down, but Piper didn't see any harm in it. It was just a rumor. It'd die on its own and Boone would get the notice he craved. Just what the youngest in the firm thought he needed to build his base in the law office.

He never visited her in Honey Creek, but when Piper was in Austin, Boone was always showing up, hanging around, even saying things like "we think" as if she and Boone had somehow locked brains.

It embarrassed her, but Piper was just shy enough not to want to cause a scene.

But then he vanished after visiting half the bars in the county Tuesday night, and the rumor of their engagement seemed to become a fact. His red limited edition BMW was found floating in the Brazos River, and no one had seen Boone since. She'd heard that he used the valley around Honey Creek to let loose, though he'd never mentioned it to her. He might not be able to get drunk in Austin without some reporter snapping a shot, but here no one noticed, or cared.

To make matters worse, the county sheriff,

LeRoy Hayes, had also disappeared. Then the deputies seemed to have gone deaf, mute, and blind, and the dispatcher declared she'd only answered the 911 calls. Everyone in town believed the deputies and the dispatcher knew something, but they were loyal to the boss.

As stories flew as fast as the north wind, Piper could almost see her career crumbling around her. Part of her felt like she was standing with the men at the Alamo. She might not win, but she wouldn't go down without a fight.

In whispers people began to talk. Some said she killed Boone because he cheated on her. Some said her father had him kidnapped just at the thought of Boone becoming his son-in-law. Autumn, her secretary, suggested that he killed himself. Piper had even heard that the beauty shop talk thought Boone hadn't been near town. His car could have been stolen and taken for a joy ride by someone who fit his description.

One old vet at the coffee shop said Boone wanted to step away from the world. Boone had served three years in the army. That'll mess with your mind. Piper didn't bother to point out that Boone was messed up long before he went in the army.

Piper couldn't deny the engagement now. She'd look like a fool. All she could do was wait until he showed up. She'd act relieved to see him, then vanish from the press. A few months later, she'd quietly break up on the first busy news day.

Piper decided not to dwell on the stories. Boone wouldn't have killed himself. He loved himself too much. Her father would never kill a future son-in-law. If he'd been turned that way, he would have murdered the guy she had married in law school and divorced less than a year later.

Dating Boone had ended some talk about her being the only mayor with a stone-cold heart. All she wanted to do was serve the people and keep her private life private. Which shouldn't be too hard since she had no private life.

Looking out on the town she loved, Piper tried to think of a way out of this mess. Of course, she could call a press conference, but that might just draw more attention. More questions.

Yesterday she'd finally called Max, not because he was a Texas Ranger, but because he was her big brother. He'd always thought his job was to tell her what to do and he didn't hesitate. He'd said simply that first they had to get the facts, and he'd send someone down to do just that. Then he'd hire a researcher in Austin to dig through every detail of Boone's life. Boone wasn't the squeaky-clean guy his family would like everyone to believe. There were whispers of money trouble in Boone's past. Gambling debts.

Max's suggestions seemed like a plan. Not much of a plan, but at least she'd be doing something besides pacing.

A hundred-year-old clock on the wall behind her chimed five times. Over the three years she'd been mayor, she'd grown so used to the sound she rarely noticed it. But now it reminded her that another day had gone by. Her career, her life seemed to be ticking away.

"You need anything else before I go?" Autumn yelled from her desk in the next room. It never occurred to the secretary to use the phone or step into the doorway to ask her question.

"No, thanks," Piper answered, feeling as always like she had no control over her one real employee. There were six more people working at city hall and several departments who reported to the mayor's office, but they all seemed to answer to Autumn.

And Autumn was loving all this drama. Piper overheard her tell someone that she felt like she was living in a soap opera.

Piper and Autumn O'Toole had graduated from high school together fifteen years ago. While Piper went away to college and then law school, Autumn married right out of high school and hired on as a secretary at the courthouse. She'd worked for the county courts and most of the city offices that filled the top two floors. By the time Piper was elected mayor, her former friend thought she ran the town. As far as the secretary was concerned, Piper was just passing through, while Autumn planned to stay embedded at her government job until retirement.

Piper waited for her once best friend to leave. She hadn't told Autumn about the man who had an appointment after dark. If she'd done that, half the town would know by dawn tomorrow. The city secretary's Rolodex mind for gossip was both a blessing and a curse.

Piper heard the click of the file cabinet. The rattle of blinds dropping. The bottom *purse* drawer opening, then slamming shut. All sounded like the last few ticks of a workday clock. At exactly five p.m. Autumn would open the door leading to the hallway and say a good night to her office.

Piper used to think the farewell was

directed at her, but the secretary never waited for a reply. Work was over. Time to get home to her husband and kids, where she'd spend all evening talking about what happened in the courtrooms downstairs and the city offices upstairs. Then she'd return to the office at exactly eight o'clock the next morning, and begin to fill every empty moment talking about how great her children were or complaining about her husband, who apparently hadn't done anything right since the day after they married. His only saving grace was that he wasn't as bad as her sister's husband. Autumn reported on him regularly.

Kicking off her heels, Piper leaned back in her worn leather chair that still smelled a bit like her granddad's pipe, and enjoyed the now-silent office. Public service was in her blood. Her grandfather had been mayor for thirty-seven years. Her dad was a state senator. Both her brothers were Texas Rangers.

She had a proud heritage, but she knew she didn't belong in this chair. She agreed with Autumn. She was just passing through. Four or five years from now she planned to move to Dallas or Houston and let someone else take over the worries of Honey Creek. She wasn't made for a small town, not in her dreams anyway. But this place flowed through her veins, slow and steady as the Brazos River wound around the city limits. Low as the wind blowing down the valley whispering of legends of outlaws and ghosts.

Her heart was here in Honey Creek even if her dreams were in the big city.

Old-timers claimed the town was a hideout back when Texas was its own nation. Over the years misfits seemed to gravitate to the place. A small band of bigamists in the 1800s. Hippies in the 1960s. Survivalists settled on farms to the north of town ten years ago. They stayed just long enough to realize that there was no Starbucks within fifty miles. A coven of witches reportedly ran the local bakery. No one knew for sure, but they made great scones.

Bonnie and Clyde were even said to have stopped for gas. But few believed it. The people of Honey Creek had one talent in spades . . . imagination. They treasured it.

Piper looked over the rolling land just beyond the town's business lights. Small farms were nestled between clusters of cottages separated by roads as rambling as streams feeding into the highway. Fishing shacks were scattered along the river's banks with dock lights already blinking. Now and then a trailer park caught the last light of day and reflected it back to her. She smiled at her view from her office window. The beauty of her town might haunt dreams with legends and stories that floated on the evening breeze, but it was also a place where ideas thrived.

Without much thought she tiptoed to the hallway and bought her fourth canned Coke of the day from a machine so old it shivered loud enough to wake the janitor. When Piper went back to her office, she didn't bother to lock the door. She read the incoming mail stacked almost a foot high as she waited.

As time passed she moved to her computer and pulled up every newsfeed she could find about what was happening in her hometown. Boone's disappearance had made a dozen papers today. She might be sitting on ground zero, but the press seemed to have all the facts. Some true. Some not.

The good news was that the number of articles was down from yesterday. The bad news, she had a feeling everyone in the state was laying odds on what really happened to Boone Buchanan. Some said he was afraid to break up with the mayor, so he killed himself. Or was so drunk he thought the river was a winding road. Or, the rich lawyer wanted better than a mousy small-town mayor, so he faked his death. Maybe her family had had him killed because he knew one too many secrets about the Mackenzies. One neighbor of Boone's in Austin even suggested his own family sent him somewhere because he had embarrassed them one too many times.

One reporter hinted that dumb lawyers, even good-looking ones, just don't make it in the capital city.

Her granddad was probably cussing in his casket. He'd left her to take care of the town, not to become a storyline for one of the TV crime shows.

Piper stood and began to pace. She needed to have her strategy ready when the specialist her brother had hired showed up. No one, including Autumn, was to know who he really was. He reported directly to her brother, and her, of course.

The man had been hired last night and was probably in town all day. He might already know more than she did.

Her office, with boxes stacked to serve as a coffee table and books lining her windowsill, was suddenly way too small for Piper to breathe.

She ran past Autumn's desk and out into the hallway. After hours, the building was silent as a tomb. She took the stairs up to the widow's walk that topped the building, making city hall look like a square wedding cake with each floor smaller than the one below.

As she stepped out on the walk, Piper felt her heart slow. She could always breathe here. Top of the world, her granddad used to say. The highest building in town. She could see almost all of Honey Creek and the river to the west. The water sparkled in the dying light, like it was winking at her, and the old cottonwood trees seemed to wave at her as they squatted on the river's edge, their bony roots looking like knees bent toward the sky.

Piper leaned on the railing, listening to the evening noises as if they were the only beat that matched her heart. Closing her eyes, she almost believed she could hear the river drifting by as the low echo of a train's whistle whispered on the breeze.

How could anything be wrong in this world? The people were hardworking and good to the bone. They cared for one another. The whole valley was known for being friendly, and Honey Creek seemed its center. The town was an eccentric day trip from Austin or Dallas with its legends and stories. Small towns like Honey Creek were where farmers' markets thrived, and barn dances made the whole valley echo with pure country swing.

Half the folks in town maintained they were either related to someone crazy or had an ancestor who was an outlaw or gunfighter. The town even had a bed and breakfast that claimed to have a ghost who hiccupped. Fishermen near the river swore there was a catfish as long as a man that lived in the muddy water downstream.

And now, she reasoned, Honey Creek had a mystery. One handsome, almost boyfriend was missing.

As the sun lowered and evening lights made the town shine like a jewel nestled in the green rolling hills, all Piper saw was trouble.

She lowered her head almost to the railing. Somehow, this was her problem. She was the mayor. The whole town would look to her to do something.

The creak of a board alerted her a moment before a low voice whispered, "You all right, lady?"

Piper battled panic. She didn't move.

Chaos whirled all around her. It might as well have a voice. She fought down a scream, but a tiny sound slipped through. Just nerves. Stand tall. Don't let anyone know you're afraid, she reminded herself.

"I'm fine," she answered as if chaos would care. After three days of having reporters and townspeople screaming in her face, she was finally cracking up. With her luck she'd go down as the first mayor to be found mad while in office.

"You are the mayor, right?" The low voice came again.

Piper turned her head slightly as she pondered the idea of lying. The shadow of a man wearing a Stetson stood between her and the landing's exit.

The stranger slowly removed his hat, and curly hair with a touch of crimson amid dark blond appeared. "I know you said we'd meet after dark, but I saw you up here from the bench across the street and thought we might as well talk here and now."

"And you are?"

"I'm Trooper Colby McBride. The Rangers sent me. When we talked briefly before dawn, you said I was to check in with you at dusk."

Piper let out a breath she felt like she'd been holding for days. "You've come to help, Officer."

"Trooper," he corrected. "And as of right now I'm working off the record. What I find will be reported straight to you with the understanding that any felony uncovered will bring in the Texas Rangers."

She could barely see his eyes, yet she saw nothing but honesty in them. Of course, she'd been fooled before. If he'd waited a few more minutes in shadows, she wouldn't have been able to make out his eye color or the sharp line of his jaw.

He seemed the kind of man she'd need on her side. Strong, straightforward, protective.

"I'm just a ghost here, Miss Mackenzie." He smiled, suddenly looking younger. "I'm an observer hired to get to the bottom of this mess. The Rangers have already examined the car that was pulled from the river. They are sending me the full report along with a list of every person who was known to have seen Mr. Buchanan three nights ago. My job is simply to put the pieces together."

Piper doubted this man would ever be *just* anything. He seemed self-assured, maybe a bit dangerous. The kind of man she wouldn't feel comfortable dating. The kind who'd run straight toward trouble, instead of away.

He wore his western shirt and blue jeans casually. He'd fit in perfectly with the locals. If he'd worked the oil fields or rodeoed, he could probably walk into any bar and learn more in an hour than she'd ever known

41

about the people in town. No one gossiped about crimes to a mayor who had two brothers who were Rangers.

From his stance to his slight twang, the man before her seemed pure Texan. He might be the type who said "yes, ma'am" to the ladies and fought his way out of a bar at midnight. But she had to trust him if she hoped to clean up this mess.

"I'm Piper Jane Mackenzie, the mayor." She realized he already knew who she was, but she needed a bit of formality in their meeting.

He smiled. "I figured that out. You look just like your picture in the press. Former mayor's granddaughter, state senator's daughter, a rising star in politics. You had plenty of press before this happened, lady. Runner-up for the cobbler cook-off when you were sixteen, youngest one in your graduating class from law school, with high honors."

He lowered his chin a bit and grinned. "Eleven months older than me, which makes us both thirty-three for one more month. You made a habit of collecting speeding tickets until you ran for mayor. Since then, not even a parking ticket. Lots of photos out there of you, none that would be embarrassing. Seems you're perfect, Miss

Mackenzie. Or at least you were until you started dating Boone Buchanan."

"I wasn't dating him, really. We were not engaged. Our families knew each other. I just asked him to go with me to a few functions in Austin and then he started showing up when I was in the capital. To be honest, I don't even think I'd call us friends." She thought of saying that Colby was more her type than Boone, but she had to keep this professional. "I don't date, Trooper McBride."

Colby shrugged. "I saw the pictures. You two looked pretty friendly to me. Also, you looked taller in the photo. Of course, you were wearing high heels then." He leaned down closer, so he could look straight at her. "That threw me for a minute. I pictured you taller." His gaze moved from her face all the way down to her feet. "Cute toes, by the way, Miss Mackenzie."

"You don't need to notice my toes, Mr. McBride."

"I thought I was hired to notice everything, Mayor. Right now, as far as I'm concerned, you, like everyone in this town, are a suspect."

She nodded once. "Fair enough. What do I call you?"

"Colby. It'll be easier when folks see us

43

talking if they think you already knew me from somewhere. In fact, that's part of the cover story we'll use. I based it on what I know of you. Don't alter the back story of us in any way, or people will start asking questions of both of us."

"All right."

Colby's amber eyes, reminding her of a wolf's stare, flashed in the low light as he moved closer. He studied her. "Thanks to the Internet I know enough to put together reasons why I'm in town and why people might see us talking. If any part of my cover doesn't fit with your approval, let me know and we can change it now."

"Should we go to my office to talk?"

He shook his head. "It's safer here. I wouldn't be surprised if your office is bugged. With the sheriff missing a day after your boyfriend vanished, leaving his car parked in a river, who knows what else is going on."

His fingertips lightly brushed her back as he guided her deep into the shadows. "The cover story is, I'm an old friend of your ex-husband. We were college buddies before I flunked out and you came into his life. At your engagement party, nice pictures by the way, I got drunk and made a pass at you. I wasn't invited to the wedding."

44

"Okay, so that could have happened, but why are you here now?"

"I decided you've been divorced ten years and might be desperate enough to give me a second chance. I've inherited a little money, so I got time to follow my dreams, so to speak. One is to hook up with you, and another is to buy land around here if things go good between us."

"Your dream is to charm me after I crossed you off the list of guests at my wedding?"

His voice lowered a bit. "How am I doing so far?"

Piper grinned as she fought the urge to kick him. "You're not my type, Colby McBride."

Colby shrugged. "As near as I can tell, Mayor, you don't have a type. Not one picture of you out on the town since you divorced. Unless you count the ones of you dancing with Boone at a fund-raiser in which you looked bored. Or a dozen shots of him hugging on you and you not even looking his direction. If you've got some secret lover out there, you might want to let me know. Otherwise as far as the town is concerned, I've come a-courting. I'm downright crazy about you."

"Dressed like that?"

45

"So, I'm the underdog type. People will want to help me out."

"That's the worst cover story I've ever heard."

"You got a better one? Everyone will either try to run me out of town or take my side. Heartsick lovers always get pulled under someone's wing. With luck I'll be able to play the fool and seem harmless. No one will notice I'm listening for clues. People tend to let the truth slip. I'll hang out at the breakfast café in the morning, bars at night, and maybe even land in church on Sunday. I'll blend in."

She reached in her pocket and pulled out a key she'd been holding all day. "Check in at Fisherman's Lodge. Show the owner, Digger, this key. Pay in cash."

"Is Digger working as my partner?"

"No, he's just helping out, but you can trust him. This key will unlock a storage room in the cabin he rents you. You'll be working alone. Let me know anything, no matter how small, that you find out." She met his gaze deciding she had to trust him. "Do you need to change your name?"

Colby shook his head. "Colby is a nick-name. No one will find a Colby McBride on the Web. If I find something, I'll try talking to you in public. Of course, you'll be polite, but distant. Then we meet somewhere in private and talk."

"Where?"

"You tell me, PJ?"

"Don't call me by my initials. I hate that."

The trooper just waited like she was a toddler throwing an unnecessary fit.

She continued. "I'll set a book with a red cover on my far windowsill, if I need to talk to you. We can meet here."

"Fair enough. I won't be hard to find," he said as he backed into the shadows. She couldn't see his face when he added, "I'll find you."

The floor near the door creaked again and he was gone.

Piper turned back to the view of her town and watched for a few minutes before she saw Colby walking away from city hall. His hands were in his pockets, his hat low. He headed straight across the street to a little diner. The *T* on the neon sign had burned out years ago, but the exas Best Coffee sign burned bright. The place served only breakfast from six to midnight, but it had a direct line of vision to city hall.

If Colby sat in the front window table, he'd be able to see the square and she'd be able to see him from her office window.

Slipping down the stairs, she tiptoed to

47

her office trying to decide what she thought of the undercover visitor her brother had sent. She knew he must be the best at his job or Max wouldn't have picked him, but the idea of spying on her own population bothered her. Plus, this Colby guy was too young. He was her age. Shouldn't he be older, wiser? Shouldn't she?

Piper closed her eyes. Maybe she was too young to be mayor of even a small town. The fact she'd run unopposed was probably the only reason she'd won. That and her grandfather stood just behind her at every public event.

This was her town, her people. How could a stranger uncover anything that she didn't already know? Hiring a man to dig up the truth about the sheriff's secrets as well as Boone's disappearance would probably be a waste of time. Either no one would talk about it, or more likely everyone would make up their own facts to prove their theories.

After all, what could a spy find that her secretary, Autumn, didn't already know?

When a cool breeze chilled her, Piper ran down the hallways that always seemed haunted after five. As always, she waved at Granddad when she passed.

A moment later she slipped past Autumn's

desk and was at the threshold of her office when she looked up and saw a man in a black suit and clerical collar around his tanned throat sitting at her desk. He was staring out the window, obviously lost in his own thoughts.

Piper froze, trying to decide to run or scream. One strange guest after dark was enough for tonight. "May I help you," she whispered as she backed toward the door.

Then, the stranger turned toward her and smiled. "Howdy," he said. "I'm Sam Cassidy. I noticed your light on and I hoped you might still be here. When I got upstairs the door was open, so I made myself at home."

Before she could answer or run, the man stood and offered his hand. "I'm the fill-in preacher at the First Saints Independent Church. Sounds to me like you people had a bit of a problem naming the place."

She should have been mad at him dropping in, but the preacher was a charmer. There was a bit of mischief in his smile and pure Southern charm in his low voice. She'd thought Colby was tall, but the preacher was another three or four inches taller, making her feel tiny standing beside him.

"We weren't expecting you so early." In truth she'd forgotten he was coming. "And

49

locals just call it Saints Church."

As she reached across the desk and shook his hand, she noticed the note stuck to her desk lamp. It said simply, *Don't forget to welcome new preacher. Take him to dinner. Autumn.*

"I'm Mayor Mackenzie."

His big hand circled around hers. "I figured you'd be back. Cold Coke can on your desk, shoes in the middle of the floor."

She pulled her hand back, moved over a few feet, and stepped into her heels.

Piper didn't miss his widening smile as she grew four inches closer to his height. "If you're up to it I'd like to show you around my town. We'll stop by the church first; then if you're feeling brave, I'll take you to dinner."

"Brave?"

She shrugged. "My last date went missing three days ago."

"Sounds like an interesting topic for dinner. Lead the way, Miss Mackenzie."

CHAPTER 4

Friday evening

SAM

Sam had waited in the mayor's cluttered fourth-floor office for maybe ten minutes. The e-mail from the church had said she was the one who would officially welcome him, but it didn't mention where to meet her.

Someone named Stella B. had sent a note after he contacted the church and said he was coming, that he meet the mayor first before coming to the church. Stella B. also said the mayor would tell him about the town as she drove him to the church to meet a few of the flock.

He watched the last glow of the sun as clouds moved in across the darkening sky while he waited.

Sam had always loved watching the ever-changing sky. Like his life, the shadows grew

51

until there was nothing to be seen. Somehow the night sky was the same everywhere in the world. It followed him, protected him, made him forget that there was once sunshine.

As a child, this Texas view was the first sky he'd studied. He'd pushed memories of lying in the grass with his dad as they picked out the constellations from his thoughts. It was too painful to remember. Sitting between his father and mother, traveling along calling themselves vagabonds for the Lord was another he'd hidden away. They'd treated every little town like an Egyptian tomb to be explored. Then, one phone call when he'd been in college, and his parents were gone. Maybe the happy memories of them would slowly fade, maybe they would stay hidden away. . . . Forgetting was easier than remembering.

This Texas sky looked like a thousand other evenings beneath stormy clouds. The last time he drove through Honey Creek, he was on his way to his folks' funeral. He'd taken the back roads southeast out of Dallas. Of all his dad's churches and all the places they'd explored, his parents had picked this valley in which to be buried. A beautiful cemetery resting between three towns — Honey Creek, Clifton Bend, and

Someday Valley. Maybe they'd picked the spot because here had been the last time the three of them had lived together.

He closed the past away and studied the small town with the city offices built square in the center of a cluster of mismatched homes and businesses. Whoever mapped out the streets must have been drunk.

He'd spent the last few months of his high school senior year here. Sam remembered feeling like a fool getting lost in such a small town. But streets dead-ended into alleys and street signs changed from block to block. At one point he believed no matter which way he drove he would run into the river.

After he left, his parents moved on to three more jobs before he came home for Christmas.

That was their life. Home was wherever they felt a calling to go.

Sam turned back to the mayor's office as he pushed the past away. He mentally listed the facts about his tour guide for the night. MAYOR PIPER MACKENZIE was engraved on the door, so he had to be in the right place. With the fresh Coke can sitting on her desk, she was probably planning to work late. She obviously hadn't remembered he was coming, which meant this was just one of the duties as mayor that she had to do.

He decided after she introduced him to the waiting church members he'd let her off the hook for dinner.

His logical mind colored in the known facts with guesses. Her black SUV, parked in the mayor's spot on the back parking lot, was clean . . . she was organized, maybe even a neat freak. Her office was packed with file boxes . . . she was searching for answers. The trash under her desk was full of empty drink cans and what looked like every snack from the machine he'd seen in the hallway . . . she hadn't had time to go out for food and she was running on caffeine and sugar.

He'd already figured out her type. Organized, driven, in charge. She would be one of those people who had to be in control. That's probably why she wanted to show him around.

She was the kind of woman who planned everything in her life and something wasn't going right tonight. He guessed whatever crisis she faced had nothing to do with him. Welcoming a traveling preacher couldn't have been high on her list.

Maybe Sam could piece together the mayor's personality, but he was baffled by his own, especially the call to preach. He'd been twenty-three when he graduated from seminary. With no relatives to attend, he'd skipped all the ceremonies and left with three friends for a summer in Europe. One of the guys was from Italy and another's family lived in England. They had the loan of a flat in London and an apartment just outside of Rome. So if their money ran out they had places to stay free.

They left laughing, hungry for an adventure before they all had to step into their serious lives.

Sam returned that summer with one friend, James, beside him. Both had wounds healing that they barely noticed. Their English and Italian classmates had been buried while Sam and James had still been in the hospital. The underground bombing in London had shattered Sam's faith and strengthened James's.

Within hours of landing back in Texas, Sam and his one remaining friend joined the army. Sam no longer felt the calling to preach. He wanted to fight evil. James became a chaplain, and Sam learned to fly.

When he was flying, the world couldn't touch him, and later, when he was fighting fires, there was no time to think of anything else. Maybe this break he was now taking would do the same thing.

When Sam had arrived in Honey Creek

that morning, he'd driven out to *his* church just to take a look. Well, his church for as long as this part-time job lasted.

Could he play this part? He did have a divinity degree even if he'd never preached a single sermon from the pulpit. By the time his fellow graduates were being assigned churches, he was in boot camp. He'd seen evil that summer and had made the choice to fight rather than reform criminals.

He heard what sounded like a mouse squeak and turned away from the window.

The outline of the mayor in a brown suit that looked two sizes too big for her stood before him backlit in the dull yellow of the hallway light. Her face was in shadow. He realized she was medium everything. Not tall or short. Not fat or thin. Even her hair, that just reached her shoulders, was medium length, medium brown. If she robbed a bank, nothing about her would stand out.

Until she turned toward him, clicked on the desk lamp, and he saw her eyes. Forest green. The color of priceless jade.

"May I help you?" she asked as she took a step backward.

"I'm Samuel Cassidy. I believe I was supposed to meet you here."

She offered her hand as she straightened.

"I'm Mayor Mackenzie. Welcome to Honey Creek."

"Thank you." He had the feeling she was playing as much of a role as he was tonight.

"We should be going. Your new staff didn't have time to plan your reception. I'm sure they will have it Sunday. Tonight they just want to meet you, show you around a bit, and hand over the keys. I'll be happy to take you out to eat when that's done."

"I know where the church is. I can drive over, and you don't have to feed me. I can take care of myself, but thanks for the offer."

"It's part of my job." She held the door open impatiently as if he were the last customer to leave at closing time.

Sam didn't move.

She brushed his arm as she reached for her umbrella and computer bag. "I'll take you to dinner to show our hospitality. It is what the mayor should do for the new interim minister in town. By the time we order dessert, word will have spread that you've arrived."

Sam picked up on the "new interim" line. "How many visiting pastors have you had this year?"

"You'll be the fourth or fifth. The last one made it three Sundays before he broke and

57

ran." The mayor hid her smile. "We seem to be hard on the clergy."

He followed her out of the office, then waited while she locked her door.

"Can you preach?" she asked as they stepped into the elevator that rattled and grinded.

"I can preach. The invitation came to me, but I suspect it was meant for my father." Sam suppressed the urge to tell her that he had given up on Heaven.

Sam never talked about his only love, or losing his friends that summer in London, or even about his parents. In fact, he hadn't said April's name aloud since the day he found out she left this earth without saying goodbye. That night seemed so long ago. He'd screamed for her as if she could hear him and would come back.

He didn't believe he'd drop to hell when he died. He was already living there now. But he'd drawn this wild card and he planned to see it through.

The mayor pushed the elevator button and they stood, staring at the crack in the elevator door as it moved down.

"Barbeque or chicken fried steak?" she asked.

For a second he thought she was asking for a password. If so, he had a fifty-fifty chance of failing. Then he remembered she'd mentioned dinner. "Chicken fried steak, of course."

"Good. I think you'll like the place I have in mind. It's a bit of a local dive, but best chicken-fry for fifty miles."

He walked her to her car, then with a nod he turned to his Audi parked three spaces away. Sam followed her the few blocks to the church. The charm of the town surprised him. The streets were clean, the breeze beginning to cool, and the church came into view in Thomas Kinkade perfection. As a teenager he'd driven these very streets, but he hadn't seen the charm.

After locking his car, Sam walked up to the driver's side of the mayor's SUV.

For a moment he saw her leaning her head back with her eyes closed as if meditating.

The lady must be dealing with a big problem. He was just a duty of her office. Once she got rid of him, she'd probably go back to her office.

He studied her profile. Memorizing the outline of a delicately carved face. Even in the streetlight's glow he could tell she had a classic kind of beauty. One of those women who could blend into a crowd without being noticed, but in the right clothes, the right makeup, she'd definitely stand out.

She had beauty and intelligence, only he wasn't interested in her or any other woman.

Her silent moment ended and she stepped out.

Sam grinned. "Little lady in a big car."

She managed a smile. "I need to haul a lot of shit."

Before he could respond, she added, "My hobby is gardening. Vegetables in the summer and greenhouse flowers in the winter."

"Sounds exciting," he lied, offering her his arm as if they were walking into a formal dinner.

By the time they reached the church steps, three greeters were standing at the door waiting. As he walked to the huge double-door entrance, the three were taking turns speaking to him, as if they'd rehearsed it.

Sam just kept smiling as Stella Blake, a slender woman in her mid-thirties he'd guess, rolled off numbers. Attendance, average age, number of days he'd be required to keep office hours, unless there was a death or hospital visit, of course. The woman looked like she'd never been outside of Honey Creek in her life.

The man on her left, Benjamin Blake, introduced himself as Stella's older brother. Their great-grandparents were one of the five families who started the church.

Sam would bet neither of the Blakes was married. Benjamin's sport jacket looked like the Penney's special from 1985. He was round-shouldered and potbellied and at least ten years older than his sister.

The third man, Tyrone Tilley, was short and had nicely wrinkled into his eighties. He said all the right things, even had a strong handshake, but something about him wasn't real. He seemed an actor playing his role but underneath he walked another path that Sam would bet had nothing to do with this life he played.

Tyrone seemed to speak only in sayings he'd heard. *It's always darkest before the dawn. Good things come to those who wait.*

Stella showed Sam the church, while her brother mentioned the flaws in both the building and the congregation. She was as shy and meek as her brother was bold and bossy.

When they finished the tour, they were back where they started. Sam spotted the mayor waiting at the front door. She looked bored as Tyrone complained about the spotty cell service in town and demanded to know what she planned to do about it.

Sam's relief at seeing Piper must have been apparent, because she gave him a sympathetic smile.

He managed to thank all three greeters, and accepted the keys to his cottage out back of the church. When Piper offered once more to take him to dinner, he quickly accepted. The last thing he wanted to do was stay around with these three.

On the way to her SUV, she whispered, "You all right?"

"You ever see that old movie, *Children of the Corn*? I just met their grandparents. Stella seemed nice, but she wouldn't look me in the eye. I don't know a woman over eighteen that is half as shy."

The mayor fought to hold in a giggle, but she didn't unlock her car. "The café is not far, want to walk?"

"I'd like that."

Within thirty seconds they were walking west, leaving Stella, Benjamin, and Tyrone still standing on the church steps.

"They do go home, don't they?"

She laughed. "I think so."

"Good." He relaxed and she slipped her hand under his arm to guide him. "I was afraid I might find their coffins in the basement." Swallowing down a few cuss words, Sam realized he was falling out of character. "Sorry about that comment," he added.

"You'll get used to them but don't expect them to warm up to you." Mayor Piper was silent a moment, then cleared her throat. "Have you heard about our problem in Honey Creek?"

"Nope, fill me in." He thought maybe they'd found mice in the church, or the last minister ran off with the church secretary, or maybe there were bats in the bell tower. There was always some crisis going on.

When the mayor hesitated, he glanced at her and thought he saw tears in those beautiful eyes.

"Just tell me. Whatever it is couldn't be that bad. The church is broke, or it's splitting apart. I'd like to know what I'm stepping into."

The streetlights were getting farther apart and he could no longer see her eyes. They were heading onto a street lined with pawn shops, bars, and weathered restaurants that were only a few blocks from the church.

He thought it odd how fast the world shifted from being a picture-perfect town to being a place where his senses became more alert.

"It's not about the church. It's about me. The papers claim I'm engaged to a man I dated a few times. He's disappeared. Everyone in town has a reason they think we *broke up,* or they think they know why someone killed him even though there is no body."

63

She straightened like a soldier giving a report. "I'm telling you this because you might not want to be seen with me."

"Damn." Gossip about her wasn't what he expected.

"Don't say damn," she said, as she stared at the road.

"What?"

"Don't say damn. You're a preacher, remember. Cussing will rank right up there with me killing my almost fiancé."

They both chuckled, and a bond seemed to form between them.

After a minute, he said, "Maybe outlaws like us should stick together, Mayor? I'll watch your back and you watch mine."

"Maybe we should, Preacher."

She pointed to a square building near the corner. The long ribbon of lights circled the roof. They blinked off and on in no apparent pattern, making the red lines seem to stutter. "Best chicken fried steak in town, I promise; but don't eat anything else here."

Sam relaxed a bit as she began telling him about the town as they neared.

"The first pioneer here settled between the Brazos River and a creek that feeds into it. Our founder, a sea captain, said if he had to move inland he'd need to see water. He built his huge house close to the creek while

64

the town grew farther inland. After all his family died off, my cousin Jessica bought it and turned the first floor into a café. You'll want to eat breakfast there or at the little coffee shop on the square. My cousin has the best French toast in town. She'd planned to make it a bed and breakfast upstairs but claims too many ghosts still live there."

"You only recommend the three?"

She raised an eyebrow as if to remind him she was the mayor.

Sam let it pass. "I think I saw the beautiful house at the edge of town when I drove around." It looked like the home belonged on the northern bay or along the Mississippi. The first floor had shined with new paint, and the wide windows seemed to be welcoming guests. The second- and third-floor windows were dark.

When they were getting close to the café, Sam turned back to the mayor's problem. "Tell me the facts about your difficulty before we go inside. I don't want to talk about it where someone might hear."

Piper began explaining her relationship with a man named Boone Buchanan, who had disappeared.

When she was done, Sam nodded but didn't comment. He'd just learned what worried her, and all he had to do was figure out how to help. After all, she was the only friend he had in this town.

When they entered the café, a long bar packed with mostly men greeted them. Several people turned to stare. A few lifted their bottles and smiled.

Piper nodded at a few but moved directly to a hallway at the back. Sam followed. Five feet into the hallway a room opened to a big dining room. It was rough, well-worn tables, paper towel rolls in the center to serve as napkins, and half a dozen scream-ing kids to drown out the country music from the bar.

He smiled. This was his kind of place.

Sam pushed his shoulders back, plastered on a smile, and started nodding at everyone looking his direction. By the time they sat down at the table by the kitchen, he was starting to feel like a bobblehead.

He commented that the café smelled like heaven loud enough for several people to hear. When he called Piper "Miss Mayor," she raised one eyebrow slightly as if in warn-ing that he was laying it on too thick.

Only, she had a part to play too. She began her welcoming lecture. Though a bit distant, she was the perfect tour guide tell-ing him the history of the town, a few colorful stories about outlaws who hid out here, and how more than one of the old homes had ghost tales to tell.

He noticed that she mentioned nothing personal. She might have let him see her true self for a moment, but now she was totally a professional.

While he ate a chicken-fried steak as big as the plate, she bragged about her town of Honey Creek.

Sam made a show of offering to pay, and she insisted on picking up not only the bill, but the tip as well.

After dessert, he followed her to the front door, calling out to everyone he'd been introduced to by name.

Once they were walking back to the church, she said, "I'm impressed. You remembered every name, even the waitress's."

"Knowing names was a skill I learned from my dad. He was a preacher and loved everyone he met. The army taught me to notice details. It takes about five seconds to really look at someone. Height, weight, approximate age, hair color, eye color, visible scars, what they are wearing. Most people don't take those five seconds."

He smiled. "For example, what color was the waitress's uniform? What toy did the little girl who walked past us three times have in her hand? And the cashier, what animal did she have tattooed on her wrist?

Piper smiled back. "Gray uniform, teddy bear, and a dove."

"Are you sure, Mayor? Would you swear in court?"

"Yes," she answered, not sounding sure at all.

"You were closer than most. The toy was a bear. The tattoo was a bird, but the uniform was blue, not gray."

"But I didn't know I'd be having to ID someone or I'd have looked closer."

"For the most part, no one does. Practice five seconds now and then. My dad claimed people are fascinating if you just take the time to look."

"Did he retire?"

"I guess you could say that. He went home. Dad and Mom died in a boating accident before I finished college. I thought I'd follow in his footsteps, but it wasn't a straight path for me."

Green eyes studied him. "There's a story there."

"Another time, Mayor. You fed me and now I've got to find that shower and bed."

As they reached the street corner, a drunk stumbled from a bar near them.

68

Piper slowed, waiting for him to pass.

He wavered right and left as if trying to remember his directions and then headed left down a broken sidewalk.

Sam watched him, as always noticing details others never saw. He might be medium built and thin, but his shoulders were muscular, rounded slightly from hard work.

As the drunk passed the alley, three little children stepped out of the shadows and began to follow him. The oldest, maybe ten or twelve, pulled an old wagon. The other two, a few years younger, walked beside the wagon. They kept their distance from the drunk, and the man in work clothes never looked back.

The mayor answered the question Sam hadn't asked. "They're not his kids. Daily Watts was only married a short time. People say that she died. He gets drunk every Friday night, walks home, and usually, no one sees him again until Monday morning when he walks to work. He's a mechanic who doesn't own a car."

When Sam remained silent, she added, "The Sanderson kids lost their father five years back. Their mom works days at the cleaners and nights at the hotel."

"So why are they following the drunk?"

She'd finally caught his interest.

Piper smiled. "It took me a while to figure it out, but I think they're waiting for him to pass out. When he does, they plan to load him in the wagon and take him home. They need a daddy."

"Anyone tell the kids it doesn't work that way?"

"Who knows, Pastor, maybe this time it might."

CHAPTER 5

Friday night

PECOS

Pecos Smith pulled his tie from his backpack and slipped it over his head as he headed into the high school gym. He had to rehearse for a graduation ceremony he probably wouldn't be attending.

The fact that he was the only kid in high school who wore a tie didn't bother him. He saw it more as the other kids' problem than his.

He was going to be somebody someday and any pictures of him would reflect that he knew that fact from an early age. He'd be rich in twenty years, and no dumb high school photo would blackmail him through life. No matter how old the picture, he'd look sharp. After all, he would be "on the job" tonight, already starting his climb to success.

As he took the school steps two at a time, Kerrie Lane caught up with him. Pecos swore he could smell her before she reached his line of sight. The blond, perfect senior smelled so good, like gingerbread cookies and honey straight from her granddad's farm.

"Hi, Pecos. You going to the dance tonight?"

"No, I'll be working."

It amazed him that she even cared enough to talk to him. Most girls looked right through him. He was six feet, bone thin, and covered with brown pimply skin.

Who would have thought a girl like Kerrie would ever bother to speak to someone like him. She was the top of the graduating class and he was holding up the other end. Her brain was probably dumbing down just smiling at him.

Her steps matched his. "You've got a job?"

"Sure, I own my own company. I'm Honey Creek's first Uber driver."

"But you drive a pickup."

He chose to look at the positive side. "I can only take two people, but I can haul lots of junk in the back. I figure all the sophomores who can't drive will pay me to drive them to the last dance of the year. Showing up to the dance in a pickup is better than having your parents drop you off. For ten bucks I'll even park out by the river for fifteen minutes before I take them home."

"Wouldn't that be a bit creepy?"

"No, I'll step out of the truck, with the keys, of course. I'll watch the river until the fifteen minutes is up. That should give any sophomore time to get a few kisses in." He handed her a handmade card. "Pass this to someone who might need a ride home tonight. After a look in to see how they transformed the gym, I'll be waiting for business in my truck out front."

She stuffed his card in her jacket pocket. "You got it all figured out, don't you?"

"No, but I'm working on it."

Just before she turned off at the door she added, "Love your tie."

Standing there watching her walk away, it occurred to him that he liked pretty much everything about Kerrie Lane. Someday, when he was rich, he'd ask her out and he wouldn't be driving an old pickup.

She'd probably turn him down, but he'd put it on his bucket list anyway. Pecos liked to think ahead and make plans. Seemed to him that if he started his list at nineteen, he'd have a much better chance of completing it by the end of his life.

Pecos turned down the handicap ramp as a dozen giggling girls headed up the steps loaded down with tissue flowers dripping with glitter. He had decided against going inside. At any minute someone might need him out here. Anyway, he'd learned about all his brain could handle.

In two more days he'd hopefully be graduating. This year wouldn't be summer break. This year would be the start of his career, his life. Time to stop planning and start doing.

With his diploma he might apply for a deputy job in town. Since he'd failed the second grade, he was already a year older than everyone in his class. Come September, he'd be twenty. That should be old enough.

He figured his chances of getting the deputy job were pretty good. According to all the gossip, the sheriff's department had been knee-deep in problems lately. He wouldn't be surprised if the feds came in and arrested them all, even poor old Miss Daisy the dispatcher. Rumor was they were covering for the sheriff, but for what no one seemed to know.

Just rumors. That's all. It wasn't likely old Sheriff Hayes did anything wrong, or that the seventy-year-old dispatcher was guilty of doing more than passing gas. She couldn't possibly be running drugs or robbing banks. Miss Daisy could barely walk to the bathroom.

If Pecos took the job, he might be sheriff in five years, mayor in another five. From what he saw, all deputies have to do is drive around. That would give him plenty of time to plan, and with luck the sheriff would let him use the squad car to make Uber runs when no crime was happening. When he got around to calling the Uber company and officially signing up, he'd ask if they minded that his car belonged to the county sheriff's office.

He had so many great ideas they were blowing off him like dandelion seeds in the wind.

CHAPTER 6

Late Friday night

COLBY

Colby McBride knew he should probably get a cheap motel, but the thought of a lumpy bed covered in thin sheets and bed bugs as company didn't appeal to him.

He'd take the mayor's suggestion of sleeping on the edge of town in Fisherman's Lodge.

Colby had walked past the rambling cluster of cabins between the river and a little creek that eventually fed into it. The place had that lost-in-time kind of look. It'd be quiet, and with luck they'd serve a decent breakfast. Plus it was only a ten-minute walk to city hall. He wouldn't bother with a car, but it might be fun to ride a bike again. Colby planned to check that out in the morning.

Fisherman's Lodge didn't have a neon

sign or even a blinking OPEN in the windows of what had to be the office, but the lights were on inside and he could see a small lobby and a check-in desk.

He took the steps two at a time. The boards were as loud as most doorbells.

As he slipped inside he saw no one, but a voice bellowed, "Come on in, stranger."

Colby scanned the room. Empty. The place was decorated in fishing décor. Half-a-dozen species of fish were mounted on wooden boards with dates below. Old fishing poles spelled out Welcome on the wall behind the desk. A bear on his hind legs took up one corner, and a wild pheasant served as a lamp ornament. Most of the chairs in the lobby looked like they rocked. Handmade doilies he hadn't seen the likes of since he visited his great-grandmother when he'd been about eight decorated every table.

On the positive side, what looked like homemade cookies were on a platter at the desk, and the place was spotless.

Colby took a step backward, then reentered.

"Come on in, stranger."

Great. The ten-pound bass was talking to him.

Colby heard a toilet flush and then an old

man stepped from the door behind the desk like an outhouse cuckoo clock.

"Sorry, son. Hope my watch bass didn't scare you. Digger is my name and this is my place."

"No, the bass seemed friendly enough. Now if that bear greeted me it might have scared the hell out of me." Colby moved closer with his hat in one hand and a Walmart bag in the other. "I was hoping you might have a room."

Colby casually laid the key the mayor had given him on the counter.

The owner shook his head. "We ain't got no rooms, but we got cabins. Built them myself. Scattered them among the trees so you'll feel like you're deep in the woods and not just at the end of town. We got the Brazos on one side of us and Honey Creek on the other."

The old guy raised one bushy eyebrow. "Sorry I wasn't in the office, but I didn't hear you drive up. That gravel is usually better than an alarm."

"I walked from town. My pickup broke down about forty miles north of here." Colby smiled. The old man was nosy, just the kind of local he needed. "Hoping to pick up a bike here. Wouldn't know where to find an old Harley that's running, would you?"

"I might. I'll make a few calls." Digger swung the hotel register around. The thick book looked as old as him. "You checking in? Sixty a night or three hundred a week. Includes breakfast. Nothing fancy but good food."

Colby pulled out the worn wallet his friend bought at the secondhand store along with the clothes and boots he was wearing. He counted out three hundred dollars in twenties.

The owner studied him a moment, then said low, "Since you're by yourself I don't reckon you'll be using much water. How about I let you have the back cabin for two fifty?"

"Fair enough." He wrote his name in the ledger. "I'm Colby McBride." The trooper began his cover story. "Used to rodeo. You ever heard of me?"

"Nope." Digger counted back fifty. "Never been much of a rodeo fan. Lost my leg in 'Nam, so it wasn't a sport I'd ever try."

"I appreciate the discount," Colby said.

At that moment a barreled-chested man walked into the lobby and headed to an old cigarette machine at the back of the lobby. The man might be a trucker, but he didn't look friendly.

Colby turned back to the lodge owner.

"I've been living lean for a while, but I'm coming into a little inheritance. If things work out, I might be buying a small place around here."

The smoker walked back out without a word, or even a glance in their direction. Digger seemed to take the big man's measure, before turning his attention back to Colby.

"What kind of place, buddy?" he said. "Maybe I can help. Know most of the folks around these parts." Digger cut his eyes quickly toward the open window where the smoker had stopped to open his pack.

For a moment Colby caught Digger's glance and knew they were both aware the big man could be listening.

Colby continued playing his part. "You know the mayor?"

"Sure, everyone knows Mayor Mackenzie." Digger pulled a key from the drawer, not the board, and laid it atop the key the mayor had given Colby.

Colby pushed his chest out a bit. "Well, she don't know it yet, but I've come to ask her to marry me." He wasn't crazy about playing the idiot or, worse, the idiot in love, but that was his cover story and he was sticking to it. "She was married to my best friend in college and I knew the minute I saw her she was too good for him. They didn't last a year."

"And you think you are good enough for her, cowboy?"

"I don't know, but I figure it's worth a try. She's the one woman I've never forgotten. I remember every word she ever said to me."

Digger scratched his spotty beard. "What was the last thing she said?"

Colby acted like he was thinking about it. "She said, 'Get lost.' "

The old man laughed. "Well, I wish you luck, Mr. McBride. I got a feeling you're going to need it. Most of us locals never set eyes on that short-term husband. They were married and divorced before she even brought him home. I should tell you, half the single men in this town have asked her out and she's turned them all down. And now with all that's going on, she won't have time for a date."

"I'm still going to try. What could be more important than finding the right mate?"

Colby picked up the cabin key and the one the mayor gave him. He linked them together.

Digger gave a slight nod. "The back cabin's quieter. You'll find all you need there."

Colby took the flashlight the old man offered and said, "Good night."

Halfway to the door he turned back. "By the way, what is going on in Piper's life? Anything I should know before I reintroduce myself?"

Digger stood a bit taller. "Nothing except that the last fellow she went out with disappeared. Most folks think his body will be floating into the Gulf of Mexico any day now."

Colby called back as he opened the door. "Well, I won't be that easy to get rid of."

By the time he stepped back on the porch, the barrel-chested smoker was gone, but a half-smoked cigarette was still glowing on the gravel.

Colby had no doubt that Digger was watching him through the window wandering around looking for the cabin. Finally, he found the last cabin on a winding road that led close to the water.

A raccoon ran across the tiny porch jabbering, then disappeared.

Colby was too tired to even be startled. He'd spent most of the day walking the town, eating at every café that was busy and eavesdropping on conversations.

He unlocked the cabin door and stepped into his new home. Surprisingly, it was neat and clean. One room with a rock fireplace in the back corner and a tiny kitchen lining the left wall. There were no windows across the back, but the front would have a clear view of any car heading toward him.

Colby relaxed for the first time since he walked out of the back door of the hospital. He pulled off his shirt. The wound on his upper side had bled through the bandage, but not the plastic bag he'd taped over it.

He stripped off the covering and began to clean the two inches where a bullet had grazed him twenty-four hours ago. A souvenir left over from the last assignment.

As he worked, he dialed his cell phone, set it on the sink, and punched speaker.

"McBride?" The Ranger on the other end shouted. "About time you checked in."

"I made it to Honey Creek. Man, this place looks too much of a postcard picture to have trouble."

"Did you contact my sister?"

"I did. You forgot to tell me your sister's hot?"

"Forget it. She's not your type."

"I've already had this conversation with one Mackenzie tonight. Just as soon not repeat myself." Colby bit his lip as he pulled the gauze away from the wound at his side. "Overnight me my service weapon and two thousand in twenties. I'm staying at Fisherman's Lodge."

"I'll have it delivered. It'll look just like any other Amazon box."

"What time?"

"That's anyone's guess. Early, hopefully." The Ranger hesitated. "Be at the office when it comes if you can. I wouldn't put it past Digger to open it."

Colby slowly cleaned blood away. "Is the old man one of the good guys or one of the outlaws around here?"

"He's harmless, but nosy. Despite his age, in a fight I'd trust him to cover my back. Word in town is that during the war he was a real hero, but after telling the story so many times Digger polished it into the Captain America version. Piper may have called and asked Digger to put you in the back cabin. I think she trusts him more than I do."

The phone was silent for a few seconds, then Texas Ranger Max Mackenzie said, "Be careful, Colby. You're just there to collect information, watch what's going on, not arrest anyone. The sheriff's office might be mixed up in this somehow and if it is, we got to find out how. Boone Buchanan may be missing, but if he turns up in Texas, someone will recognize him. He's tall, good looking, and rich. Plus, he loves getting his picture in the paper. If I didn't know better I'd swear he was running for some office ten years in the future, and if you start asking too many questions you might find yourself in trouble."

"Believe me, I'm not planning on being used for target practice again. I'll check in with any news tomorrow. Someone in this town knows what's going on and I plan to find out who. If Boone Buchanan is hiding out in this place, it shouldn't be too hard to flush him out."

Colby clicked off the phone and dropped the bloody washcloth in the sink.

When he turned to pull out the supplies he'd bought at the pharmacy in the local Walmart, something moved just inside the back door of the cabin.

Out of habit he reached for a weapon. It wasn't there.

The shadow moved again, into the light.

Colby relaxed and tried to hide his injury. "Evening, Mayor. Glad to see you found your shoes." She had on sneakers now that didn't go with her boxy brown suit at all.

"Shut up and sit down on that bed." She advanced. "Why didn't you mention you were injured?" She lifted his arm so she could examine the wound on his side.

"Because your brother wouldn't have

hired me even though he knew I was the best man for this job." Colby faced her straight on. No use trying to hide the wound. "It's not as bad as it looks. Just a scratch, really."

She leaned down to stare at the bloody wound. "You've been walking all over my town bleeding?"

He sat on the bed. "Sorry I'm leaking on your perfect little town. I'll tell that street rat who shot me in the alley last night that you won't have me dripping all over your nice, clean sidewalks."

"Why did you take on this job? You look like you should be in the hospital." Her hand pushed his fingers away so she could see.

"I'd already accepted the assignment. The bullet was just a stray. No one noticed I was shot. It was a wild bullet and both guys firing in the gang war are dead. I figured this was as good a place to recuperate as any."

"You're crazy. It won't be worth the money you'll make if this gets infected. And you'll be in big trouble when you get back. Bullet wounds have to be reported."

"I'll worry about that later. Right now I'm here to make sure you are not in danger. I'm your guardian angel, Mayor."

"Then I'd better get you patched up."

He couldn't help but notice how anger made her green eyes darker.

Colby watched her go to work like he was a practice dummy at the first-aid station. She wasn't gentle, but she was efficient. This wasn't the first wound she'd treated, he'd bet. "I'm not doing this for the money or the thrill. I figured this might be my chance to get into the Rangers a few years sooner. Plus, I couldn't miss the opportunity to help you. Word is you'll run for governor one day."

Heading off any more questions from her, he added, "How'd you find me, and what are you doing here?" He considered making some kind of joke, but she was all business.

"I saw you going into Walmart as I was heading home from feeding the new preacher in town."

He fought down a yelp as she lathered antiseptic around the wound.

She continued, ignoring his protest. "I watched you through the store window. A man with no luggage buying bandages. No great brains needed to figure out you were hurt." She ripped tape to place over the fresh bandage. "For a moment I thought it was my fault. I brought you here, left you alone for an hour and you're wounded. Then I realized that couldn't be right. You couldn't have blown your cover that easy. Which leads me to one other conclusion. You showed up damaged." She ran tape across the bandage. "Where is the return ticket so I can send you back?"

Colby ignored the pain and stood. "You ever stop talking, PJ?"

"I . . ."

"I know. You don't like initials, but at the rate you talk that may be all I have time to get in between your lectures." Before she could comment, he went on. "I'm fine. Just a graze. And while we're on the subject of secrets, why didn't you tell me that old man Digger is in on our game?"

"What makes you think that?"

"Give me a break." Colby pulled on his shirt. "He switched keys when he noticed the keychain you gave me."

"All right, he was watching for you. I may have called and told him to give you this cabin. And if he saw the key I gave you, he'd just think you were going to use some of the fishing gear my brother stores here." She frowned. "But that's all he knows."

"Maybe my cover story convinced him," Colby added. "I'm just a man looking for love."

Colby went to the closet door along the back wall and unlocked it with the key she'd given him.

Inside, three stacked file boxes had been shoved in front of random fishing gear.

"I thought you'd like to read up on every detail we've found." The mayor smiled. "Have a good night."

After she left, Colby locked the storage closet and lay down on the bed. He was too exhausted to take off his clothes, or even turn off the light.

He realized he hadn't heard a car start or even footsteps on the gravel road.

One surprising fact. The mayor had come by boat. She was making sure no one saw her.

CHAPTER 7

Friday, almost midnight

PECOS

The school dance didn't turn out to be the moneymaker Pecos Smith thought it might be. Seems Honey Creek was too small a town to support even one Uber driver. He'd put up a dozen flyers and no one called.

Everyone knew Pecos had a pickup and no one wanted to ride in it. Over the whole month he'd had six jobs. One was to drive the Moody sisters to bingo. They were so large they wouldn't fit on the seat with him, so he had to make two trips both ways. One ride was for an old man from the nursing home who just wanted to drive out and look at his land. Two were calls from people who couldn't get their cars started.

One mother said she couldn't drive and hold her sick toddler, so she had Pecos take her to the clinic. The kid threw up all the way to the doctor and coming back. The mom didn't even give Pecos a tip.

He'd thought the last high school dance before summer would be his big night, but he simply sat outside watching kids go in and out of the gym that had been decorated in paper flowers and blinking lights.

Pecos had figured out in the past few weeks that most people who need rides spend the journey complaining. The Moody sisters complained about each other on their separate rides to bingo, then refused to pay for both trips since they'd only ordered one round-trip. The old man claimed his sons were ruining his land. The guy whose car wouldn't start swore it was his wife's fault, and that he was being slowly driven crazy.

Pecos had waited all night for a job to come through and not one pickup. Apparently everybody had someone to bring them and take them home.

Every time someone walked in or out of the gym doors he could see the flashing lights and hear the music from the dance. He thought about going into the dance, just for a few minutes, but what would he do. Dance? Not likely. Pecos was too tall and too thin. His hands and feet looked like they should belong to a man two sizes bigger. If he danced, he'd look like a string puppet with a few extra joints built in.

When his phone rang, he almost jumped high enough to hit his head on the roof of his pickup.

"Hello." This wouldn't be an official Uber job because it wasn't texted in; he hadn't figured that out yet, but he'd take cash if someone needed his service.

"Pecos, can you take me home?"

The girl on the other end sounded like she was crying. Great. Another complainer.

"I'm outside the front door ready to drive. Who is this?"

"Kerrie Lane. I'm at the back door of the gym. Can you drive around?"

"I'm on my way."

Pecos gunned the engine and circled the school. He was there before she closed the gym door.

She looked so small in the shadows.

He started to open his door to help her in, but she climbed up onto his bench seat before his boots hit the ground.

"Kerrie, you all right? You're shaking." Pecos had never seen her like this.

"Get me away from here," she whispered.

"Will do."

As he pulled away from the building, she took a deep breath and added, "Take the back way through the parking lots so we

92

won't pass the front door."

"I'll do that," he answered again. "It's almost eleven o'clock. Except for a few fights on the parking lot, the dance is pretty much over. I've been watching kids leaving since ten." He was rattling, but this quiet Kerrie made him nervous. He'd watched her for years and she was always sunshine. Not tonight, though.

"I know where you live." He wasn't sure if that knowledge was helpful or a little creepy to admit. He just wanted to be accommodating. Let her know she didn't have to talk if she didn't want to. "It's not far. I'll get you home fast, Kerrie." He glanced over at her, but her blond hair hid her face. "No charge for the last ride of the night. I was about to go home anyway."

That didn't cheer her up. In fact, she hadn't made a sound. She just stared out the window at the sleeping town.

"Did you like the dance?" Dumb question. If she'd liked the dance, she wouldn't be slipping out the back door alone. Which reminded him, where was her date? Girls like Kerrie always had a date to everything. But then, when she'd gone in, she hadn't been with anyone.

"I don't want to go home yet, Pecos," she finally whispered. "You said rides could buy fifteen minutes out by the river. I want to go there."

"All right." He turned toward a spot on the Brazos where fishing boats embarked. It was small and seldom used. Only, on a night like this when the thin moon reflected off the water, the place past the bend in the river looked haunted. Probably half the kids in town had gone out there at some time to tell ghost stories.

When he pulled off and parked, he cut the engine and took the keys. She caught his arm before he could step out. "Stay inside. Watch the water from here with me."

"Sure." He closed the door and they became no more than shadows. Well, she was a stone shadow in the night. He was more like a twitchy shadow.

To his surprise, Kerrie reached across the bench seat and took his hand. She didn't say a word; she just sat beside him with her fingers laced in his.

Imaginary conversations fired off like firecrackers in his brain, but he didn't say a word. He could be her partner, her confessor, her counselor, her friend. Maybe he was just someone to be there so she wouldn't be alone. He could be that. Company. He could be that too. Hell, he'd even kiss her if she wanted him to, though that seemed like a long shot.

Pecos didn't move. He just held her hand.

Finally, she pulled her hand away and said, "I'm ready to go home now."

He started the pickup and backed off the loading dock. He stared straight ahead until he pulled up to her house.

Without a word he climbed out and walked her to her door. Just part of the service, he told himself.

On the porch, she turned and said, "Thanks."

"Anytime," he answered.

Just before he headed back to the pickup, she leaned near and kissed him on the cheek. "You won't say anything, will you?"

"Nope."

He didn't look back until he was at the street.

She was gone. Had she really been there? He should have sworn he'd take her secret to the grave, but then, he wasn't sure what her secret was. Going home alone? Being sad? Holding hands with the only senior who'd never had a date? Not a great last night of high school for her.

Pecos closed his fingers of the hand she'd held. He thought he could still feel the warmth of her touch.

We shared a moment, he thought. I was

there for her. They might never mention it, but they'd remember. In a small way they had a bond.

CHAPTER 8

Saturday, May 26
Dawn

SAM

Sunshine cut between the thin curtains like shards of crystal slicing in, then shattering into tiny bits of glass on the polished wooden floor.

For a moment Sam Cassidy woke not knowing where he was. The facts came back one at a time.

The mayor had walked him back to the church after dinner last night.

She'd told him to drive around back and he couldn't miss the church's guest quarters. Then she waved, climbed in her huge SUV, and drove away.

He'd found his way around to the guest cottage for visiting preachers. He remembered seeing a sign as he unlocked the front

97

door. It said, May Your Time Be Blessed Here.

The only blessing he wanted was peace and he doubted he'd find it anywhere, even in this little town. He'd been here one day and hadn't felt one ounce of the peace his father talked about.

Calling himself a preacher, or a firefighter, or even a soldier didn't change anything inside, where his heart had once been, but he'd play this adventure out.

The bungalow looked like it was one foot too big to be a tiny house and had way too much gingerbread trim.

He'd been so tired he'd barely said good night to the mayor. He felt like his brain was already asleep and his feet were still walking, mindlessly searching for a bed. When he finally bumped into one, he whispered "Timber!" and was asleep before he hit.

Now, shading his eyes, Sam rolled over and swore. He'd slept ten hours and still felt bone-tired. Hell, he had a job to do. Tomorrow he'd have to give his first sermon. He was trying to wear his father's life and it didn't fit.

Slowly, he opened one eye. Last night he'd only turned on the hallway light to find the bedroom.

He forced himself to look around. It was worse than he'd thought. Cute, crafty, heavenly stuff was everywhere. The bedspread was made of quilt squares of cherubs playing harps; the night lamp was a waterfall flowing from heavenly clouds down to forest animals praying.

Sam flipped to his back and forced himself to look up. Yep, it was there. *Creation of Adam.* God touching the first man's finger. Worst rendition of Michelangelo's painting Sam had ever seen.

He closed his eyes, wishing he could go back to sleep. Sometime this morning he'd have to mention how cute the cottage was, and lying wouldn't come that easy. It did occur to him that the place had probably been decorated by the Over-the-Hill Sunday school class, and they must have all thought it was just darling.

Or, maybe the church hated single ministers. Sam guessed staying here would drive even the most determined bachelor to marry so he could get into the family parsonage.

He glared at his watch. It may be Saturday, but by nine, people would be expecting to see the new pastor. Sam had stepped into this fantasy of glimpsing back in time. Living his father's life for a few weeks. The problem seemed to be, everyone would be watching. He'd have to live a life that he'd once thrown away.

He'd been educated to do this, Sam reminded himself. Five years of seminary. He'd watched his father. How hard could it be?

No more cussing. No more three-day drunks. No more picking up a date for the night and then forgetting her name at dawn.

For the next two weeks he needed to be always smiling. Be interested in people. Hell. That wasn't going to be easy. He'd spent years walking among all kinds of people and being little more than a ghost in the crowds.

Tomorrow, he'd be at the front with all the congregation staring at him.

He stumbled out of bed and stormed toward the bathroom.

Time to get started. Maybe a shower and shave would help him look a bit more heaven bound.

The house had been built in a square. The living room, kitchen, and bedroom were equal fourths of the place, with the bathroom and closet taking up the last fourth. This plan made all the rooms seem small, except the bathroom, which was just about the right size for his over six feet height.

Sam barely noticed the decorations and paintings. Every room was lined with plastic plants, statues, and colorful boxes stacked in corners so not one inch of the baseboards showed. The effect made each room look a few feet smaller than it was.

Closing the bathroom door, Sam relaxed in the one room that had space to breathe. He'd spent so many years in dorms and barracks, anything but the basics seemed too much. He half expected to see bars of soap in the shape of crosses and Bible verses on the toilet paper.

Surprise, nothing. Just a simple bathroom with white towels.

He stripped and showered until the water turned cold. Then, he walked nude around the house, letting his body air-dry. He found his suitcase just inside the front door. Three changes of clothes were all he packed. One casual slacks and a white shirt. One dark suit with a proper collar, and a clean pair of jeans and western shirt with a bolo tie. One pair of boots. One pair of black shoes.

The lean wardrobe reminded him of his father. His dad had been a traveling preacher like his father and his father before him. The first Cassidy rode a mule from town to town in Missouri; the next one started preaching in the Oklahoma Territory.

Sam's father would take on a congregation for a few months until they found someone, or he'd fill in during illnesses. Now and then they'd travel all day to some church having a revival. Sam had loved those times. It was like a vacation. They usually got to stay in a hotel and everyone seemed to want them to come to dinner.

His dad never owned more than three suits or two good pair of shoes, but his parents had been happy. His mom used to say that they made friends wherever they went and she was right. At Christmas time they'd string cards all around the living room, then his mother would talk about each family they'd met along their journey as if they were kin.

Dressed in the white shirt and slacks, Sam walked over to the back door of the church still thinking how this life must be in his blood, but he couldn't hear the calling.

Saints Church wasn't anything big or fancy, but there was a polish about the place. The building had been lovingly cared for over the years.

The office was to the right when he stepped in the back entrance, and to his surprise the rooms were empty. Sam expected to find at least one of the greeters from last night waiting.

When he walked back into the hallway someone came through the back door loaded down with boxes. Boxes and legs were all he saw before she plowed into him.

"You all right?" a female yelled.

"Yeah," he answered.

"Then get out of my way." Whoever was behind the box was angry.

Sam decided to take off the top box.

One look and he stepped back. He hated redheads. This one was short with flaming red hair brushed tumbleweed style and anger flashing in her blue eyes.

"Well, don't just hold that box. Help me carry it into the office." She pushed past him, poking him with the corner of the box she carried. "I would have made it fine by myself if you'd had the brains to get out of the way."

Sam thought of saying he was sorry, but he didn't want to show any weakness to this creature. He followed her into the office and dropped the box where she told him to.

Finally, she turned to face him, straightening as if she could grow a foot to his height. "I'm Anna Presley and I'm on a mission to make the world a better place. Who are you and what do you do beside act like a hall monitor?"

Sam laughed. She had to be one of the nuts in town the mayor mentioned. "I'm Reverend Cassidy and I mostly just try to talk others into saving the world."

Anna turned toward the door. "Well, if you ever want to make yourself useful, I run a suicide hotline weekday mornings in the basement, host AA meetings on Wednesday night, and manage an after-school program from three to five during the school year. I'm getting the fall curriculum set up today."

"It's May."

She raised an eyebrow. "You read that somewhere?"

Sam couldn't stop smiling. "Cut me some slack, lady. This is my first day."

"I don't have time to waste my time. There is too much to do. Before long we'll have to start the school supplies drive. Then the fall coat drive. Before that's finished the church needs to collect presents for the . . ." She frowned. "Oh, never mind. You'll be gone long before then."

"One question, Anna Presley." Sam felt he had to get in one question. "You have a lot of suicides on weekday mornings?"

"Not many, but I'm standing ready if they come in. Besides, that's the only time I have open."

"Can I help you with the boxes?" If he believed in reincarnation he might think he was looking at Joan of Arc.

"No." Anna grabbed a pile of mail out of a nook and bumped her way past him. "You just go on about your hall wandering. I'll check on you later to see if you need water." Then she was gone. Sam blinked. Anna Presley was too short, redheaded, bossy, and definitely crazy, but she was also interesting.

He walked on down the hallway to a small kitchen that opened into a parlor set up with a dozen long tables. One of the boys he'd seen following the drunk last night was sitting alone at one of the tables. In the light the kid looked about nine or ten. Dirty. Thin.

Sam grinned. "Where'd you park your wagon?"

"Outside." The kid didn't look up. "I'm supposed to be here."

Sam moved closer. "I'm not. You going to kick me out?"

The boy raised his gaze, a smile fighting to keep from breaking out. "No, I'll let you stay, but I doubt Miss Stella will."

Sam pulled out the chair across the table from the kid. He had sandy hair and intelligent eyes.

Might as well meet the natives, Sam decided. Maybe it would be best to start with a little one. "I'm new in town. Don't know nothing. Does this café serve coffee?"

The kid shook his head. "You are lost. This isn't a café. This is a church."

"Oh, thanks. I didn't see any sign when I came in the back door." Sam stood and walked to the kitchen. When he opened the refrigerator door, he wasn't surprised to see a dozen boxes of juice.

"How about we have a snack while we wait?" He grabbed four boxes of apple juice and two bags of chips. "It's all right. The mayor told me to help myself."

When he set his loot in the center of the table, the kid nodded his head. Sam asked, "What's your name?"

"Gabe. I work here. Every Saturday I deliver bags to the shut-ins." He pointed to a line of paper grocery bags on a counter. "I have to wait until Miss Stella gets here and tells me the route. It's the same as last week probably, but I still have to wait for orders. Miss Stella says that's the way things work."

"What's in the bags?" Sam opened one of the juices and passed it to Gabe.

The boy drank it before he answered. "Milk, oatmeal, three cans of soup, a small

106

loaf of bread, cookies, and tuna. Sometimes a dozen eggs from the Moody sisters. They got more chickens than they can count. Sometimes honey from the Lane Farm or leftover scones from the bakery."

"You get paid for the deliveries?"

Gabe shook his head. "No, but I get one of the bags to take home."

Sam found the kid fascinating. "You mind if I go along? I'd like to meet a few people in town. Besides, Miss Stella hasn't told me what to do today so I might as well tag along with you."

Gabe tilted his head. "You aren't long on praying, are you? I got a dozen deliveries."

"Nope. Was the last guy?"

"Yeah, I was thinking the next Saturday might roll around before we finished the deliveries." Gabe frowned. "He wasn't as bad as the stand-in who came next. That preacher sniffed at the end of every sentence and he squirreled away tissues by the dozens. I wouldn't have been surprised if he didn't have a few stuffed in his socks."

"You call the preachers the stand-ins?"

"It's easier than trying to remember their names. I don't know if none of them want to stay or if the church doesn't offer them a long-time job. Near as I can tell they all walk out faster than they walked in."

Sam rarely talked to kids, but he figured if he hung around two weeks he'd probably learn a great deal from this one. "Any other rules I should follow if I tag along with you?"

"You pull the wagon half the time." Gabe grinned. "The first half."

"Deal." Sam passed the chips and another juice across the table.

Five minutes later they were loaded up. The wagon was packed and Stella had leaned her head in the parlor long enough to tell Gabe to get going. Same route.

She didn't say a word to Sam, but her thin eyebrows raised. Probably because he was still in town.

He couldn't help but wonder what it was that drove preachers off. Maybe her stern looks.

Gabe stood. "I'd better get going. You still coming?"

"Of course." Sam picked up four bags. Gabe picked up one and led the way to the back door, where his wagon waited. Two more trips and two more juice boxes and they were on their way.

Gabe walked beside Sam and told him all he knew about each person before they reached their house.

"The first was a trucker before he got the

big C. He's always asking me to move something or climb up where he can't reach. Then he gives me a dollar and says a man should be paid for his work, so I take it."

Sam talked to the man while Gabe put up groceries and took out trash. Sam kept the prayer to one minute.

A half block later the next delivery went about the same, only the ninety-year-old woman didn't offer Gabe money. She just sat in her rocker and knitted while Sam fought the urge to count the cats wandering around.

As they walked away Gabe said, "Last Christmas she made me a blanket. Real pretty one."

The next house was old and rambling. They passed through two unlocked iron doors to get to the back entrance. Gabe whispered, "This is Mr. Winston's home. He's rich, they say, and he got there by never wasting a dime. He put in for the weekly bags and the church don't ask any questions so he gets one."

An old man dressed in a worn suit finally answered the door. "Hello, young Gabe," he bellowed. "Please come in." Watery gray eyes looked up at Sam. When he smiled, the old man seemed to have wrinkles on top of wrinkles. "I see you've brought a guest. I'll pull down another cup." Winston stepped back as if he were the butler and not the owner of this house that had to be worth a great deal. "Come in, gentlemen. I'm honored to have company this fine day."

While the old man pulled another cup from an open shelf, he motioned for them to sit around a table pushed into a small bay window off the kitchen.

"It's not cold today, but I thought there was enough of a breeze to have our last cup of tea before summer." Winston smiled at Gabe. "I've been letting yours cool, young sir."

Winston removed the tea bag from the first cup.

Gabe straightened as a wrinkled hand moved the cup toward him.

Winston dropped the tea bag into the second cup.

The old man turned to Sam. "I'm Mr. Winston, sir, and you must be the visiting preacher. The fifth in six months, I'm thinking. I do believe, and the first to visit me. Of course, I'll be seeing you tomorrow. I come every week."

"Thank you for welcoming me into your home." As Sam took his seat, Winston moved the second cup in front of Sam,

110

pulled the tea bag once more, and plopped it into the third cup of hot water.

They talked of the weather and Winston wished Sam well. Then Gabe helped put up the food and carried the three cups to the sink. Everything Sam could see was old and worn, but still polished clean.

When Sam and the kid reached the sidewalk outside the big house, Gabe whispered, "Next week we'll get lemon water with ice. It's summer."

On and on they went. Each house welcomed Sam. When Gabe pulled the wagon back toward the church with one bag left, Sam smiled down at the kid. "I'm glad I came along with you. I learned a great deal. Will I see you tomorrow?"

Gabe shook his head. "Sunday is my mom's only day off. We all spend the time together. She sleeps late. We help her do all the errands and chores. Then we play games or go for a walk down by the river. She says she thinks all week what she's going to do with our time."

Gabe turned off a block from the church, pulling his wagon behind him. Sam smiled thinking he'd just gone on a journey into kindness.

When Sam went back to his real job and saw people in trouble, he'd think of Gabe.

Maybe it would give him a bit of peace.

He was almost to the steps of the church when he saw the woman who was perched on the top step. At first glance she looked like a teenager with jeans and a T-shirt tied just above her waist on one side, but as he moved closer he saw she was older, well into her twenties.

"Are you lost, miss?"

She frowned at him. "I don't need saving, Preacher. Go away."

Sam almost laughed, but she didn't look like she was joking. "I was thinking more of giving you a map if I could find one."

"Oh. I thought . . ."

He smiled. "I know what you thought." He sat down about five feet away. "I'll ask again. Is there something I can do to help you?"

She stared at him. "I don't need any preaching. I'm not planning a wedding or a funeral."

He could see anger in her eyes and there was a nervousness about her, but Sam had no idea what to say.

She looked down. "That's not true. I may need a funeral. I am planning to kill someone if I could find him. But I can't go look because my car is across the street out of gas. Just my luck, it stops in front of a

112

church and not a gas station."

Sam wasn't sure if offering to push her car to the nearest gas station would count as a good deed or a bad one. He decided to change the subject. "Who are you going to kill?"

"My secret *boyfriend*. I've texted him a dozen times to come get me and bring gas. We've been *dating* for months. He said our love was too special to share with anyone. Now he doesn't share it with even me. He hasn't answered his phone in three days and this weekend was going to be special."

"Well, if he's your boyfriend and you've been dating, maybe you'll need the wedding. After all, several months is plenty of time to get to know him." Sam did his best to look innocent. A "do the right thing" kind of preacher.

"I know him real well and I don't want to marry him. He's handsome, but his best feature is his wallet. He's fun to go places with, but I'm not the kind of girl to marry for money."

"That's good to know."

She nodded. "My momma told me once that a woman who marries for money will have to earn every penny. She's been married five times so she should know."

Sam figured if he talked to this woman

much longer, his brains would be scrambled. "I've got a gas can in my car. I could give you enough to get to the station, then you might want to think things out. You might decide never seeing this guy again would be a blessing."

"Only problem is my boyfriend has vanished before I got the chance. It's even on the news like he was some big shot or something. How are we going to keep our love a secret when his face is in the paper?"

Sam stood and offered his hand to her. "Good luck . . ."

She took the hint. "Marcie." She accepted his hand and didn't let go. "You won't tell anyone that you helped me, will you, Preacher? It's in your job description. Right?"

"Right." He stood and added, "I'll get the gas for you and if you need to talk anytime the next few weeks, I'll be here."

She nodded once, then stretched her long legs over several of the steps as if preparing for a wait.

When he returned, Marcie and her car were gone. Sam sat back down on the steps thinking about her. She looked worried, fighting mad, but in her eyes there was pain. This no-good secret boyfriend had hurt her, and Sam wished he'd known what to say to make her feel better.

CHAPTER 9

Noon, Saturday

PIPER

The mayor did her Saturday morning duties as if it had been an ordinary week. No
make-believe fiancé disappearing, no sheriff
wandering off, no undercover state trooper
practicing to be a detective.

She could almost believe all was well in
her little town.

Her first duty for the weekend was simple
but not easy. She appeared on the local
eight o'clock radio talk show for five minutes. Her mission — to announce what was
happening in Honey Creek. She usually
mentioned any charity fund-raisers, wed-
dings, or the recently departed. Nothing too
heavy, the station manager had said, but it
seemed he forgot to tell the DJ. Rattling
Randy seemed to enjoy making his guests
uncomfortable, if not downright angry. He

had few friends in town, but his ratings were the highest the station had ever had. He tended to ask the questions no one else would.

As soon as Piper had read the weekly happenings including the Fair on the Square to welcome summer, Randy jumped in with his first question. "According to the Dallas papers, you were involved with a man named Boone Buchanan, a big-time lawyer. Folks out there in the land of honey are talking about why this lawyer went missing this week. His bright red two-year-old BMW was found floating a mile downstream from Honey Creek. Want to tell us what you know about that, Mayor?"

Piper had been preparing for this question all week, practicing her answers with every person who walked in her office. "First, Randy, thank you for letting me set the facts straight. Boone is a friend. Our grandfathers were friends and I've seen him occasionally since I was a child. We have attended a few charity and political functions in Austin together, but nothing more. We are not romantically involved."

She straightened. She'd told the truth. Now all she could hope for was that someone was listening. A memory of Boone at the age of ten flashed through her mind.

They'd spent the afternoon playing Monopoly. When he'd lost, Boone had upended the board, sending all the pieces flying.

Randy didn't let a breath pass before he shot the next questions. "Have any idea why he was in town? Was he coming to see you? Driving in for a wild weekend? Maybe he made a wrong turn and simply dropped into the Brazos River."

"I didn't know he was in town last week and I'm not familiar with his driving skills."

"What about the sheriff? Did you send him out to find your boyfriend?"

"I thought part of the sheriff's job was finding people. If Mr. Buchanan was in town and driving his fancy car when it went into the water, it makes sense that the sheriff would go looking. I, however, did not send him, nor do I have any idea of the sheriff's or Boone's whereabouts." She stared the DJ down. "And, once again, Buchanan is not my boyfriend."

Randy showed his teeth, this time predator style. "By the way, Mayor, I'm sure our listeners would like to know who your last lover was? Don't you think you're a bit old to have a boyfriend?"

Piper hadn't lived with three generations of politicians without learning a thing or two. "I'll be happy to let the people of

118

Honey Creek know when Mr. Right comes along. Until then, my first and only love is my hometown, Honey Creek."

Randy frowned as he glanced at the clock. He didn't have time to ask another question.

The last minute the mayor always answered questions from callers. The town was so small Piper recognized most by their voice.

Two people complained about the drainage problem on Main when it rained. One asked her to repeat the library hours, and the last one, toothless Harry Sizemore, asked her for a date.

She left the windowless box of a radio station and walked a block to the weekly farmers' market. It was too early in the season for many fruits, but vegetables packed the booths, along with honey, soaps, and all kinds of handmade goods. Here people were friendly and conversations floated along with the smells of fresh flowers and homemade fried pies.

People came from all over the valley to sell their goods. It was easy to tell the locals from the tourists from the big cities like Dallas and Austin. The locals bartered with money rarely changing hands. Tourists paid the asking price and walked away, marveling at their finds.

"Morning, Mr. Winston." Piper smiled at the old man dressed in his summer blue suit with a gray linen vest. The collar of his white starched shirt might be a bit frayed, but his shoes were polished and his beard perfectly trimmed.

"Good morning, Mayor. May I say you look lovely today?"

"You may." Winston might be more than twice her age, but he still had a twinkle in his eyes for the ladies. "I'd like one of your baskets full of cherries."

"For you, half price." He winked.

Everyone knew Mr. Winston bought his berries from the produce manager at United. Winston simply took them home, washed them, put them in cute little paper baskets, and sold them for double the price to the tourists. Near the end of the market morning, he'd trade two baskets for a dozen eggs, one basket for a homemade peach fried pie or a fourth pound of homemade butter.

Surprisingly, he also bought a small flowering plant. It seemed odd because he had only weeds growing around his big Tudor home that had stood out in the town for more than fifty years.

"Thank you, Mr. Winston," Piper said as

she carefully slipped the cherries into her shopping basket and turned to finish her walk along the west end of the small market.

A shadow blocked the sun and Piper looked up.

She forced a blank expression as if she didn't know the man who'd stepped up behind her. Worn jeans, western boots, and a plaid shirt. His curly hair brushed against his collar as his amber eyes studied her. Wolf eyes, that she hadn't seen clearly last night. A touch of cinnamon color blended in his curls.

Trooper Colby McBride was handsome when he wasn't in shadows or bleeding.

"May I help you, sir?" Winston said from just behind Piper. His tone more formal than friendly now.

"No, thank you, partner. I'm just here to say hello to this pretty lady. It's been ten years since I've seen her and I swear she's more beautiful than I remember."

Piper continued to stare at Colby Mc-Bride. Of course she knew who he was, but she did her best to pretend. She'd talked to him on the widow's walk last night atop city hall. She'd patched up a bloody wound in his cabin. He'd been all business, all professional on the top of her building. Later he'd been angry when she slipped into his cabin.

Now he was grinning and rocking back on his heels as if he were waiting for her to give him a hug.

Except for that comment about her having cute toes, she'd thought him well trained with a bit of kooky mixed in. Only now she decided he wasn't as polished as she'd thought. This part he was playing might turn out to be hard to handle. She wanted him to solve this mystery, but she didn't know how far she wanted to play in to his goofy cover story.

Today he was all smiles, and those magnetizing eyes seemed to be looking at her with longing. His voice had more of a country tone. The wide grin made him look like he'd drowned one too many brain cells with whiskey.

"Oh, come on, darlin'. Surely it'll take more than ten years for you to forget me."

She had the urge to slap that grin off his face. The man was looking at her like she was dessert.

"Ten years ago," his voice rose slightly like a growing echo, "you were about to marry my best friend. I thought I'd get one kiss in before you two tied the knot. You didn't take it well as I remember. Banned me from your wedding." Colby lowered his voice slightly as the people turned silent so they could

122

hear. "Now, was that fair, darlin'?"

Piper nodded a polite farewell to Winston and started to walk away, but Colby followed her, sidestepping like a salesman determined to make the deal. He didn't seem to notice that all locals within ten feet were watching.

"Oh, come on, Piper. Give me a break. I drove halfway across Texas to see you again. You're the one girl that I could never get out of my mind. You didn't even give me a chance to say I was sorry. It was just one kiss, but it stayed forever in my memory."

Piper knew this was a game. Nothing more than an act to give Colby a reason to be in town, to ask questions, to be seen with her. But he was so corny she had to fight to keep from rolling her eyes back.

She managed to keep walking, playing her part. "Go away. I'm not interested in getting reacquainted." Even if they weren't acting, she wasn't interested. Her husband had left too many scars on her heart.

When Colby kept following behind her, she suddenly whirled and said in a voice just loud enough for several people to hear, "What do you want?"

Colby looked confused, as if he hadn't thought that far ahead. "I just want to talk to you," he finally said. "That's all. I'll be a perfect gentleman. We'll stay out in public. I just want to get to know you so you'll figure out I'm not some nutcase." He made his goofy grin again. "Maybe kiss and make up after all this time?"

When she didn't laugh at his joke, he wheedled on. "You don't have to go out with me, just have a cup of coffee. I'm available for anything from an ice cream to a one-night stand, Piper."

Now the crowd of locals was circling them as though they thought the mayor and the cowboy were putting on a street show. Half had paused, ready to jump in if they needed to protect her, and the other half looked like they felt sorry for the poor guy standing in the middle of the farmers' market with his hat in his hand.

"All right, I'll have coffee with you, but if you touch me in any way, I will file assault charges on you. Do you understand that, Colby?"

He nodded so fast she feared his head might be loose. "At least you remembered my name. Any chance you've thought of me over the years?"

"Not once," she snapped. "Wait for me just outside at the Honey Creek Café. It's at the end of the road if you head toward the creek. You can't miss it. I'll be there within an hour and we will have one cup of coffee."

He crammed his hat on his head and walked away whistling. Then, as if doing an encore, he looked back and added, "One cup of coffee might turn out to last a lifetime, darlin'."

"Idiot," she whispered. He'd made a fool of himself in front of half the town.

She turned to the crowd and realized all were watching him leave. Colby might have played the part of a love-sick cowboy, but he'd won them over. Maybe he wasn't as dumb as she'd thought. Her loyal neighbors would probably help him if they got a chance.

The gardener who sold tomato plants and aprons made out of grain sacks whispered, "Give him a chance, dear. It won't hurt to talk to him. He's a good-looking cowboy. A curly-haired man with amber eyes wouldn't be bad to wake up to." She chuckled and moved away.

Piper took her finds to the car, aware that people were talking about her. His show had only given them more to gossip about. The people in Austin might think she was engaged to Boone Buchanan, but the locals knew differently. They'd seen him in the company of her father in papers, but his fancy sports car had never been parked at her office or at Widows Park, where she lived with her grandmother and half a dozen widowed relatives. Buchanan had never taken her out to dinner anywhere around here or people would have talked. And last, Piper rarely left town on the weekends. A woman, even a mayor, would take a few days off now and then if she had somewhere to go.

All the people in town would have to do was look up at her window to see that she was working late. Weekdays and weekends.

Piper pulled into her parking place at city hall and went up to her office.

After an hour, she drove over to the Honey Creek Café. If he was still there, she'd play his game and talk to him.

More than likely the trooper turned investigator had decided to give up. She wanted him to do his job, not get involved in her life.

To her surprise, Colby was sitting out alone at the gazebo, his chair facing the water. Since it was Saturday, and too late for breakfast, most of the café was empty. Three men stood beside him, talking low.

When Colby caught sight of her, he rose, dusting blueberry muffin crumbs off his shirt. "Mayor Mackenzie, I'd like you to

126

meet my three new friends. They happened to all be named Jeff."

Piper nodded. "Good morning, gentlemen."

As she stepped closer, Colby pulled out her chair and said to the Jeffs, "Thanks for the advice. I'll fill you in later if any of your ideas work. Right now, if you don't mind, I'd like to talk to my lady alone."

The oldest Jeff in the crowd whispered to the other two, "How about we meet up at the Pint and Pie after five." He slapped Colby on the back. "That is, if you don't have a date."

The other two Jeffs laughed. Then they all moved off, leaving Colby and Piper to their meeting.

"I'm not your lady," Piper said under her breath. "You're laying it on a bit thick."

Colby simply shrugged. "We're far enough away that no one will hear us now, but you can bet they are watching." He kissed her on her head as he passed behind her and she batted him away as if he were a fly.

They sat in silence until the waitress took their order of coffee and brought two cups. As she took her time refilling the waters, Colby murmured just loud enough for the waitress to hear. "I've been hoping you might kiss me hello and we could make up.

127

Ten years is a little long to hold a grudge."

He reached for her hand, but she pulled it away.

Colby tried again. "Being here with you is like a dream. I measure every woman I meet to you and none come close. I swear, Piper, I could drown in your green eyes."

Piper scanned the windows of the beautiful home-turned-café behind Colby to see if anyone was watching.

As the waitress walked slowly away, Colby added, "I promise if you give me a chance, I'll love you till the day I die."

"Not even one chance, cowboy," she whispered.

Colby winked at her. "How about a one-night stand, Mayor?"

Piper fought down a laugh.

Colby sat with his back to the audience, but she saw them all smiling. The gardener's words drifted through her mind. *A curly-haired man with amber eyes wouldn't be bad to wake up to.*

It had been so long since she'd waken up to any man. Boone had asked once if she'd like to end the night at his place. She'd said no and he'd shrugged as if he'd suggested going for ice cream.

Maybe her rejection hurt his pride. Men like him must rarely go home alone. The only time he drew close was when cameras were near, and she'd figured out early that Boone would never love anyone but himself.

Colby's voice came low and direct, pulling her from her thoughts as he leaned closer. "Is it working? People have left their tables and are practically lined up watching."

"Why am I not surprised? How about we give them a show?" She touched his jaw thinking he truly was a good-looking man but somehow she got the feeling he didn't know it.

Colby grinned and leaned an inch closer. "Everyone will want to talk to me after this. I plan to let them coach me on how to court the mayor, who they all love by the way. Then I'll start asking about the town and the people like I might settle here if you ever smiled at me."

"Be careful, Trooper. Half the people in the town would walk around the truth to tell a good story. Honey Creek may sound sweet, even innocent, but we were founded by outlaws and people who didn't fit in to the standard for their time."

"I know, but usually there is an ounce of truth in even gossip. I can play along. I've got a gift. I can spot a lie."

"You've studied the subject, have you?"

She glared at him and folded her arms as she sat back trying to look like she was arguing with him now.

"Sure. It's called interrogation. By the way, folding your arms over your breasts is telling anyone watching that you're not interested in what I have to say."

"What do you have to say?" She didn't move her arms. "And, I'm folding my arms over my chest."

"Oh, sorry. Maybe we could address that subject at a later time."

"Not likely." Something about him brought out a violent side in her. The urge to knock her coffee cup against his head flashed in her mind. If there were more men like him, she might become a serial killer.

Colby, totally unaware of her thoughts, leaned back in his chair and waited a long moment before leaning forward and whispering, "I walked the river at dawn." His voice was direct. Facts, no pretend.

She frowned. "A dozen investigators have already done that. I thought the area was roped off."

"Where they pulled the car out was marked 'No Trespassing.' So was a place where it looked like someone crawled out of the water, but no one was around. I was careful not to contaminate those spots." He

130

drank his coffee and slowly slid his hand across the table until their fingertips touched.

She jerked away.

Colby straightened and kept his voice low. "What kind of shoes did your boyfriend wear?"

She fired up. "He's not my . . ." Realizing Colby must have heard her on the radio this morning, she answered simply, "I have no idea."

"Any hint what he was doing around Honey Creek?"

"No. As far as I know he never came here. We're not a stopover place to anywhere. Once, when we were kids, he came with his dad for a barbeque at my granddad's ranch. You know the kind where they roast a pig and sit around a campfire. Smoke, fire ants, and snakes. I was about eight. I threw a fit and refused to go. A photo of Boone and my grandfather made the Dallas papers."

"I can see that happening."

"The picture hitting the Dallas paper?" she asked.

"No, you throwing a fit." He smiled a real grin. "Back to our problem. According to the reports you delivered to my cabin last night, Boone had been in court until after seven the day he disappeared.

"Assuming he drove straight here, and the car was discovered in the water a little before midnight, there is a good chance he didn't stop to change clothes."

"Makes sense."

"But according to the footprints found, whoever climbed onto the bank and walked away was wearing sneakers."

"Maybe he had the shoes in his car, or maybe he stopped and changed clothes." Colby seemed to be putting the pieces together in his mind. "If he left Austin at say seven, the traffic might still be slow. An hour to get out of town, three or four hours to get here depending if he was speeding. Almost midnight. Plenty of time to run the car in the river and climb out and be long gone before the car was seen."

She shook her head. "What does changing shoes have to do with anything?"

"If he changed shoes, he planned it all. And, for some reason despite the long day in court he had to do it that night."

"Or he stopped somewhere and another person drove the car into the water. Boone doesn't seem the type to get muddy."

When she remained silent in thought, Colby leaned closer to her and whispered, "Good point. Question is, why did he pick that night and why here? There are lots of lakes or streams near Austin."

They heard a laugh from behind them. "Sit back in your chair. Everyone watching thinks that you're making progress whispering in my ear."

"Am I?" He remained close.

"We've got a date tonight, Mayor. We're going out to where the car was found. We're going to walk the bank just like he did four nights ago. We're going to see what he saw, or maybe see what he couldn't."

She nodded. "I'll pick you up at eleven."

"Come by boat. I'll be waiting behind my cabin." He stood and leaned in to kiss her cheek.

She turned away as she stood.

So low that no one could have heard him, he added, "Don't wear a suit, PJ. Wear jeans."

As they walked away, Colby made an okay sign with his fingers and yelled at the men who'd been talking to him. "See you at Pint and Pie tonight."

When they reached the street, she stood away from him, making it plain that they were not *together.* "Don't you already have a date with me tonight?"

"Yeah, but the boys I'm meeting will be too drunk to follow us by nine. Then I'll be alone with you so I can fill you in on local theories on what happened to your last boyfriend."

Piper gave a quick wave and turned back toward her SUV. She didn't correct him again that Boone was not her boyfriend or that Colby was not or would ever be her new boyfriend. She could tell the trooper got a kick out of needling people.

Or maybe it was just her? If she wasn't so worried, she might have to admit it was fun pretending.

CHAPTER 10

Late Saturday morning

PECOS

Pecos Smith slept until almost noon on Saturday. Something he never did. He'd made it home by midnight, but he couldn't get to sleep. His almost date with Kerrie Lane still floated thick in his mind. Some might say it was just a job taking her home after the dance. His one fare for the night, but she didn't offer to pay him. It could have been just a favor, but she'd kissed him on the cheek and held his hand.

Now that sounded more like a date, he thought, as he rolled out of bed and scratched his wild hair. Glancing in the mirror, he decided it looked almost as good as it would have if he'd used a comb. So he pulled on last night's clothes and headed downstairs.

Reliving every moment of being with

Kerrie in his mind, Pecos stumbled into the long ranch kitchen decorated in garage sale finds. "Got any breakfast left, Mom?"

His mother, round as she was tall, frowned at him. "No. What do you think this is, a diner? I got better things to do than keep a skillet warm in case you wander in. You're finished with school now, so it's about time you pulled your weight around here."

As Pecos sat down, she walked by and slapped him on the back of his head as if he were a kid and not a grown man about to graduate from high school. "You've got chores to do before you have lunch so you might as well get to it."

Pecos knew there was no use arguing. Mom's sunny disposition vanished years ago, probably about the time she had him at forty-four. He stood, took an apple from the bowl on the counter, and walked out into the cloudy Saturday.

He had four older brothers, two in the army, one in the marines, and one was lost somewhere in California. They all left home soon after high school and he was starting to see why. His parents considered them free labor on the farm as soon as they were old enough to feed the chickens. From there the chores piled on until the next brother could help.

All the boys could plow and work the small fields where their dad raised grain by the time they were twelve. When his first son Tucson was old enough to milk cows, Dad decided to buy a barn full.

His brothers reminded Pecos every time they came home that being in the army was easier than farming and in the army you got days off even from war.

As a slow rain began to fall, Pecos stayed around the barn working. He knew his dad would be mad at him for not getting up to help with the milking at dawn. The two men he'd hired were not near as good as Pecos.

Every time a brother left, more chores were added to Pecos's workload. There were times when he'd missed school to get it all done.

His oldest brother, the marine, came home one Christmas and saw what was happening. The morning before he was leaving for his second tour of duty overseas, Tucson followed their dad out to the barn.

Pecos silently followed them through the freezing dawn just to see what was going on.

Tucson looked like a warrior in his uniform. His bag was packed by the door, but there was apparently one last thing he needed to do.

From the back of the barn Pecos couldn't hear much of what he said. His nose was two inches from their dad's as he talked.

For the first time Pecos thought Dad looked old, very old. He was now shorter than all his sons, and the anger lines on his face dug deep into his tanned skin like tattoos.

As Pecos watched, their father's face turned red and his arms rose and lowered at his sides as if he thought he could fly. But the old man never struck his oldest son like he had when Tucson was small.

The marine wouldn't have taken it now. To his credit, Tucson never raised his voice. He never lifted a hand, but his words came fast. Dad seemed to shrink a bit. When Tucson turned and marched away, Pecos saw his father lower his head, beaten without a blow.

The old man never mentioned the barn conversation to anyone, as far as Pecos knew.

After that, Dad let Pecos go to school. They sold most of the cows and leased out all but one field. Maybe his parents were tired of farming, as well as parenting, or maybe they were just slowing down, but they seemed to forget about their youngest.

For the past two years the only time they

noticed him was on Saturday and then their communications were usually notes of to-do lists on the refrigerator and another on the barn door. If he didn't finish on Saturday, he'd work Sunday.

If Pecos didn't make it home for a meal, there were never leftovers waiting. Any allowance was forgotten. Sometimes he felt like he was invisible or less important than a chicken. They knew he'd fly the coop as soon as possible and they didn't seem to care.

Thank goodness his brothers had passed down the old pickup. Pecos often hauled feed for the neighbors. One day's work hauling would buy his school lunches for a month. Any other jobs would buy clothes or pocket money.

Pecos figured he liked being ignored more than being yelled at. Most of the time he worked alone, and if his dad did show up he usually complained. Only today, his dad left the barn as soon as Pecos showed up, and headed back to the house.

By six the rain had stopped and Pecos finished both Dad's and Mom's lists. After moving in and out of the rain all afternoon, it felt grand to take a warm shower. He dressed in clean jeans, his best T-shirt, and a jean jacket that was a hand-me-down from

Tucson. He had nowhere to go, no friends he wanted to hang out with, but he wasn't staying home.

With ten dollars in his pocket, he drove the three miles to town. The air smelled of more rain, but he rolled the windows down and let the cool breeze blow over him. Some of the seniors were having graduation parties tonight, backyard barbeques, or pool parties. Some had relatives coming in for the weekend just to watch them receive their diplomas. His parents hadn't mentioned going to the ceremony, so he was sure there would be no party.

Dad commented that he'd seen one graduation and they were all the same.

Three of his brothers sent letters saying they couldn't get leave to come home. They also each sent a hundred-dollar bill with the letter. Pecos had hidden the three bills with the six hundred he'd saved. He'd walk before he'd spend his someday money even on gas.

He was going to be somebody one day and he'd need money to start. He'd build an empire, design his own house by the river, marry at forty, and have half a dozen kids before he turned fifty.

When Pecos reached Honey Creek, he drove down Main, waving at anyone he knew. He'd made a habit of getting to know every old person in town. At first it was so he could offer to do odd jobs for them, but later he just liked talking to them. There was a great deal of good advice under gray hair.

He'd heard someone in the hall at school say once that Pecos might be nineteen in body, but in mind he was already forty. After all, what kid wears a tie to school?

Pecos just thought of himself as mature before his time.

Tomorrow, a few hours after church was over, the school auditorium would open and the graduating seniors would walk in. For some it would be the last time they set foot on campus. They'd cry and vow they'd all stay friends, but Pecos planned to simply leave. After all, he had the rest of his life to start.

Pecos had his cap and gown, but he still hadn't made up his mind whether he'd go to the ceremony. There would be no relatives cheering him on. He'd feel like a flagpole standing out on the grass afterward with no one hugging on him and the Texas wind blowing his gown.

By the time he got down to the dock where he and Kerrie had parked last night, the dying sun had started to make a show.

Just enough sunshine to make the clouds look like they'd been polished with diamond dust.

Cutting through the thick undergrowth and trees, he reached the river's shoreline about a hundred yards down from the dock. This was his thinking place, and tonight he needed to spend some time here.

This spot probably looked the same now as it had back in 1836 when Texas was fighting for its independence. Somewhere upstream Fannin's men had been captured and held in a mission called Goliad. History recorded that Santa Anna's army marched the newly formed Texas troops to the river's edge on Palm Sunday, then had the men fighting for Texas line up to be shot. One volley fired and then the soldiers had to reload. Fannin's men who weren't already shot bolted for the river and jumped in before a bullet found them. A few lived to tell the story.

Pecos climbed out on a huge rock that hung over the water. In his mind he could hear the rifles. Hear the men diving into the Brazos. Those who lived joined Houston's army and fought later at San Jacinto.

A small band of ragtag Texans won over Santa Anna's army in that battle. They attacked the camp yelling a cry that still

142

echoes today. "Remember the Alamo. Remember Goliad."

Pecos was born a Texan. The blood of both sides of that battle ran in his veins. He liked to think that the courage of those early fighters was in him. No matter what the odds, he'd fight and win. He didn't know exactly what he wanted in life, but he wouldn't become his parents. He'd be someone who was looked up to. He'd be important. He'd be loved. And if he ever found a girl to marry him, he'd have kids and he'd love every one of them.

He could see himself being one of those men who ran and jumped into the raging water, and lived. Here, on his private rock next to the river, he could dream and plan. There were just enough trees behind him that anyone on the dock wouldn't see him, and the river below blocked out any noise from the road. Perfect for meditation. He'd found this spot the day he drove to town to get his driver's license.

Sheriff Hayes had met Pecos at the double doors of the county offices. He knew, like everyone in town did, that farm boys drive before they come in to take their test. As long as they don't speed, no one troubled them. But today the old sheriff must have been feeling bothersome. He stopped Pecos at the door and whispered, "You fail the test, kid, and you'll be walking home."

Pecos was shaking, but he answered, "I won't fail, sir."

An hour later when he'd passed, Pecos shook the old guy's hand, then drove out to the river to think about becoming a man. It just seemed like getting his license was the first step.

That was a good memory, he thought. Pecos made a list of those. It was like he hid them in a box in his mind. Whenever he felt low he'd just pull one out.

Last night with Kerrie would be one of those memories.

For a while he remembered every detail of being with her after the dance. Kerrie's strange call still echoed in his mind.

Pecos walked through all that had happened. He'd pulled up at the back door of the gym. He thought she looked so small coming out. She'd held his hand laced in hers. Then she'd thanked him for taking her home with a kiss on his cheek.

Later he'd think about what he should have said or done, but right now he wanted to remember every moment pure. Not *what could have been or what he wished for,* but the time just like it happened. If he kept the memory exact in his mind, maybe it would last longer.

Movement in the bush behind him drew him out of his thoughts. The sun was at the top of its setting glory, but what stood behind him held his gaze.

Kerrie Lane in yellow shorts and a white top with one shoulder bare. She just stood there staring at him. He couldn't breathe, or form words. He wasn't sure he could even blink.

"I saw your pickup and realized you were out here on my spot."

He managed to whisper, "It's my spot."

She laughed and stepped onto the rock.

Pecos couldn't take his eyes off her. Last night she'd seemed so fragile, so small, and now she was brighter than the sun. She stood legs apart, fists on hips, as if she were a female Peter Pan about to fly.

"Have a seat," he said. "We can share."

She sat down a few inches from him. "I found this place when I was about ten. Now and then when I need to talk to myself I come out here."

"What do you want to talk to yourself about tonight?" It was probably none of his business, but he had to ask.

She shrugged. "When I got in my car I just wanted to leave the dumb party my parents are throwing me. They invited all their friends. The few of my friends I invited are having parties with their families. So I'm watching my parents and a bunch of their crowd sit around, get drunk, and talk about their high school days."

"That must have been terrible." He tried to sound serious, but even a party of middle-aged drunks sounded better than being home watching his parents sleep while the TV blared.

She rested her hand on his knee. "It was dreadful. I know you think I'm exaggerating, but I'll take you home and show you."

He'd patted her hand resting on his jeans and hoped she didn't think he was doing anything wrong. After all, she touched him first. But then, she'd kissed him first. It was on the cheek, but maybe he could kiss her back. On the cheek, of course, maybe a little closer to her mouth.

Which he noticed was moving and his ears weren't listening.

"I told my mother it was my party and she just laughed. They'll be so drunk when I get back they'll all be jumping in the pool with their clothes on. No wonder my grand-dad wouldn't leave his bees. He'd rather talk to them than my parents. They both think they're so funny when they drink."

"I'd like to see that." Pecos tried to join

146

the conversation.

To his shock, she grabbed his hand and tugged him to his feet. "Well, let's go."

Before he thought of an excuse, he was in the new midnight-blue Mustang her parents had bought her for graduation and heading back to town.

Kerrie talked. In fact, as near as he could tell she didn't even stop to breathe until she pulled into the driveway.

Same girl, same house as last night. But all had changed. Every light was on; the lawn and out back looked bright as day. He heard music from the nineties blasting from speakers in the back. Voices blended in the heavy night air, some yelling, bits of conversation floating, and someone who couldn't remember the words to "You Are Not Alone" was trying to sing.

Pecos tried to slow his steps, but Kerrie dragged him along. She didn't seem to notice he didn't belong here. He wouldn't know how to act, what to say. His own parents didn't talk to him, why should someone else's?

They stepped inside and the talking became a roar.

Pecos realized he was an alien stepping onto an uncharted planet.

Then, he grasped one simple fact. He was

147

also invisible.

All the people were busy, acting like they were dancing with their drinks in one hand or having heated debates or, worst of all, flirting with little more skill than sophomores.

As she pulled him through the laughing and cussing people, and of course the group singing Madonna's "Take a Bow," Pecos couldn't decide if he should run or laugh.

"You want something to eat?"

"Sure." All he'd eaten today was the apple he picked up in his mom's kitchen at noon. "I could eat." He knew if she'd suggested they jump off the roof, he'd go along with it.

Kerrie smiled up at him. "Let's try one of everything."

"Sounds like a plan."

She picked up two plates and they moved around a long dining table decorated in a Maiden of the Sea theme for some reason. Half the food he'd never heard of, but he gave each a try. Fish that didn't look cooked and tiny pies with different flavors of pudding inside were his favorites.

When they moved to the backyard, Kerrie collected a plate of ribs and two beers. They sat in a dark corner swing and watched adults acting like they were teenagers again.

Only they were doing a terrible job.

He watched for a few minutes, then decided his eyes would get stuck on bug-out setting if he didn't turn away, so he moved with Kerrie to a bench that faced the field behind her house. "See that light way off in the distance?" she asked.

"Yeah."

"That's my granddad's place. I'm an only child of an only child. My granddad keeps that light on to let me know he's there in case I need him. He's a grumpy old man, but I kind of think of him as my guardian angel."

She set the ribs between them and handed him a beer. "Do you drink beer?"

"Yeah," he said. "When my brothers come home for Christmas they always buy a case and leave it in the barn. After my folks go to bed, we sneak out there, freezing cold, and drink. Tucson and my second brother, Worth, claim it's the only way they make it through the week at home."

"You have four brothers, right?"

"Tucson's kind of my guardian angel. He's a marine. Worth, number two brother, and Claude, number four and closest to my age, are in the army."

She held up three fingers. "You skipped one."

149

"My mom says Houston is lost somewhere in California like the state was a jungle he accidentally wandered into and one day he'll walk out of and come back home."

She slid over, closing the distance between them. "What do you think?"

"I don't think I'll ever see him again. He was two years younger than Worth. Three months after Worth finished high school, he signed up to be in the army. About a month after he left, I remember hearing Houston and Dad yelling. The next morning, Houston was gone. Two years later, we got a letter that said he was in California and doing fine, but I remember thinking how sad it must have been to turn eighteen so far from home."

She took his hand. Pecos thought that was probably the most downer story he could have told her. Kerrie didn't want to hear about all his brothers.

She smiled at him as if she'd read his mind. "Where'd you get your name? The Pecos is a river."

"Dad always said he didn't remember why they named me that, but Tucson said we're named after where they conceived us. Tucson, Worth for Fort Worth, Houston, and Claude. They must have slept out by the river about twenty years ago."

"But Claude isn't a name of a place?"

"It's a little town not far from Amarillo. My dad worked a farm there for a year before he moved to Honey Creek."

She laughed softly, then apologized for asking questions.

Pecos didn't know whether to be embarrassed or happy about making her laugh. He couldn't believe a guy like him was even sitting beside her.

She finally took pity on him and changed the subject. "Are you going to leave home soon? Army, marines, or California?"

"I don't know." He'd been thinking about it, but where would he go?

She leaned closer as if giving away a secret. "My folks want me to go over to the junior college at Clifton Bend for a year before I go away. They said it would save them a ton of money and it's only a thirty-minute drive." She pouted. "But it's such a cowboy town and I won't know anyone on campus."

"I was thinking about going there, too. You'll know me." Pecos was lying. No college would let someone from the bottom fourth of the class in. Besides, lots of millionaires get rich without going to college.

"Maybe we could share a ride. Most of the classes are at night." She reached across the plate of ribs that neither one had tasted, and touched his hand again.

This was definitely looking like a date, he thought. Kerrie Lane hadn't touched him in the ten years they'd been in school together and all at once she was patting on him like he was a new pet.

Pecos forgot about the party around them and the graduation tomorrow and even what would happen Monday when his dad figured out his youngest son was no longer in school.

All his brain could register was her fingers touching his.

"Pecos, can I ask you something?"

"Sure, anything." This was about time for her to tell him to leave. He'd have a long walk back to his pickup, but he didn't mind. She probably had a lot more important things to do than talk to him.

He looked up and realized she was talking again and he hadn't been listening.

Her big blue eyes were staring at him as if she'd just asked another question.

When she waited, he thought, *Yep, she's asked something and I haven't caught one word to hang an answer on.*

"Would you mind saying that again?" He felt like a suicide hotline volunteer who'd just got an obscene phone call and the message wasn't registering. Worse, he was asking to hear it again.

Looking down, he decided not to look at her when the bad news came. This was close to the best night of his life. All through school he'd been that kid who everyone knew but no one wanted to hang out with.

"I said, would you want to be my boyfriend?"

He looked up. Yeah, she was still there. This beautiful girl who was a cheerleader, who sang solos in the choir, who was popular, and who was valedictorian of their class. Hell, if Kerrie Lane hadn't lived in Honey Creek, the class yearbook would be the width of a menu.

"You won't hurt my feelings if you say no. I'd understand if —"

"Yes," he said.

"Yes?"

He straightened a bit and closed his fingers around her hand. This might just last a day. She might be joking or doing this to upset someone like her real boyfriend or her parents. He didn't care why. The answer was yes.

She stood and stepped in front of him. "Thanks, Pecos."

A hundred questions came to mind. Should he give her his senior ring? He'd have to buy one first. Should he kiss her? Could he tell anyone, or was he a secret boyfriend?

All he could think to say was, "You're welcome."

Her knees bumped his as she moved nearer. He stood and was so close to her they were touching.

"Would you hug me?" she whispered.

He gently put his arms around her shoulders, and to his surprise she moved even closer. She rested her head on his chest as he tried to take in all the feelings that were exploding inside him. Fear, panic, love, need.

Then he felt something wet against his neck and realized Kerrie was silently crying.

He had no idea why or what he was supposed to do, so he patted her lightly on her back and whispered softly, "It's all right, Kerrie. It's all right. I'm here."

Somewhere, over the noise of the crowd, he heard someone yelling her name.

Kerrie straightened but didn't turn his hand loose. She tugged him toward the pool area.

Pecos had grown up knowing who the Lanes were. Kerrie was an only child of the man who owned Lane Flooring and Carpeting. Since it was the only one in town, he

154

got all the business. Her mother ran all kinds of societies and fund-raisers.

It seemed like the Lanes had everything. It made no sense that Kerrie would cry. Only she had and he'd been the one she turned to.

Kerrie's mother stood on the patio smiling as they neared. Luckily, she didn't seem to mind that her only child was attached to him.

"Everyone! Everyone! Our baby will be graduating tomorrow afternoon. Thank you all for coming to help her celebrate a milestone in her life."

The hired-for-the-night kitchen staff of five in their bow ties and white aprons were passing out champagne in tall, thin glasses.

Kerrie's dad raised his glass. "To our Kerrie."

Everyone wished her a glowing future as they surrounded her. In the crowd, he lost her hand. Then, he lost sight of her.

Pecos just stood there holding his glass. Not drinking. Just waiting. This might be the shortest time anyone in the history of the world ever had a girlfriend. He backed away and stood in the shadows, watching and waiting.

When he finally set the glass down, still full of the first and only time he'd probably

155

ever get the chance to taste champagne, he didn't feel much like celebrating.

He told himself that someday, when he was rich, he'd buy a case, have it shipped all the way from France, and drink it all. But Kerrie was lost in the crowd and had forgotten where she'd left him.

"Well, hello, Mr. Smith," a very formal, low voice said from behind him.

Turning, Pecos smiled. "Hi, Mr. Winston. I didn't see you among all the guests."

"Oh, no, no, I'm not a guest. I just live down the block and when I saw so many people parking up and down the street and heading this way, I figured the Lanes wouldn't notice one more guest. I'm the party crasher, you see. All the best parties have at least one."

"I'm the boyfriend, or I was for a minute or two. I'll probably never see Kerrie again."

Mr. Winston laughed. "Follow me. I've crashed enough parties here to know the lay of the land."

They slipped through a side door into a game room with a bar. Mr. Winston picked up a handful of nuts from the bar as they passed, then Pecos followed the old guy up half a staircase to a kind of balcony that looked over a huge living room. Everything below was either glass or leather.

156

Kerrie was sitting on the floor opening presents. With each gift a few of the guests drifted away. She was almost finished when a scream came from the pool followed by a splash. Everyone headed out through the patio doors, leaving Kerrie alone with wrapping paper all around her.

Mr. Winston motioned for Pecos to follow and they walked down another half stairs into the living room.

"You got some great stuff." Pecos picked up one of half a dozen pen and pencil sets.

"And to think, all I wanted was a stuffed armadillo," she answered.

He offered his hand and helped her stand. "I was going to walk Mr. Winston home. There are not many streetlights around his place. You want to go with me?"

"I'd love to."

Mr. Winston talked all the way to his house with Pecos and Kerry on either side of him.

Afterward, when they were on their way back, Pecos asked, "Am I still your boyfriend?"

"You are."

"Want to tell me why?"

She squeezed his hand. "Does it matter?"

"No." Pecos shortened his steps to match hers. If she was just using him for some reason, he didn't care. He was a willing sacrifice.

Laughing, she whispered, "You're kind, Pecos. You always have been. Like walking old Mr. Winston home when no one else thought of it. All my life I've seen you do kind things. You gave your milk money to a kid who'd lost his. You're always hauling band equipment for free. You talk to kids that no one talks to."

He thought of mentioning that he didn't much like milk and that he felt part of something when he helped the band and he'd talk to anyone who'd talk to him. But he decided to keep quiet.

They didn't go back to the party. She drove him to his pickup as they talked about the next day. When he mentioned that he wasn't sure he was going to graduation, she made him promise that he would.

When she pulled up beside his pickup, he thought of leaning over and kissing her, but this was too new. "I'll see you tomorrow," he said as he stepped out of her car.

"After the ceremony, I'll find you." Kerrie waved and was already pulling away when he closed the car door.

CHAPTER 11

Late Saturday night

COLBY

The highway patrolman turned investigator had been in the shadows behind his cabin for twenty minutes waiting for the mayor to show up with her boat. Colby had a dozen things he'd found out about her missing person's case, and a few of them she might not know. He'd hoped to tell her in the light so he could study her face.

He'd noticed that her green eyes darkened when she went on alert, which was pretty much every time she saw him. Everything she was thinking flashed in those eyes, even when she thought of clobbering him. But it was too risky for them to be friendly this early. For all he knew she was in on this almost crime.

She'd mentioned that Boone might be doing his disappearing act to draw attention.

159

Maybe just claiming he was engaged to Piper hadn't been enough.

From the things she'd said, Colby sensed that Boone had wanted the press to think that they were more than friends. Or maybe it was all some sort of plan to gain control over Piper. It occurred to Colby that if Boone could influence Piper, he might also be able to influence her father. A senator is far more powerful than a mayor.

But Colby's guess was that Piper was a woman that no man would ever control. She saw right through Boone Buchanan.

Colby figured most politicians play games of control, but Boone wasn't a politician, he was a lawyer. Piper hadn't publicly denied the lie about Boone and her being engaged. For all he knew, maybe she was in on this deception.

Colby rejected that thought. Every cell in his body told him she wouldn't be involved in this mystery.

A man driving his BMW into the river wasn't a crime. Maybe the sheriff had picked up Boone and they'd decided to go south for a long weekend. The guys he'd met at the bar seemed to think Sheriff LeRoy Hayes was vanishing more and more lately. Maybe he had a lady friend or maybe he was fishing. He'd never been a great sheriff, and now he was slipping.

Several people said that Hayes didn't keep regular hours. He was known to not come into the office until midmorning, and work the midnight shift just to pester the dispatcher. He even claimed having regular hours only benefits the criminals. Now that he was a short-timer, maybe he was becoming more erratic.

Boone had been missing four days now. Lawyers like Boone, who had a court schedule, would at least need to call in. One of the Jeffs told Colby that earlier, on the night his car took a swim, Boone had been seen in Bandit's Bar over in Someday Valley. The wide spot in the road about thirty minutes away wasn't more than a cluster of trailer parks and bars. Locals in Honey Creek claimed even rats didn't hang around the town.

Why would a rich lawyer be there?

Witnesses, who were probably drunk and not too reliable, reported seeing him drinking with a tall woman. He wasn't drunk and the woman wasn't Piper. She left and he had two more drinks, they reported.

A couple celebrating their two-week anniversary in the parking lot claimed a man who was about Boone's build cussed all the way from the bar door to his fancy car. The lovers claimed they would have confronted him for ruining their date, but he was gone before they could get their clothes on.

The accounts of his activity pretty much blew the theory of carnapping. Colby had heard other theories whispered around, but they were all simply guesses.

For the most part, Colby couldn't believe how great what the mayor had called *his dumb cover story* had worked so far. Every store he went in wanted him to court the mayor. From the mechanics in the garage where he bought an old Harley, to the ladies having tea at the bakery, everyone agreed. Their mayor needed a man in her life, but it had to be the right man.

One farmer downing coffee at the town's only coffee shop stared at Colby and felt the need to add a comment. "You're a good-looking guy, but you ain't her quality. Our mayor needs a partner, not a pet."

Colby growled at him and the old guy growled back.

Piper Mackenzie was wonderful, everyone told him. One of the best mayors the town had ever had. Some said even better than her grandfather. She worked late at night and weekends, and she cared.

They also agreed Boone Buchanan was not good enough for her. Though most had never seen the guy, they read the papers. He was nothing but a gold digger, a playboy. Boone could see how she shined and he wanted to ride on her coattails.

One lady in the bakery said everyone knew Piper would someday be governor. She needed a man who'd support her goals. Someone smart enough to always be good to her.

Another lady eating her second éclair pointed her pastry at Colby and said she didn't know if *this one,* meaning Colby, was smart enough to marry Piper either. Most men who drove a motorcycle had scrambled their brains at least once.

To his disappointment, the éclair eater's friends agreed.

As the day passed, he'd visited every business, sat on half the benches on the square, and bought things he didn't need in shops. Colby slowly became one of them. He listened to the stories about the early days in Honey Creek and how the local football team almost won state last year.

Finally, an hour into talking with the boys at the bar, who'd all done research for him, Colby turned the tables on them and began to ask questions.

He slowly put the pieces together. Piper, Boone, and the sheriff.

Sheriff Hayes was easy. The guy had been a lawman too long. He'd be retirement age before the next election rolled around, and no one expected him to run for another term. Most didn't like him much, but they'd voted for him. He reminded Colby of that old saying that the devil you know is better than the devil you don't.

The sheriff never took bribes or roughed up a suspect. In fact, as far as Colby could tell, the man had gone his entire career without ever pulling his service weapon.

But something about Hayes wasn't right. The first twenty years in office he'd been married and done his job. After his wife died, he started sleeping around and drinking. Some said he even slept with Daisy the dispatcher before she went on the walker. Then, in his late fifties he cleaned up his act. No wild nights. No heavy drinking. Of course of late he had been disappearing at odd times.

A bartender at the Pint and Pie who overheard them talking said he'd seen Boone Buchanan last month. Said Boone had been coming through Honey Creek headed somewhere west for several months. He'd stop by for a few six-packs and a large pizza. There was a high-stakes poker game the first Wednesday of every month at a ranch farther down the valley. Word was Boone never missed it. Several months ago, he'd gotten friendly with one of the waitresses when he'd stopped by late one night.

She said he was easily forgettable except for one fact. He'd bragged that he was dating Piper. She also said he mentioned he'd lost at poker that night but he still had money to burn. The waitress and Boone must have not hit it off because lately all he dropped in for was beer and pizza now and then.

He guessed that Boone was at the poker game for some reason other than gambling. He was playing a game, but it didn't involve cards. Boone probably thought he was the hunter but he might find he was the game.

Colby checked his watch as he waited for Piper, listening for a boat. He hated people who couldn't be on time. The mayor was now thirty minutes late. He'd sworn when he got out of college almost a dozen years ago that he'd never marry a woman who couldn't read a clock.

That might explain why he was still single.

The low rumble of an engine echoed through the trees near the dark river.

He slowly looked around, trying to see through the moonless night. Limbs of hundred-year-old trees bent over into the water. Dusky-purple brush grew almost as high as a man in places, and the lazy breeze made all the foliage move like an ink drawing floating around him.

A splash sounded from ten feet away. The wet scrape against the wet grass and river rocks sounded like a boat being pulled to shore. Then, the outline of a woman dressed in black materialized.

As she walked toward him, he could see her outline in silhouette. Perfection without the boxy jacket. Now he had two things to admire about her, but she'd probably fire him if he mentioned either her eyes or her body. Her black shirt and tight black slacks made him aware of her every curve.

When she was three feet away, he whispered, "About time you showed up, PJ. We don't have any time to lose if you want this solved."

She shrugged as if she couldn't care less that she'd kept him waiting. "I guess my love-sick cowboy didn't show up tonight. The trooper is back."

"The cowboy is just an act, Mayor, nothing more. My dumb cover story, remember. I spent a few weekends trying to win money riding bulls. That doesn't make me a cowboy. Don't get the pretender mixed up with me."

166

"I agree. All business between us, nothing more, but you did give me a laugh when you winked at me on the street. A dozen people saw you pat your heart. A little corny, don't you think?"

"How about we head downstream?" He didn't have time for small talk. "You can critique my performance later."

She turned and headed back toward the water. "You can tell me what you learned as we drift with the current."

Without a word, he walked beside her down to the tiny boat, pulling branches out of her way as he moved. Once she slipped on the wet grass and he caught her by the arm. She didn't bother to thank him.

She lifted a paddle to use as a rudder to guide them in the current. When she climbed in, he pushed the boat away from the shore and they slipped into the river as silently as a tree branch migrating south.

They sat so close their knees were touching. Colby told himself to think of her as just a job, not a woman, but it wasn't easy when she was so close. Even in the darkness he could feel her nearness.

"Fill me in," she ordered, removing any hint left that he was attracted to her. "What did you learn?"

Colby watched the banks, making sure no

one saw them pass.

"Your boyfriend was two-timing you with a waitress who works over at Pint and Pie. It seems that Boone was also friendly with some woman thirty miles down the road in Someday Valley."

"I know about that first part. That waitress and I were friends in grade school. She felt guilty, so she came and told me about how he hit on her several months back. When I explained I wasn't interested in Boone, she got mad that he lied. Claimed she'd spill a drink on him the next time he came in at the Pint and Pie." Piper lowered her voice. "What's next?"

Colby moved on. "You know about the sheriff's odd hours?"

"Everyone knows about his weird habits. He'll disappear for an hour, then pop up again and claim he didn't hear his phone."

"Do you think the sheriff and Boone are together somewhere, or it's just coincidence that they both disappeared the same night?"

"It might just be. They don't seem to move in the same galaxy, much less the same circle. I'd be surprised if they even knew each other."

"I can think of a few things they have in common."

"What?"

168

"They both disappeared on the same night. Both drank. They both know you." He began to recognize the terrain. One more bend and they'd be where Boone's car had been found.

Colby pointed to the left bank. "That's where they found footprints. Not sure it was Boone. One, the car could have drifted some and two . . ."

"The fresh prints were tennis shoes?" She finished his sentence. Another thing he hated about her.

"Right, Mayor. Only in the report, the investigator added that they were cheap rubber soles. Your boyfriend wouldn't be wearing anything cheap."

"So you think someone else was driving Boone's car?"

"Maybe. Or someone else could have been out there watching when the BMW hit the water. Whoever was standing on the bank saw the car floating and didn't want to get involved." Colby stared at the darkened bank that he'd examined completely before sunset.

"If there was someone watching, or involved in some way, he might know if Boone was driving, or if he went under, or if he swam away?"

"I'm leaning toward the person watching

more than your rich boyfriend buying cheap shoes. I found a beer can about five feet away from the bank beneath a barberry bush. It was half-full, which suggests to me that someone was watching when the accident happened. Or Boone climbed out of his BMW, swam to shore, and stopped for a drink before he walked off."

Piper huffed. "I don't care what he did. I just want to know where he is. Every day the press makes it a bigger story. One account claimed I was pregnant and killed him because he was two-timing me."

For a few minutes they just drifted. Colby figured she was thinking of her career, and in truth his future was on his mind as well. If he could find Boone, crime or not, her brother, Max Mackenzie, would remember him. All his life he'd dreamed of being a Texas Ranger. He loved being a trooper for the Texas Highway Patrol, but he wanted the Ranger badges. Few people know that when troopers are promoted into the Ranger Service they're given two badges — a silver badge made from a Mexican coin and a bronze, silver-plated badge to carry in their identification case.

"You thinking of catching the bad guys, Trooper?" Piper's sexy voice drifted through the night just to bother him. "Maybe Boone and the sheriff are dope smugglers. You might get the chance to shoot one . . . in the leg, of course."

"Yeah, that's what I was thinking, PJ." He wondered if that midnight voice ever whispered something sexy. He wouldn't mind hearing that.

Probably not. Piper never dated, and anyway she was way out of his league.

They drifted another half mile downstream, both watching the shoreline. He'd already walked the area, but if Boone was floating at night something might have caught his eye. A light from a house? A road?

Piper whispered, "We might want to turn around. The shore up around that curve is pretty populated, folks laying trotlines by the midnight light might see us."

She reached for the cord to start the little motor. The engine didn't turn over. It didn't even hiccup a cough that sounded like the beginning of starting.

Piper tried again, then again. Colby even tried twice.

"I guess we're walking home. It would take hours to paddle upstream," Piper announced as if it was her call. "It'll take forever if we follow the bank. There's a road that runs a few hundred yards from here. It winds right past your cabin and then into town."

They both fought the flow of the river with splintery old oars until they were four feet from the bank. Colby jumped out, sinking to his knees, and tugged the boat to shore.

To her credit, Piper joined him when they were a foot out and helped him pull the boat in. She slipped once forward in the mud and again backward against him.

Colby pulled the boat onto dry land and offered his hand to her. Muddy fingers grabbed his. When she squalled, he laughed, then pulled her up the bank.

Once-white sneakers were now covered in mud, and her black clothes now looked camouflaged with brown mud and wet green leaves.

"You got someone who'll help you get this tiny yacht home?"

"I'll figure it out," she answered quickly, making it plain she didn't need his help.

"No, I'll figure it out," he snapped. "If you ask for help, people will gossip. If anyone sees me with this boat, I'll just tell them that I had to go fishing to get my mind off of you and I accidentally stole your boat."

"Great." She fell into step with him as they reached the road. "Your new bar friends will probably riot if I try to file charges against you. I dock my boat by the old Honey Creek Café and everyone in town knows they can borrow it for an hour."

"You wouldn't ever press charges against me, PJ. I saved your life."

"When?"

"If it wasn't for me catching you, our beloved mayor would be dead in the water or look like a walking mud-man right now."

"Thank you for that. I can swim so I doubt I'd die," she said. "But if I arrived in town covered in mud you can bet it would be on the radio by eight."

He laughed. "I never would have guessed you were so picky about your appearance. When I met you, you didn't even have shoes on."

"There was a time when a woman was considered insane if she wasn't dressed properly."

He looked at the mayor's clothes spotted with mud. "There must be millions of crazy people hanging out at garage sales and discount stores, but, PJ, you're not one of them. Even muddy and wet you look great."

She laughed and stumbled over a bump in the road.

He caught her hand and didn't let it go. "For safety's sake," he told her.

173

CHAPTER 12

Midnight

PECOS

Pecos was so busy thinking about seeing Kerrie tomorrow that he almost didn't see the couple walking down the center of the farm-to-market road between town and his folks' farm.

He hit his brakes, and the pickup swung crossways in the road. Leaning his head out the window, he yelled, "Are you crazy? Get out of the road!"

"Sorry," the man shouted. "I was just walking the mayor home."

Pecos jumped out of the pickup. "The mayor? Are you all right, Miss Mackenzie?"

"I'm fine, Pecos. Any chance you could give me and Colby a ride back to town?"

"Sure, but I'm an Uber driver so I'll have to charge you."

The man with the mayor swore under his breath.

Pecos decided he didn't like the stranger. "Half price for the mayor but full price for you, mister."

"We're going the same way, kid."

"I don't care. Since I drove the Moody sisters around I charge by the person. And I'll expect enough tip to cover the cost of having to wash off the mud you'll leave on my seat."

The stranger didn't say a word. He just walked over and opened the passenger door. Pecos thought the man probably figured out the price was not negotiable after midnight. If he decided to complain to the Uber company, they'd just say they never heard of Pecos Smith. After all, Pecos hadn't gotten around to telling them he was working for them.

The outsider offered his hand to the mayor, but she didn't take it.

Pecos was too curious to not ask. "How'd you two end up out here this time of night together? This ain't a sidewalk. I'm probably the only person who drives this road after dark."

The man opened his mouth, but Piper spoke first. "I like to motor out and think at night." She looked at her companion. "I ran into this idiot fishing. The motor got tied up in his line and Mr. McBride did nothing."

"It's dark out there." Mr. McBride answered like he thought the whole thing was her fault. "Who in their right mind would go boating on a moonless night?"

That ended Pecos's guess that they were lovers. He started the pickup and waited. "You have to pay first since you didn't use the app." He didn't mention that he wasn't on the app.

The stranger handed Pecos a twenty. "Will this get us the couple of miles back to town preferably without any more questions?"

Pecos held the bill up to the dashboard lights. "I don't have change."

The man swore. "Keep the change, kid."

For some reason the mayor thought this was funny. She poked at the stranger like he was a blow-up toy that needed air.

Pecos figured the pair must be drunk. Even if he told someone about finding them out here, no one would believe him.

They rode back to town in silence.

He let them out half a block from Widows Park, figuring she might not want the stranger to know her address. Her home where all the Mackenzie women lived wasn't far and Pecos didn't really care how far it was from where Colby McBride stayed.

The mayor headed toward town and Pecos figured the guy was heading toward Fisherman's Lodge. The old lodge and the Honey Creek Café were the only two things down that road.

Pecos parked and watched them for a few minutes. She didn't turn around as she walked toward the huge old Victorian house that had been turned into the Honey Creek Café, and the cussing man didn't look back as he strode the other direction. In a blink the mayor disappeared behind the trees lining a driveway. Pecos figured she knew a shortcut home.

Pecos turned his truck and started back home, passing the stranger. Smiling about the twenty he'd just made, Pecos waved.

The stranger didn't wave back. If he and the mayor had been out on a date, it must have been the worst ever. They hadn't even said goodbye.

CHAPTER 13

SAM

The almost preacher walked the sidewalks of Honey Creek by the low streetlights' glow. Like the town, the concrete was uneven and broken in spots, forming interesting clusters of shattered pieces. Earthy mosaics reminding Sam of his life. The pieces didn't fit together like a puzzle, but seemed more forged in place. The simple childhood, the quiet seminary, the constant march of the army and thrill of jumping into fires.

He was thirty-eight. What next?

Tomorrow he'd give his first sermon and the possibility frightened him more than going to war. Maybe he should just stick with some general theme like "we should all love one another," but Sam had seen enough in

178

the army to believe it could never be that simple.

Hell, he didn't even want to love himself most of the time. When he was fighting fires, he had a mission. He had a reason, a quest. But preaching to people who probably weren't listening didn't make much sense. How could it have made his father so content?

Sam remembered how his dad used to hum as he walked, like he could hear the hymns of Heaven whispering down from above.

Maybe Sam could preach about following the Ten Commandments . . . only he'd broken several of them. For a few years he'd used the ten dos and don'ts as a playbook on leave.

This living another life for a while didn't seem to be working out. Maybe that saying "You can never go back home" was true. Sam had been nuts to think he could change his life so drastically.

As he walked to the edge of town where farmhouse lights sparkled like grounded stars in the distance, he thought about leaving Honey Creek before dawn. He could drive back to Denver and go to work. Vacation over/experiment done. No one could go back in time and live the life he first planned. No one.

He turned toward the church. Maybe he could leave a note that said he'd had a family emergency. A lie to cover a lie sounded about right.

But he had no family.

He had nowhere to go but back to work.

As he passed a bar across the street from where he and the mayor had eaten last night, he considered going in for a few drinks. But no, that didn't seem right either. His collar seemed to tighten a bit around his neck.

A man almost as tall as he was was walking toward him. Sam recognized him as the guy who'd changed from scrubs to western clothes in the truck stop restroom the other day. Sam had been told by one of his new friends that this fellow was new in town. Looking to buy land. Courting the mayor.

"How's it going, cowboy?" Sam said.

The cowboy seemed taken aback to see another person out in the night. "Fine, Preacher. And you?"

Sam stopped walking when they were three feet apart, and so did the cowboy. It was dark enough so that neither one of them could see much of the other's face.

Total honesty ruled the darkness. More to himself than to this stranger, Sam said, "I don't think I belong here."

"Me either," came the other man's words. "Did you ever try to help someone who didn't want your help?"

"That seems to be my new job description. A few hours ago a man asked for some advice about his drinking problem with whiskey on his breath."

The cowboy nodded in understanding.

An old story popped into Sam's mind. Three robbers were burglarizing a home. Two went in. One dressed up like a policeman and walked the city street outside the window where his friends had disappeared. He liked talking to the people, tipping his hat, being smiled at. He liked being an officer of the law. When his companions slipped out of the home's window, the pretend lawman forgot he was one of them and blew his whistle. *Clothes Make the Man.*

But Sam didn't think this was working for him. He'd been lost so many times in his life that he didn't have any idea how to find himself. Here in the darkness he knew he'd met a mirror man in this stranger.

The stranger gave a salute, then continued on his way. Sam did the same. The cowboy melted into the night.

A few minutes later, when Sam turned onto the tiny walkway beside the church, he saw that all the windows were dark as if blindly staring at an imposter walking below them.

All but one.

The last one, Stella B.'s tiny office, where she kept the books.

He told himself that he'd slip by, not look over. If she was still working, seeing him pass might frighten her. Maybe she'd simply left the light on.

In spite of his best efforts, when Sam walked by, he looked in.

Stella's head rested on her arm on the desk. The muffled sound of weeping seeped through the thin glass.

Sam swung up the steps and opened the unlocked back door. Five steps later he was in her office.

"What's wrong?" He sounded as panicked as she looked. "Has something terrible happened?" His brain was swearing and praying at the same time. Praying he didn't have to preach a funeral for someone and cussing himself for being so self-centered.

Stella gulped back tears and tried to speak, but only a squeak came out.

"An accident? A murder? A fire?" He felt like he was on a game show and had no idea what the question was much less the answer. "A tornado. Someone robbed the church?"

She shook her head.

He moved around the desk and gently took her shoulders. "Stella, you have to tell me. Are you in danger? Are we in danger?"

"No," she finally whispered. "I've run away from home. Will you help me, Pastor?"

CHAPTER 14

1:30 a.m., Sunday morning

COLBY

After talking to the preacher, Colby walked to the nearest bar. It might be half an hour until closing, but he could drink enough to wash away a few memories of tonight.

He hadn't slept in two days, the wound at his side still throbbed, and he hadn't made any real progress on the case. This idea for putting himself on the fast track toward becoming a Ranger didn't seem to be working, and the mayor was one step away from hating his guts.

Boone Buchanan was still missing, and no one seemed to care except the press.

After two beers, Colby switched to whiskey. He kept wondering why he'd said that to the preacher. Just because they once passed each other in a roadside restroom didn't mean they had to be honest with each other.

What kind of preacher says he doesn't belong here? Maybe he was living a lie, too, playing a part just like Colby. Most preachers were out of shape, even a bit rounded, but Sam Cassidy looked like he worked out. Most preachers had a sunshine smile even when it was raining. Colby had never seen Cassidy smile.

The preacher was hiding something. No doubt. Come to think of it, half the folks in town looked like they needed to stand in a lineup.

Maybe he was an ex-con planning to act like a preacher so he could break into homes. After all, everyone opens the door for a man of the cloth.

Colby turned his thoughts back to the mayor. All he was trying to do was help her out of this mess, but it often felt like she was fighting him. Maybe she just didn't like him. But which side of him? The guy who was trying to court her, or the trooper trying to locate her boyfriend.

Who wasn't really her boyfriend, or so she said. He'd looked at the press photos. She did look bored in every one.

Colby ordered a double and rolled the empty glass across his throbbing forehead.

He couldn't think. Or actually, he couldn't stop thinking — memories of Piper flashing across his mind like ground lightning.

Holding her hand. Pulling her up against his chest when she'd almost fallen. Putting his hands on her waist to lift her up. How could a woman so proper feel like dynamite in his arms?

It was like cell memory from a hundred lifetimes ago. He knew the feel of her. Even when they were arguing, he cared for her, protected her.

It made no sense. He liked women . . . for a short time anyway. Then they started asking too many dumb questions, like "How do I look?" There is no winning on that one. Even if you say great, they get mad because somehow that wasn't good enough. Or, like "What are you thinking?" Better to say *nothing* and let her think you don't think than mention anything.

Most men who count the number of dates before they plan to break up have had their hearts broken, but not Colby. He'd figured out from the beginning that falling in love was a trap. The first few dates are great, but once she says "I think I love you," it's all downhill from there. Before she settles into a "happy ever after," she wants a remodel of you. Then when you change for her, she

186

reminds you as she walks out that you're not the man you used to be.

Colby stood, leaving his last drink untouched and a twenty on the table. When this was over. . . . when all was solved. . . . it still wouldn't be over between them. Not for him, anyway. Mayor Mackenzie would still be in his thoughts long after this job was finished.

He'd made it almost to the door when he recognized the other customer in the bar — it was the mechanic who'd worked on the Harley he'd bought. "Evening, Daily."

The man looked up with eyes so bloodshot Colby wondered if he could see.

"Evening, Colby. You get the girl?"

Colby stepped into cowboy mode. "Nope, she hasn't come to her senses yet. She thinks she can do better than me, but I plan to put up a fight for her heart."

Daily was mumbling something about having a girl once who died in a car wreck. His words weren't clear, and Colby didn't try to untangle his meaning.

As Colby helped the mechanic make it out the door, he noticed three little kids sitting in a wagon across the street. "Those yours?"

"No," Daily said. "They're not real."

"They look pretty real to me, Daily."

The drunk turned away, and headed down

the street.

To Colby's surprise the three kids started following Daily. Colby shook his head. Another mystery he didn't have time to look into.

Now, as the moon passed behind clouds, Colby began to walk back toward town. In a little while he passed a big, old house close to the water. After a moment he recognized it as the café where he and Piper had coffee this morning. From the sidewalk, the place was so overgrown near the road he wouldn't have seen the turnoff if he hadn't been walking.

And now that he thought of it, hadn't Piper been walking in this direction when they had parted ways earlier?

Only one light was on near the back of the house. He wouldn't have noticed it, but the reflection floated on the water like a spirit who'd met a watery end. The big three-story home of a sea captain was almost enveloped in hundred-year-old trees from this side. As he walked closer to the water he saw a balcony one floor up with open French doors to let in the night air.

A small sign by the mailbox had said, "Honey Creek Café. Open ten to three for brunch on Sunday. All other days open till breakfast runs out or the cook gets tired."

He had a strange hunch that he might find Piper here. Right up there where that light was. He knew that the mayor's official residence was the massive house in town known as Widows Park that her grandfather had willed her. Every person in town had mentioned that to him. The place looked big enough to be a sorority dorm just off a college campus. One of the guys at the bar said the mayor would always be safe once she was home. Her house used to be called Mayor's Park because of the gardens that surrounded the place, but Mackenzie women all outlived their husbands and moved in, so now locals called it Widows Park.

As Colby stared at the light hidden from anyone driving by, it came to him that this was PJ's hideout. She'd mentioned that the café could have been a bed and breakfast but her cousin Jessica used the bottom floor because the upstairs was haunted.

Piper had laughed and added, "They say now and then you can hear the ghost stomping around or hiccupping or swearing."

Colby smiled. He'd solved one mystery. He knew who the ghost was.

He couldn't resist circling the house until he could see her window light clearly. Silently he watched as she stepped out on the balcony almost hidden in honeysuckle vines and climbing yellow roses. In one white towel wrapped around her body and another crowning her hair she looked more like a spirit than a real woman. It was too dark to see her face, but she was leaning back as if watching the sliver of a moon say hello to its reflection in the water.

Colby, who considered himself a rational guy, figured the honeysuckle lattice offered the perfect ladder.

By the time he'd scratched all his arms and legs several times and probably scraped the wound on his side enough to start it bleeding again, she'd closed the door and gone back inside. The trellis hadn't proven as friendly as he'd thought and he wasn't at all sure, now that there was no light coming from the bedroom, that he could get down without breaking his neck.

Dumbest thing he'd ever done, next to riding bulls in college.

He managed to stab himself with a broken lattice board as he swung onto the balcony. Fighting down a yelp, he walked slowly across her balcony trying to think of one logical reason he was standing on the mayor's balcony after midnight. His boots were covered in river mud. His clothes were dirty and still wet. The only shirt he had with him was ripped in several places. He looked more like a Halloween scarecrow than a state trooper.

She'd turned off the light, but there was a bit of light filtering past the drapes. Probably a night-light so she could read till she fell asleep. Great! She was already in bed.

Being a total idiot was all he could think of for the reason he was here. Or, he could claim he was more than half drunk. At least that would be true. No, insanity would work better. After all, maybe she'd feel sorry for him if he was nuts.

He might as well play the wild card.

Colby knocked.

He heard movement, light steps of bare feet, then she pulled back the curtain just far enough for him to see one eye.

And that one eye was glaring at him.

He stepped back, reconsidering the fall he'd take if he jumped. Maybe she hadn't recognized him yet.

"Colby? Is that you?"

Too late. "Yes, Mayor, it's me."

After a long pause, the long French door opened. "What are you doing here?"

He straightened as if on official business. "We'll get to that later, Miss Mayor, but first I feel it is my duty to tell you not to open doors in the middle of the night. In

191

fact, don't open a door if you are alone unless you know the person outside very well."

She stepped back a foot. "Again, Trooper McBride, what are you doing here?"

Colby's only hope was to stay on topic. "You should scream if someone even walks past your window, or call the police. You should not step back as if inviting him in." Colby stepped over the threshold as if demonstrating.

She moved back again.

"I could be here to attack you. Aren't you afraid?"

"No," she answered as she raised her arm and flipped on the overhead light.

Colby glanced down to notice the thin nightgown she wore, but before he could speak he saw the Colt .45 in her hand. It looked old enough to have been used by Jesse James.

She smiled. "I'm not afraid at all, Trooper."

Colby raised his hands in surrender. A woman with a gun was twice as dangerous as a rattlesnake with two rattles, but dang he couldn't stop looking at the pale-blue nightgown. If she was planning to shoot him, he'd like to have the sight of her as his last memory.

Why would a woman wear oversize suits

in brown to work and baby-blue gowns to sleep alone? This wasn't a good time to ask her that question.

"Before you start another lecture, let me remind you that I have two older brothers who taught me to shoot before I started school. This might be a hundred-year-old weapon, but I clean and oil it regularly. Now, I suggest you tell me why you're here."

He could lie and she'd see right through him, or he could reveal the idiot that he was and hope she didn't fire him.

He looked at her face and realized she was enjoying this. He'd go with the idiot.

"I just had to make sure you are all right. I know you think you're safe here, but something could happen."

She didn't lower the gun, but she did smile. "Keep talking."

He raked his fingers through his dirty hair. "I know you think I'm all about the job, but I was worried about you. All I wanted to know was that you were all right." She was fresh from a shower and he was dripping sweat and mud. Only good thing was he smelled like honeysuckle. "Also, I wanted to tell you that I've been reading up on Boone. The guy looks great, comes from a good family, is educated, but make him mad and he goes crazy. Beat up a fraternity brother after an argument. Almost killed him. He's had four assistants this year and all claimed verbal abuse as the reason they quit."

She put one fist on her hip and glared at him. "I may be clumpy in wet sneakers, but I assure you I can take care of myself."

But Colby could see that she was rattled, and not by him.

"Next you'll be telling me Boone is a nice guy," Colby whispered. "That's what all the neighbors always say about serial killers."

"I can take care of myself," she said again.

The mayor might be afraid, but she still wasn't buying his reason for being here. Colby tried again. "All right. The flat-out truth, Mayor. I've been reading about how great you are and half the town telling me how wonderful you are, and I think I'm falling for you. I've never met a woman like you."

She didn't look impressed. He'd run the idea by her again. "I've never talked to a woman like you. I'm falling hard so maybe you should just shoot me now and put me out of my misery." He thought a bit more wouldn't hurt. "I swear I've never said anything like this to a woman."

If that didn't work, he'd try getting her drunk. Or better yet he should get drunker. Drowning in beer was probably the only way he'd get the sight of her in that night-gown out of his mind.

He looked down just to confirm the view was as fantastic as he remembered it had been five seconds ago.

Colby figured he might as well throw out a dying wish while he had time. "Any chance you'd kiss me before you pull that trigger?"

Suddenly, she set the gun down and took a step toward him.

For a flash he thought he'd finally said one thing right.

But she grabbed him at the neck of his tattered shirt and jerked, ripping it down to his waist.

He was about to close his eyes and pucker up when she yelled right in his ear. "You're bleeding again. I swear you've got to stop bleeding all over my floors."

She pulled him to the bed and pushed him down when he tried to escape. "I see several bloodspots and that left leg has a steady drip. Take off those clothes while I get the first-aid kit."

Any hope of some kinky game of playing doctor and nurse vanished when he saw her eyes. Annoyed didn't begin to describe the look she gave him.

"I swear I should shoot you and put you

out of your agony." She vanished into the bathroom.

He tugged off his boots and jeans, and found three places bleeding on the right leg and a shallow gash that bubbled out like a mini volcano with every heartbeat. The bandage at his side was bloody again also.

When she returned, she was wearing a robe that left most of her legs bare. He followed orders and leaned back on a towel. Her hair was straight and still wet from her shower. It brushed over his skin now and then as she examined each wound.

"I'm surprised you're not covered in scars as often as you get hurt."

"In ten years of work I've only had a few injuries on the job and they were minor."

"So what's wrong now? What's different about this job?"

"You," he answered.

She went to work on his side. "So, you're saying I'm your bad-luck charm?"

He flinched as she washed over the wound. "That hurts. Where did you learn to patch people up?"

"The Internet. I Google anything I think I might need to know when I can't sleep. Fixing cars, plumbing, speaking Spanish, cooking, making soap. After work it's the only way I can relax." She pulled the tape off without saying "This is going to hurt."

He moved in agony again, knowing he needed to stay still and not let her see how much pain he was experiencing.

She pulled a tiny branch from his hair. "You've got a touch of the Irish in your blood. Sunshine brown hair with a brush of red blended in."

He knew she was trying to distract him, but it wouldn't work. Even when she patted the other side of his chest he knew what she was trying to do. She was simply waiting for him to relax so she could hurt him again.

"I tell you what, Trooper. If you make it through my nursing without yelling out, I'll give you that kiss when I show you the door. I don't think you'd survive another adventure with the honeysuckle."

Colby leaned back and closed his eyes. The vision of her little nightgown seemed to push the pain away as she worked her way from one cut after another.

"You still with me?" she asked as she moved a cool cloth over his chest. "In a few hours it will be dawn and you need to be out of here."

"One question," he whispered. "Will you be wearing just that nightgown when you kiss me goodbye?"

She smacked him on the forehead with

the palm of her hand. The only part of his body that wasn't already hurting.

He decided to keep his mouth shut.

As she worked, he relaxed for the first time since he'd answered the Texas Ranger's call.

A moment before he drifted into sleep Colby thought he felt her fingers lightly brush his hair back. Not exactly a doctoring touch. Not quite a caress.

CHAPTER 15

Sunday, three hours before dawn

SAM

Stella sat at the tiny table in the bachelor parsonage. She was still crying even though they'd finished a pot of coffee.

Sam had no idea what to say to this shy young woman. She'd told him she was thirty-two, but she seemed more like a frightened teenager. Her older brother had finished raising her after their mother died. No father seemed to be in the picture.

"Benjamin doesn't want me to leave . . . ever. He says he can't manage without me and I'd never be strong enough to face the world on my own. I do the books at his office and keep the accounts for the church, but I have no money of my own to manage."

"Maybe he could get married to an accountant," Sam suggested. "Then she could

199

take over your jobs and you could go look for work." Maybe logic would work?

She looked confused. "I don't see how that would help. He says none of the women here in Honey Creek want to marry him and I don't have much education. He's right. I'd probably be unable to find a job."

"What do you want to do, Stella?" Sam smiled. He was making progress. He'd thought of a question. Hell, if this preaching job didn't work out maybe he'd try being a life coach.

Sam fought down a smile and tried his best to look thoughtful, but a shy woman finally leaving home didn't seem like the end of the world to him.

"I want to go to school and study music. My mother always said I had the voice of an angel. I already teach the children's choir and I practice every morning for an hour after Benjamin leaves. Once a month I sing the solo on Sunday. Sometimes more often than once a month, because people say they feel closer to Heaven when I sing."

"That's a gift, Stella. If music is what you want to do, that is exactly what you should do. Your brother can't stop you. You are of age." A thought occurred to him. "He wouldn't physically try to hurt you, would he?" Sam wouldn't hesitate to beat some sense into the brother if he was hurting this gentle creature.

"Oh no, but he'd not be happy. It would cost money to go to college. He might get angry. I can't stand it when he yells at me."

Sam thought of telling her to find a backbone and yell back, but that wouldn't help the problem. "You got any friends you can get to help you talk to him?"

"Anna Presley. She'll help me." The crying stopped. "She helps anyone in need. I think she's a saint looking for a quest."

"Great. I'll drive you over to her place. We'll wake her up." Anna deserved a late-night visit after she called him a hall monitor just because he didn't get out of the way fast enough. Plus, he couldn't wait to see what the little redhead looked like before she combed her hair.

"I'll get the car. You get your things."

Stella was waiting when he pulled his car around. Her laptop case was slung over one shoulder, her purse over the other. An old suitcase waited at her side.

Once they were driving away, she said, "I'll still do the solo in service tomorrow. Be sure and tell Paul."

"Who is Paul?"

"He's filling in as the choir director. Drives eighty miles every Sunday to offer his services free. He's also the only one around who can play the organ. He'll be at the church early tomorrow. We sometimes have coffee after we practice and before people start coming in. It's a settling time for us both, I think. I look forward to it."

"You mean today, Stella, not tomorrow. It's long after midnight." His news didn't seem to cheer her up. She was thirty-two and frown lines were already forming at the corners of her mouth. "Tell me about Miss Presley. I only bumped into her once in the church hallway and she seemed bothered that I was in her way."

Stella smiled. "She's always in a hurry. Anna is a few years older than me, but I remember she was usually rushing around in school. Ran the school newspaper, was an officer in every club, and protested everything she thought was wrong. I recall once she stood out all night protesting the fact that everyone had to have a date to prom."

"Did she win?"

Stella shook her head.

"Did she go to prom?"

"No, I wasn't there, but I heard the principal wouldn't let her in. She just turned around and started yelling. Someone said her parents had to come pick her up."

Sam turned down a dirt road with a lone house built far back near the trees, one porch light flickering to guide his way.

Stella lowered her voice as if Anna might hear. "My brother felt sorry for her a few years back. He asked her out."

Sam slowed the car. "Did she go?" He couldn't imagine the spitfire going out with dull Benjamin Blake.

"She looked right at him and said, 'Sure, when toads fly.' Maybe she dated when she went off to Austin to school. Knowing her, she decided dating wasn't worth her time. Sometimes I think she can hear her life clock ticking down and she has to finish everything she can before she hits zero."

Sam fought down a laugh as he pulled in front of Anna Presley's home. He wasn't sure what he expected, but a tiny house out here in the middle of nowhere wasn't it.

Before he could get out of the car, Anna Presley stepped around the front door with a shotgun cradled in her arm. "State your name or I'll take aim."

"Anna," Stella called, "it's me. I've run away from home."

The little redhead set the weapon down and ran to her friend. Sam watched them hug and pat on each other as they both cried. No one who saw them would ever doubt that Anna had a heart.

Just as he figured, Anna Presley's hair looked just the same as it had yesterday morning. A tumbleweed on fire. Both women broke apart and laughed while the tears were still dripping.

Finally, Anna looked over at Sam. "Thanks for bringing her here, Preacher."

"You're welcome, Miss Presley."

As the women moved inside, Sam collected the suitcase and assumed he was invited in as well. If not, he guessed there would be the barrel of a shotgun pointed at him. A silent guard dog.

He dented one board of gingerbread trim along the roofline. Elves must have built this place.

The girls didn't notice the damage. As Stella told every detail of how she decided to leave home, Anna was asking questions about Stella's future. The shy bookkeeper had stopped crying and was taking notes on what she needed to do.

Sam looked around the house, which took him about three steps in every direction.

Modern furniture made of sticks so thin he wasn't sure any of it would hold his weight. Most of it was made to serve more than one purpose. One chair flipped over to make a ladder. A table turned into a twin bed. The small loft looked barely big enough to hold a full-size bed, and he was pretty sure he couldn't even get in the bathroom. The place was decorated in bright colors. Maybe meant to make the place look bigger, but in truth it was more like a rainbow got trapped in the house and exploded.

Sam decided he'd rather sleep outside. And go to the bathroom there as well. And take a shower only when it rained. Anything was better than bumping around in this dollbox she called a house.

The only plaque on the wall was a diploma from UT.

"You're a lawyer?" Sam said the words aloud.

The women stopped talking. Anna's voice came fast and sharp. "Look, Stella, he can read." Before he could answer, she added, "Is it that hard for you to believe that I've got an education?"

"No, I'm just surprised. I would have guessed you were a social worker or something like that."

"Keep wandering, Preacher. Make yourself at home and try not to break anything." The women went back to talking.

An hour later Sam was sitting on the tiny porch with his legs hanging over the railing, when Anna came out. Walking out a few feet, she stared up at the stars. "Beautiful, isn't it?"

He leaned his head sideways and looked inside. Stella was asleep on the table, correction, the guest bed. He straightened, in no hurry to go.

"Yeah, I love the stars this far from town. To think there are folks who never get far enough from lights to see how crowded the heavens are." He was looking at Anna now. She was far more interesting than the stars.

Dang if she wasn't growing on him. Anna had said all the right things to Stella. She'd calmed her down, told of her rights, and even made her laugh by describing Benjamin doing his own laundry.

Sam kept his voice as low as she had. "I'm not as dumb as you think I am, Anna."

"I know," she admitted. "I just came out to tell you that you can go. Stella's staying with me for a few days. Do her a favor and don't tell her brother where she is."

"I won't say a word."

When she didn't answer, he added, "I've figured you out, Anna. That quick wit is a defense. Strike before you get hit. Reject before you're rejected. Right? Maybe you've been hurt and don't want to let people close. Maybe you hate all men. Maybe I remind you of —"

206

She moved so fast he barely had time to set the front legs of his chair down before she was nose-to-nose with him. He braced to be yelled at, but her voice came soft. "Don't try to figure me out. Just stay out of my way."

If she'd been a man he might have shoved hard, but the porch light flickered in her eyes. Behind the anger was a pain so deep it might shatter her into a thousand pieces if she admitted it was there.

Sam stood, climbed in his car, and drove away. All the way back to the church he told himself that he'd give Anna her space, but deep inside he knew he was lying.

The fiery little redhead was the first woman he'd been attracted to since April Raine.

Getting close to Anna might burn him more than any forest fire he'd ever been in.

But if he could get close, it might be worth all the scorches he'd endure on the journey.

■ ■ ■ ■

SUNDAY

■ ■ ■ ■

SUNDAY

CHAPTER 16

9:00 a.m.

PIPER

The clatter of pans in the kitchen below her room rattled Piper awake. As she rolled out of her covers she fell, her bottom hitting the floor hard.

"Ohhh," she whined as she gripped the timeworn settee that had served as her bed.

Piper froze as all movement on the first floor below stopped.

After a moment, she rubbed her bruised bottom and smiled. The staff would have another ghost story to tell this morning. She tried to be out of the house long before eight when the pastry and bread cooks came in. On Sundays they came in early to make enough for the after-church crowd.

Piper had promised Jessica, the owner and her second cousin, that she would do her best to remain silent if anyone was downstairs, but sometimes she forgot. At first sweet Jessica had been annoyed by the resurgence of ghost stories, but she was more forgiving when that turned out to be good for business, drawing in traveling strangers.

Piper and Jessica were the only two Mackenzie women under the age of sixty. They had to stick together. Officially Piper lived at Widows Park, but she liked her retreat on the second floor of the Honey Creek Café, and it also allowed her to watch over things after Jessica went home to her tiny farm where she raised most of the food used in the café.

Piper stood up and kicked the settee for the poor night's sleep it gave her. Speaking of strangers, there was one in her bed whom she needed to get out of not only the bed but the house.

She tiptoed over to the bed. Colby was still there. Sound asleep. He was on his stomach, arms and legs out and taking up most of the space.

For a minute she just stared at the muscles along his back and his arms. He was well built, all tanned except for his bottom, where a bathing suit must have kept the sun away.

Piper started, creaking the floor again. The

man in her bed was naked. Naked!

She'd dated in college. Even married. She'd seen men before. But not like Colby. He was perfect except for a few white patches she'd taped over wounds.

Slowly she sat on the edge of the mattress and poked him.

He didn't move.

She poked him harder.

He growled like a hibernating bear.

"Wake up. Get out of my bed. Don't make a sound."

When she poked again, he twisted and caught her hand. Sleepy amber eyes met her stare. "Stop that, PJ."

His whisper was low and gravely. "I'm awake. Why do we have to be quiet?"

She leaned closer to him and softly said, "They think we're ghosts."

He sat up and pulled the sheet over his middle. "Oh, thanks for explaining it." He scrubbed his face. "So what do we do? Make a little noise, then wait till they come up, or stay in bed until they are gone. I feel like I could sleep all day."

"No, you have to get up very quietly and get dressed and get out of my room."

"I see a few problems with that plan. One, you ripped my shirt off last night, so what do I wear? And two, I'm not going down the honeysuckle again and the only other way out appears to be that wide staircase that leads to the main dining area."

She gave him a look that said this was all his fault. "We're stuck here. Jessica doesn't close until three."

"You wouldn't happen to have some of your ex-boyfriend's clothes lying around?"

"I don't have any ex-boyfriends."

"Really?" He'd heard the rumor that she never dated, but he didn't believe it.

"Really. The last guy I dated I married, and that was one mistake I do not want to repeat." She leaned against the headboard, crossed her bare legs, and pouted. After a few minutes she figured out that the wounded, naked man beside her wasn't going anywhere. "What about you. Have you ever found a woman willing to marry or even date you?"

"I like women from a distance mostly, you know, dressed up to party in a low-cut, almost see-through blouse and one of those short skirts girls only wear in bars. My kind of date."

He grinned.

"Then, over a few dates we get to know each other. Maybe we'll sleep together for a month or two if I don't see them too often. But women have the shelf life of yogurt. No matter how good they look or taste, after a while they turn bad. Asking all kind of questions, wanting you to do what no man wants to do, like go visit their grandmother or get matching tattoos or cook together."

She shook her head. "I can't believe you're not married." She didn't have to ask. She knew he had no tattoos.

"I'm smarter than most men, I guess. Women treat boyfriends like pets once their claws are in. They tell their friends, 'My boyfriend does the dishes . . . buys me whatever . . . takes me wherever I want to go . . . brings me breakfast in bed . . . sends me flowers.' If he's good enough, does enough tricks, they marry him and keep him."

She raised an eyebrow. "You certainly changed from last night when you wanted to kiss me."

"I was drunk." He shrugged as if the one sentence explained everything. "But . . . I still wouldn't mind kissing you. You got lips that look like they haven't been kissed near enough."

"But women sound like the enemy in your life, cowboy. Haven't you given up on them?"

"I have. I'm like the guy who smokes. I've given up a hundred times."

She stood and tiptoed over to the wardrobe. "I do have clothes, so I'm getting dressed. We've got plenty of time to talk. You know, Colby, I'm suddenly interested in what you have to say. I have a feeling you're a dying breed."

"You like my theories about the opposite sex?"

"No, but I do wonder how you've managed to stay alive this long."

Just as she pulled a sweatshirt on, a light knock sounded at the door. The knob turned. "Piper, you still . . ."

Jessica poked her head in and saw Colby in bed, the sheet now up to his chin.

Piper loved her cousin because she never judged people, but from the look of her rounded eyes she'd assumed the worst.

"How can I help get you two out of here? We'll talk later." Jessica set a breakfast tray beside the bed and focused on Piper as if she was the only person in the room.

Bless her heart, Piper thought. "We need to disappear fast. He has no clothes and no one can see me, or that will be the end of my hiding place."

Jess tiptoed to Piper and whispered, "What happened to his clothes?"

Colby grinned that grin she hated. "The mayor ripped them off me."

"I was doctoring him." Piper knew that one sentence wouldn't cover it, but they had no time.

Colby was nice enough to drop the sheet to his waist so the cousin could see the bandages.

Jessica walked to the bed and addressed the naked man in the room, "Can you cook?"

"I make a mean grilled cheese sandwich with bacon."

Jessica turned back to Piper. "Get dressed, Sunday best. I'll make an announcement in thirty minutes and you can slip downstairs while everyone is looking at me."

She whirled back to Colby. "You're my new cook. I've got a uniform I ordered for a man about your size who quit before it came in. I'll leave it on the landing. Before I make the announcement in the dining room that we're serving kids free cheese sandwiches you start down the back stairs that leads to the kitchen. When you hear me talking to the staff, you slip in. I'll put you on the grill."

Piper shook her head. "This will never work."

"Sure it will. Who doesn't love grilled cheese with bacon for free?" Jessica turned to Piper and whispered, "Don't worry, your man won't get hurt. I'll have an assistant at his side."

"He's not my man."

No one was listening. Piper felt like Colby was a lost dog following her around. If she didn't do something, she'd end up taking him home and feeding him.

CHAPTER 17

Morning

PIPER

Piper tossed clothes around as she tried to think of what to wear. It was Sunday. Church clothes. Lunch with her grandmother and the other ladies at Widows Park at one o'clock. All was back to normal . . . Right?

Of course not. Her almost boyfriend was still missing. Stories, none to flattering, were beginning to come out about him. It seems he wasn't the big-time lawyer he claimed to be, and there were rumors of another woman. People would think she was a fool for dating him and feel sorry for her at the same time. Could it get any worse?

To add to her fears, memories of her childhood circled like stagnant water blown by the wind. She remembered how peevish Boone had always been. He'd wanted all the attention, and he always knew how to make sure he got it.

Meanwhile, a trooper who had slept in her bed last night might be trouble, but she did believe he had her best interests at heart. All her life she'd felt protected, by her brothers, her father, her grandfather, but now, none of them were near.

Reluctantly, she smiled. Even a beat-up, naked, irritating bodyguard was better than none. Piper knew trouble was coming. She could stand alone, but it helped to know that Colby had her back.

Of course, Colby could become the problem all by himself. She could almost see the headline. Mayor caught in a secret hideaway bungalow with a naked man.

She'd live that one down. Her career wouldn't be over. Every time she ran for office, if she ever did again, the rumors would fly, but it wouldn't be too bad. She wasn't married. People would forget that gossip. Boone, on the other hand — if he did something crazy she might have that hanging over her head forever.

She pulled out one of her three brown suits, then put it back. Church clothes. A spring dress and heels. Her mother had always liked to see her in pretty dresses. Though her mother died when Piper was eight, she'd never felt unloved. Her brothers were in college, her father covered his sorrow in work, but she had her grandfather for a while and all the aunts to help her grandmother raise her. Granddad had left Piper the huge old house as if saying that now was her time to look over the family. But that didn't mean she didn't enjoy her private space above the café.

Piper slipped on the dress and stepped out of the bathroom.

Colby was gone. He must have put on the uniform, then gone down to the kitchen in his muddy boots to cook. No one would bother to ask questions. A good-looking man can get away with anything, even crashing a kitchen.

She sat at the tiny makeup table and tried to figure out the trooper. Like any logical person, she started with the facts.

One, she didn't like Colby McBride. He seemed very efficient in his job. He'd done his homework yesterday, but he bugged her. He called her PJ and he didn't hesitate to argue with her. He wanted to kiss her, well maybe he still did, even though she obviously didn't want to kiss him. She'd only suggested it to keep him still so she could doctor his wounds.

Maybe he'd forgotten that promise. She

221

hoped so. But then, if he remembered, she'd carry out her promise even though she didn't want to. She couldn't very well call her brother and tell him to fire the trooper just because he didn't seem the least impressed with her being mayor.

As she buttoned up her satin summer Sunday dress, she thought of another problem he had. Last night he'd touched her several times. Well, once she did fall into him when she'd slipped climbing out of the river, so that might not count. But twice he held her hand and once he'd slid his arm along her side to steady her.

Then when she was doctoring him in her bedroom, she'd touched him a few more times than necessary. Just making sure he hadn't developed a fever.

Maybe that was nothing to him, but she was very aware that Colby had handled her. No one touched her. Not the way he did. It was like he cared for her. Like he'd always touched her, protected her.

She needed to inform him she didn't need any help. She could take care of herself.

Besides, the last thing she needed in her life was a man who cared for her.

Since her divorce, Piper never let men close. As soon as they got out of this mess, she'd give Colby a piece of her mind. She'd set boundaries.

By the time she was ready for church, she had settled down. He had just been helping her. That's what he'd been hired to do. She was surely imagining anything more. Maybe the fact that she was attracted to the man was not due to what he said or how he looked, or anything he was doing on purpose, but to the way she felt when they touched. That might explain why she'd touched him a few times more than she needed to.

It was almost as if they were communicating on another level. Maybe by touch she was saying she needed him. Maybe he was silently saying he was there for her.

By the time she heard Jessica start an announcement in the main dining room, Piper was ready to sneak down the front stairs. She was cracking up. What chance did she have of slipping into a roomful of people without any notice?

One two-year-old turned to watch as she moved down the stairs, but all other eyes were on Jessica.

Since she was two hours early for church, Piper decided to have a light breakfast at the café, then work at her office for a while. As the diners clapped for the new addition to the menu, Piper slipped into a seat near the windows. She'd pulled off the impossible.

She'd just finished an omelet and coffee when she heard Colby's voice.

"Morning, PJ." He stepped around the waitress. "How's my sexy mayor this morning."

That urge to slug him was back, but Piper managed to smile. "I'm not sexy and I'm not yours. Don't tell me you got a job in this café."

People were listening and Colby stepped into his character. He did look the part of a cook. He even had a stain on the uniform.

Colby whispered something in her ear that she couldn't make out, and Piper noticed the three couples at the next table all smiled. Then aloud he added, "I'd do anything to be here with you. You want one of my grilled cheese? I'd make one special for you, darlin'."

"No, thanks."

Ten minutes later and without being asked, he came out and sat down at her table with a plate loaded down with today's special. "You don't look like you got enough sleep last night, darlin'. I'll share my breakfast if you're still hungry."

He wiggled his eyebrows suggestively and she kicked him under the table.

"I'm the luckiest man in the world to get to see you this early. How about we spend the day together? You could show me your town and I could talk you into loving me. I'm definitely lovable. Just ask my mother, she'll tell you."

A few feet away, they had an audience, who was now chuckling.

"Not happening." She stared at him as she folded her arms. "What are you wearing?"

Colby straightened his uniform. "I'm the new chef. I got a real job. I think that's worth one kiss from my sweetheart."

Several nearby diners laughed. The waitress refilled Piper's coffee. "Go ahead, Mayor, give the poor guy a kiss. He's been working hard in the kitchen."

"Not happening." She looked straight into Colby's amber eyes. "He may be cute, but he has the IQ of a flea. Go away, cowboy."

"Mind if I finish my breakfast first. I'm on my break."

"You haven't been working an hour." She hoped her voice didn't travel past him. "Go away."

He moved his hand over hers and got in one pat before she pulled hers away.

He had the nerve to give her a puppy-dog sad look.

She looked up at their audience and sensed that the diners were on his side. "All right, you can finish your meal and drink your coffee, and we only talk about the town, nothing more."

Colby nodded. He didn't say a word while she told him about the new preacher in town and how tonight would be the Fair on the Square. Lots of fund-raising booths just like they have at carnivals. There would be food trucks and dancing by sunset. "It's a fun way to usher in the summer."

As she talked she felt Colby's leg brush hers. She thought it was simply an accident until his knee pressed against hers again.

He kept his expression blank when her eyes met his. But he knew exactly what he was doing. Get her angry. Then she'd react. Make a scene.

Piper refused to play this game. She didn't move.

He scooted down slightly in his chair until his knee was touching her thigh. She tried to smile and keep talking about the town as her face grew warm.

Piper leaned closer to him and whispered, "I'm going to murder you as soon as I get you alone." She shifted, moving sideways in the chair and crossing her legs.

He leaned across the table and whispered

226

behind his coffee cup. "Why don't you slap me and walk away?"

She glared as she whispered, "Unlike you, I don't want to make a scene."

He smiled, his nose now only three inches away. "We already are the scene."

Piper didn't have to look around to know he was right. She straightened, having no idea how she'd get out of this mess. She wanted to be the mayor, a good daughter, nothing more. Anxiety built. She didn't want to be the person everyone was talking about. "Help me leave, Colby." The words were out before she realized she'd said them aloud.

The wish was spoken so softly she was surprised he'd heard it. Colby leaned back, dug a bill out of his uniform pocket, and tossed it on the table. Then he stood and offered his hand.

"I guess it's time for you to head to church, Mayor. Thanks for having breakfast with me, but I'd better get back to work." His words were clear and polite so anyone around could hear.

She stood, calm as if they were strangers. "Enjoy your visit in our town."

As they walked to the door Colby rested his hand on the small of her back. Just like he had last night, he was protecting her now, doing exactly what she'd asked him to do.

She knew he'd been trying to ruffle her earlier, give the folks something to talk about, but he'd gone too far. It was fine if he acted like he was love-sick about her, but Piper wanted to always remain professional. He must have realized she didn't know how to handle a scene, so he helped her.

When they were out of sight and hearing of the guests at the café, she turned on him ready to fight, but he spoke first. "I'm sorry. I may have gone too far."

The fight in her cooled and she took a deep breath. "You did. Don't do it again."

"I'll try, but I'm playing a fool in love." He gave her a slight smile. A real smile that was nothing like his acting grin. "You're an easy woman to rile."

"And you are the first man I've ever wanted to slug. I was angry but now I think I'll have to admit you are quite an actor. You almost had me believing you."

"So, PJ, should we kiss and make up?" The love-sick cowboy was back.

She punched him on the shoulder and walked away. She couldn't help but smile, though, when she heard his soft laughter behind her.

"I'll pick you up at Widows Park at three.

228

We'll dance on the square."
She pretended she hadn't heard him.

CHAPTER 18

10:45 a.m.

SAM

The church bells rang loud enough to travel down the valley and echo back again. Sunday. For the first time since he was more boy than man, Sam Cassidy stood and simply listened to the day begin. He closed his eyes. Cars were parking outside. Doors slamming. Children running along the gravel. And somewhere a baby cried.

Sam heard people moving up the wooden stairs to the choir loft, their shoes tapping almost in rhythm.

Stella had been right about the music director. He arrived early and was playing the organ as if it needed warming up. Sam couldn't see her, but he bet Stella was sitting near him getting ready for her solo.

Sam couldn't wait to hear her sing like an angel, just like her mother had told her she could. He had a feeling folks were probably coming more for the singing than his preaching. Since he got back from Anna's house so late he'd only had time to jot down a rough draft of his sermon last night before he fell asleep. It was nothing grand, but it would do.

The walker cluster was already seated on the second row left. The church always let their Sunday school class out early so the old folks could be seated first and, of course, have the pick of the donuts because row two was a direct line to the parlor. All walkers were lined along the wall.

Miss Daisy, the old dispatcher, would be among them.

Stella had told him that the widows from Widows Park always sat on the second row right. Tradition.

Sam closed his eyes. He'd had three hours sleep, but he was as ready as he'd ever be. He'd pieced bits of sermons together from what he remembered. His father often preached the same sermons several times because the congregation was always new. Once he had circled back to a town too soon and accidentally preached a repeat lesson. Only one person mentioned he'd heard it before.

Sam would start with how people should

love one another. As near as he could tell these folks were already doing that. Then he'd go over the commandments. Since he wasn't a priest, there was no confession, but several members hadn't hesitated to mention other people's weaknesses. They seemed to think they were doing the poor sinner a favor by confessing for him.

He hadn't been in town three whole days, but Sam was becoming convinced that coming here had been a bad idea. You can't go back fifteen years and start living the life you once wanted. But, like it or not, the past few days had changed him. He didn't know if it was for better or worse, but he had a feeling it was forever.

"You ready, Sam?"

He turned and was surprised to find Anna. "I'm ready. Did Stella make it here?"

"She did. I haven't seen her brother. Probably still home trying to figure out how the toaster works. She did everything for him, even bought his clothes."

"Is she penniless?" Sam had spent most of the way home fearing she was.

"Right now she's got a few hundred, but the house is half hers. I'll start digging in the morning when the courthouse is open. I bet half of her parents' inheritance is still in the bank. I might stop there first."

232

"Who will man the suicide lines if you go to the courthouse and bank?"

She grinned. "I'll have it routed to your number. Make sure you're in your office by nine."

Sam hoped she was kidding, but he didn't have time to worry about it now. The bells had stopped. Time to step up.

Anna walked with him down the hallway to a small door that opened a few feet from the pulpit. She patted his back. "Look at the bright side, Preacher. Good or bad, you'll be gone in a few weeks."

"That's comforting." He looked down and saw a green bow pinned in the mass of hair. "One question. Would you take me to the Fair on the Square tonight? I have no idea where it is or what to do."

Anna tilted her head. "You asking me out?"

"No, I'm asking for help."

"Then sure. You bring the leash and I'll walk you around. Stella could probably use a night to think about her next move. I'll pick you up at six, but you're paying."

"Fair enough."

Sam started down the little passage. As he walked, the congregation came into view a bit at a time. Second row. A line of mostly old ladies with hats. Families bunched

233

together sharing hymnals.

He could hear his heart picking up speed as if he were starting a marathon.

Next step closer. Mr. Winston was there. Third row center. He was all dressed up in a summer blue vest and a shiny black suit. People seemed to have given him plenty of room, but everyone nodded as they passed him.

Sam felt his stomach growl and his head start to pound.

He forced himself to look out over the congregation. Sam didn't know most of the faces, but they were a mixture of summer flowers and weeds. For just a moment he wished he could stay around and get to know them all.

The drunk he'd seen the first night he arrived was hunched down on the last row. His head hung low as if he didn't want anyone to see him, but for some reason he was there.

Sam reached the pulpit and grabbed on as if it was his only life raft.

As he straightened, he saw Stella standing in front of the organ, waiting.

Tyron Tilley rose and asked the congregation to stand and sing the first hymn. After that, he reminded them there would be a reception to welcome Samuel Cassidy after the service.

Sam could hear him leading the people through the opening, the welcome, the prayer, but he couldn't focus on the words. It dawned on him that he'd forgotten his notes and he couldn't remember even the first sentence of what he planned to say.

He broke out in a sweat. He thought he might be having a heart attack. After the army and all his jumps out of airplanes it would be Saints Church that killed him.

He'd been a fool thinking this would be easy. He'd rather fight a forest fire alone than preach.

Then Stella's high-pitched voice rose to the roof and pounded down on the crowd like hailstones.

Sam raised his head, praying that wasn't her singing. She was terrible. No, worse. She was so bad it was almost painful to hear. The organ was loud, but it couldn't drown out her voice. Sam knew he'd hear Stella's singing as background in every nightmare he'd have for years to come.

He forced himself not to move. Not even twitch. Instinct screamed for him to take cover, but he couldn't.

Then he looked out at the people. Her people. They were all smiling as if listening to the Mormon Tabernacle Choir, and he knew they were either all tone deaf or they loved Stella so much no one would tell her she couldn't sing.

Even the music director turned and smiled at her.

Stella had spent her life being kind, and in a small way they were paying her back.

Sam spotted Anna's red hair on the tenth row and smiled. She nodded slightly as if to say, *You figured it out.*

When the song was over, silence truly seemed golden for a moment, then a few Amens echoed.

The congregation settled in, waiting for Sam to start talking.

He was so blank he thought about asking Stella for another song. As he was making a show of turning to the right page in the hymnal, a racket came from the double doors at the back of the church.

Everyone wiggled on the benches as a big man with white hair and a little lady wearing a slightly wilted rose corsage came through the entrance. The man hadn't seen a razor in days and the woman looked a bit lost, but they were dressed for church. The lady wore sensible shoes and a dress she'd picked off a rack at a discount store. Both were in their sixties and to Sam's surprise they were holding hands.

The man's suit jacket flew open as he stormed the place, and Sam saw the flash of a badge on his white shirt. This was the lost sheriff the whole town had been talking about.

Halfway down the aisle he noticed folks staring at him. "Howdy, everyone. I'm sorry. I thought we'd be on time. Since Miss Flo started her English class on time for thirty-seven years, I guess I'm the one who's at fault."

No one responded. As far as Sam could tell no one even breathed.

The sheriff looked totally out of place, but the little woman with him pushed him with her shoulder. Her black purse bumped against her ample hip. "Come along, dear. We've got explaining to do."

The sheriff took control. "Miss Flo and me went to Vegas to get married the night she finally said yes. I wasn't taking any chances on her getting away. It's not easy to find a virgin in her sixties, but I got to respect her being so picky. We'll be coming to church every Sunday from now on. The missus insists on it." He looked around. "Any objections?"

Everyone seemed to take a breath at the same time, as if the sheriff might shoot the first one who objected.

A heartbeat later, Sam figured someone must have yelled "Go nuts!" and he missed the signal. Everyone started talking and moving toward the sheriff. Miss Daisy grabbed her walker and started doing a jig as she laid claim to having introduced the couple. Most seemed to know sweet Flo because they were hugging her before they spoke to LeRoy.

He might be a cranky, old sheriff, but she must have been a much-loved teacher.

Then Paul, in the choir loft, started playing the wedding march, and Tyron Tilley announced everyone should move to the parlor for a reception of donuts and coffee to celebrate the wedding.

Sam went straight to the last word of his sermon: "Amen!"

He'd live to panic another day.

Chapter 19

COLBY

Colby had left the café as soon as Piper pulled away. Dressed in his uniform with butter smeared on the front, he drove off on his motorcycle. He managed to find clothes at the local Walmart and got dressed in the public bathroom without anyone noticing, or caring.

If Piper was going to church, he was going in to watch her. Her brother had left a text early this morning saying that the news would be releasing evidence that Boone Buchanan was in debt over gambling losses. Reporters would be coming after her for a statement as soon as it was released.

The mayor would be facing trouble and he wanted to be there to stand guard. Now might be the time to say she was no longer involved with Buchanan, but the press

239

would still hound her. How much did she know? Was his unfaithfulness the reason they broke up?

The sunshine boy of the Buchanan clan was looking worse with each passing day.

Colby slipped into the church just as the singing started, and sat in the back pew with Daily Watts. From the looks of it, the mechanic hadn't bothered to change clothes since he'd left work Friday. He must have had a bad weekend. He'd been drunk both nights and now he was sleeping through church.

By the time the woman stopped singing, Colby was wishing he was drunk. Maybe he could wait out by the mayor's car for the service to be over. Before he could decide, the back doors bumped open as if someone had charged the door.

Colby went on full alert. On instinct he reached for his weapon. It wasn't there.

Two people entered the church. Colby slid down the bench. If they were trouble, he could come up to them from behind and stop any attack. There was too much random violence for him not to prepare for the worst, but this pair didn't fit the profile.

Then he took in a few things. The man was six feet tall. Three hundred pounds and then some. Most of his hair had slipped down to his sideburns.

The sheriff. Colby had looked at enough photos to recognize the man even in profile. Half the case was solved.

Colby texted the Rangers while the sheriff was explaining where he'd been. Then the whole place went crazy. Colby left Daily Watts asleep on the bench and joined the crowd moving to the parlor. He saw PJ up near the front. She was walking with two old women, her arms linked with theirs.

People flowed into the hallway like logs on the river, moving toward what he assumed was a big parlor in the back of the building.

He kept Piper in sight but once in a room with wing rooms to make more space, Colby moved to the back of the crowd, keeping near the wall as much as possible. Before long he bumped into the preacher, who'd arrived in town the same day he had.

"Hi, Pastor. Enjoyed your preaching."

"It was rather short." Sam smiled.

"Shorter than the shortest verse. I think that was 'Jesus wept.' "

"You know your Bible."

"Not really. I heard it on *Jeopardy!*"

Sam's smile melted. "We're about the same level of scholar. I'm thinking of giving this career up."

Colby shrugged. "Are you still thinking you don't belong here?"

"Maybe. But I am doing some good by helping a few people, so I guess my time hasn't been wasted. I helped a thirty-two-year-old woman run away from home, and I tried to help another one, a waitress, whose boyfriend had disappeared." Sam laughed. "She said he wanted to be her secret lover. No one was supposed to know." Sam shook his head. "Now he's so secret, even she can't find him. I can't believe she was naive enough to fall for it."

A lot of boyfriends seemed to be disappearing. "This guy she liked, was he a gambler?"

"I don't know. She said his best feature was his wallet. Seems he lives somewhere else and only comes through town now and then. Then a few days ago he stopped taking her calls."

Colby lied, "I might know this guy. She's better off without him."

"Yeah, but she has a right — a moral right, at least — to know why he dumped her. To just vanish like that is really tearing her up. She believed he really loved her and now she's got to find him."

"Tell me where to find her and I'll talk to her. If she describes this guy I know, I'll tell her where to find him so she'll have a chance to tell him off. That's a thing I've noticed about women. They like to say goodbye, usually rather loudly." Colby thought of his last girlfriend. She'd called to break up so many times it was still echoing in his head.

Sam shrugged. "I didn't help her much. She shouldn't be too hard to find, though. She's a waitress at a bar around here. I'm sorry, I can't remember which one. Long hair, long legs. Her name was Marcie."

Colby tried to act casual, but in truth he was itching to pull out his pad and write everything down. Only he didn't have a pad. He felt as naked as he had in Piper's bed this morning, but he didn't plan on admitting that to the preacher.

"If I talk to her, she may end up feeling even worse, and you may have to help her out with some counseling. If it's the same guy I know, he's bad news. Keeps more than one girl on the line at a time."

When Sam wandered off to refill his coffee, Colby leaned back against the wall and began to put the pieces together. It seemed Boone did have a woman — and it wasn't Piper. And if he did, she might know what went down in the hours before the BMW went into the water and the big-city lawyer disappeared. Maybe Boone had given some clue away and she didn't even realize she was holding it.

It didn't make a whole lot of sense. Why would a man who seemed to crave attention just disappear? Colby had read enough about him to figure out that he was probably living one life in the light and another in the shadow. He played the part of golden son of one of the oldest families in Texas, yet he drove over a hundred miles to drink and gamble and consort with waitresses.

He was getting a very bad feeling about this.

For once, PJ showed up at his side without him having to go looking for her. It took Colby a few seconds to switch from serious investigator to love-sick cowboy.

"Are you following me?"

He continued watching the crowd and didn't look at her.

"Yes," he whispered. "You look great, by the way." Still, without facing her, he asked, "Where are you going after this?"

She hesitated, and then gave a small shrug. The fact was, Colby could probably ask anyone in the room where she was going, and he'd get the same answer. She went to Widows Park every Sunday. Piper was very predictable and everyone knew it.

244

Which was why her secret hideout at the café had surprised him. The people in town thought they knew all about her. She worked late. She always showed up on time. She took care of all the widows. She loved her town, the city hall her grandfather had built.

PJ poked him as if she was waking him up. "I'll be at Widows Park until about three; then I plan to walk down to the fair."

"Good. Stay with the ladies until I get back. I've something to check out first; then I'll go with you to the fair. Hopefully we'll have good news before dark. Oh, PJ, don't talk to the press. Not a word unless I'm at your side."

After leaving the church gathering, Colby rode straight to Fisherman's Lodge and found Digger sitting on his porch. As always the place looked deserted. "Morning, Digger. You counting cars going by?"

To his surprise, the old man said, "Sure am. Ten years ago we didn't have half as many on Sundays. Before long they'll build one of those interstates and we'll start having traffic twenty-four/seven."

"You're right." Colby couldn't imagine being so bored that he'd have to start counting cars. "I got a strange question."

Digger leaned back in his rocking chair. "I

ain't asking any questions of you, son. But I might answer a few. If I was doing the asking, I might ask why you didn't come home last night, or why your jeans still have the price tag on them? Probably be an interesting story, but I ain't asking. Course, I'll have to charge you for the night even if you were in someone else's bed."

"Fine. I'll pay and thanks for not asking. I was out on the river with a lady. I followed her home and she didn't kick me out. That is all the details you're going to get. Now, to my question."

Digger leaned forward as if Colby was about to test his skills.

Colby decided to be direct. "You wouldn't happen to know where a woman named Marcie tends bar. I need to ask her a few questions."

"You ain't planning to pester her, are you, son?"

"I'm doing this for the mayor. Piper needs her help."

Digger was silent for a few rocks of the chair, then he said, "She's over in Someday Valley. Ain't nothing but a jumble of trailer parks and bars in that spot in the road they call a town. Her folks used to own a place called Bandit's Bar. First bar you pass heading into town. Don't know if they passed it to her and her brother. Marcie comes from bar room royalty. They say her granddad ran whiskey during Prohibition."

Colby stood. "Thanks." He now had a direction to head.

"Course she ain't there today. It's Sunday."

Colby deflated. He should have guessed that it wasn't going to be that easy. "Any idea where she lives?"

"Nope, you might want to wander through the trailer park yelling her name. If she ain't shacking up with some guy, she might stick her head out and answer. Might not. Somebody sleeping might just shoot your head off for yelling. Most of the folks living out there are nightwalkers. Probably vampires. You know, like *The Walking Dead*."

"Digger, those were zombies." Colby couldn't believe he was having this conversation. "Well, thanks for trying to help me."

The old man shrugged. "Sorry I don't know, son, but I do know where she'll be tonight."

"I thought you said the bar was closed."

"It is, but she's one of the backup singers with the band playing for the dance on the square tonight. She ain't great, but those long legs dancing onstage make me, with only one good leg, think I should twirl her around the floor a few times."

Colby grinned. Finally, the answer he needed. "Thanks, Digger."

"You might want to talk to the sheriff. He's back, you know."

Colby raised an eyebrow. "I know, but how did you know? The reception is still going on."

Digger laughed. "I always listen to the sermon on the local radio channel. It was so short this morning they had to play a half hour of Elvis hymns to round it out. Tell that new preacher I really liked his message. Amen is my favorite part. That and Miss Stella's singing." When Digger saw Colby's frown, he added, "It's an acquired taste for the ears."

Colby fought the urge to back away from the old guy. He had a chilling fear that he was starting to understand the people of Honey Creek.

Before long he'd be counting cars.

CHAPTER 20

Early afternoon

PECOS

Pecos stood on the lawn outside the high school auditorium living his nightmare. Families were all around him, hugging, laughing, taking pictures as if making it through high school was a grand achievement.

One family had even brought a ten-foot banner painted with three-foot letters: "Happy Gradation." No one seemed to notice the missing *u*.

The wind blew his huge paper gown around his thin body, adding the finishing touch to his bad dream. His parents hadn't come. All around, families were celebrating while he stood there like a flagpole. Out of place like always. How had he become that guy that everyone knew and no one was friends with?

He thought about leaving, but that would just draw more attention to himself. Plus, he'd promised Kerrie that he'd walk across the stage. Too bad, because even sitting home with his dad watching golf was better than this.

He heard his name being called. "Pecos!"

He turned around and saw Kerrie running toward him. Her diploma in one hand and her hat in the other. Her long blond hair waving behind her like a superhero's cape.

Before he could react, she ran into him, almost toppling him as she hugged him. Her hat hit one side of his head and her diploma edged into his shoulder, but he barely noticed. She was hugging him right there in front of everyone.

He kissed the top of her head. "The speech was great. You're really going places, Kerrie."

"No, it wasn't that good." She laughed. "I forgot to say the last line."

For once he didn't think about who would see or if he was doing the right thing. He just kept hugging her because this one hug had to make up for all those he didn't get.

Maybe she hadn't been making fun of him last night when she'd asked him to be her boyfriend. She liked him enough to give him a hug, and that had to be a sign that they were really at least friends.

"Let's get out of here," she said, smiling up at him.

Before he could answer, she was pulling on his hand, and then they were running toward his old pickup. She jumped in and slid over close to him. "Let's do something wild. I want to be free and still a kid for one more day."

"Name it, babe."

His smile was so wide he could feel the stretch on his cheeks. He was finished with school and he had a girl beside him whom he could call babe. Life was grand. This felt more like a movie than real life, and all he could do was hope it would never end.

"I know, let's go to our rock and dive off in the river."

"We can't do that. We don't have our bathing suits."

"We don't need them. No one will see us."

Pecos's mood plummeted. Even he didn't like to see his body, so he definitely didn't want Kerrie seeing it. He was so thin she'd be able to count his ribs. He had one spot of chest hair and legs that looked like hairy pipe cleaners. "I don't know about that."

Then it dawned on him that he wouldn't be the only one taking off his clothes. He'd

251

seen girls in bikinis lots of times, but he'd never seen what was beneath. Not a real girl anyway, only pictures. He'd seen his mom in her underwear once and he'd thought about cramming his toothbrush in his ear and scrubbing the memory out.

But Kerrie nude? That picture would be worth bronzing and letting it roll around in his brain for the rest of his life.

Kerrie put her hand on the back of his neck and whispered, "Come on, Pecos. It'll be fun. It'll be something we'll always remember."

Five minutes later they were on their rock surrounded by trees so thick no one could see them. Kerrie turned her back and stripped off her clothes, then jumped in. Pecos just watched. He'd seen her back. All of her back.

He'd barely started undressing before she shrieked his name. Panicked, he threw off his clothes and jumped in. The current was strong and he might have to save her. What if she couldn't swim? What if he couldn't swim strong enough? He'd dived in Honey Creek, but never the river.

There was no going back. He jumped. When he closed his eyes, all he saw was the back of her running toward the water.

A moment later they were swimming. For

252

the first time in his life he felt totally free. The day was hot and sunny and he was with the smartest, most beautiful girl in school. Life didn't get any better. If he died right now, he'd take this one memory with him into the next life. It was too precious to leave behind.

She laughed and splashed him. "You're so tan."

"I was born tan." He laughed. "I got the blood of everybody who ever walked across Texas in me."

She wrapped her arm around his neck and let her body brush his. "I think you're beautiful, inside and out, Pecos."

If she'd have stayed any longer against him they might have had sex. He had no idea how long it took, but he knew he was ready if she'd just stay close.

He would have been willing to give anything a try, but she swam away before he could figure out what to say or do?

When she swam underwater, he called out, "Watch out for the catfish that's as big as a man. I've heard lots of fishermen see him, but no one ever catches him."

She came up spitting water. "That's just a legend."

"What if it's not?"

"Then he'll eat you first and I'll live to

tell the story." They both laughed.

When they were both exhausted, they climbed out of the water and dried each other with a blanket from the back of the truck. Pecos tried to act like this wasn't the first time he'd seen a naked girl, but he couldn't seem to form words. Her breasts seemed bigger now that they were free and Kerrie wasn't thin. She even had a bit of a tummy he hadn't noticed with her clothes on. It seemed she was rounded in all the right places.

When she put on her underwear, a lacey bra and panties to match, he still couldn't take his eyes off her. He'd seen his mother's underwear on the line and those had been nothing like this.

He put on his shorts and they lay in the sun like lazy turtles. This was the best few hours he'd probably have for the rest of his life. If she'd thought he was too thin, she didn't comment.

Kerrie closed her eyes as she held his hand. He thought she might be asleep until she suddenly sat up.

Pulling her knees to her chin, she started to cry so softly he barely heard her.

He had no idea why she was crying — this girl who had the perfect life. He should have asked *what* or *why,* but he held back. Guys like him didn't get to just walk into her world. She'd given him a memory; he was grateful for that.

She was someone he'd watched ever since they started school all those years ago. He'd loved the bows in her hair, a new one every day. Now and then she'd smile at him like she knew he was staring at her. When she was older, Pecos remembered watching her do her cheerleader thing more than he watched the games.

Now he remembered how she'd cried that night he'd picked her up from the end of the school dance. Maybe it was just a habit of hers and he'd never noticed it before.

Finally, she stood and began to dress. They both knew the wild time was finished.

Maybe if he'd thought they had a chance of making this real, he might have been mad or hurt, but all he felt was hollow. The movie was over, it was time to leave the theater and step back into the real world. He'd go home and thank his parents for the new work gloves and the fifty dollars in a card. School was over and except for these few hours his new life didn't seem in any hurry to begin.

"You should get dressed," she whispered so low he barely heard. "I'm sorry I cried."

"You all right now?"

"Yeah." She stood. "You ever get the idea that things are changing and nothing is ever going to be the same."

"I'm hoping that's the way it will be."

When Pecos dropped Kerrie at her car, she asked him to come to an early dinner at her house. "When it cools off, we can walk down to the square. My grandfather is selling his honey at the fair, and I try to always help him for a few hours."

"I'll go home and clean up." He could think of nothing he'd rather do than spend more time with her. He realized he had always loved her. She never laughed when he wore his tie and she always smiled at him.

When she got out of his truck, she kissed him on the cheek like it was the most natural thing in the world to do. Pecos waited until he was out of sight to touch the spot. By his count, she'd kissed him three times.

When he walked into his parents' house ten minutes later, neither of them greeted him. They didn't ask about the graduation or where he'd been. Mom was on the phone to her sister, and Dad was stacking up empty beer cans by his chair. Typical Sunday.

Pecos showered and packed. What he took didn't fill the suitcase. He wasn't sure where he'd sleep tonight, but it wouldn't be here. He left the new work gloves his dad handed him yesterday on his bed. When Pecos had first seen the gloves, he'd asked, "This for graduation?" and his dad had said, "Yeah, kid, come Monday your life is going to be work. No more goofing off or going to school. Things will be changing."

For once his old man was right. Pecos was about to change. He figured he had no way to go but up.

When he walked out of the house, no one even looked in his direction. He didn't look back. This wasn't somewhere he wanted to be. Not ever again.

CHAPTER 21

Sunday afternoon

SAM

Sam stayed in the parlor a long time after everyone left the church. He helped with the cleanup and visited with the sweet ladies called the kitchen crew.

Even the people who didn't like the sheriff seemed happy for him. LeRoy had told everyone who'd listen that he'd been attracted to Miss Flo every time he saw her. She retired and moved to Clifton Bend to take care of her mother, but she'd substituted off and on in several schools over the valley.

LeRoy bragged that she wouldn't go out with him until he cleaned up his act, and that had taken him more years than it should have. He claimed he kept driving the thirty miles to her place to ask for editing help with his legal papers. She'd always

258

serve him coffee and pie. He said she must have finally figured out that he was too dumb to live alone and so she agreed to marry him.

In Sam's eyes, Flo simply looked like a little old lady, but everyone could see that from the sheriff's view she was perfect. He admitted that his deputies had to know where to find him if an emergency came along, so they knew about Flo. Only they didn't consider a car floating down the river that important; after all, there was no body and the flights LeRoy booked weren't refundable.

The sheriff admitted he planned to retire soon, and he and Miss Flo were going to see the world. They might go as far as California.

As Sam walked through the church, he decided the whole service this morning was grand. Most folks mentioned that the sheriff was a hard man to get along with, but he was Play-Doh in the little grade school teacher's hands.

When Sam entered the side door of the church, he heard people talking. Stella and Paul were both sitting on the organ bench in the loft. While he watched unseen by them, they rose and headed down the stairs discussing where to eat lunch.

Sam stepped back out of sight.

When they closed the front door and disappeared, Sam walked down the middle aisle. Now he had a whole week to work up a sermon. Maybe he'd do a better job. Then he remembered, he'd already decided to go back to his life fighting fires. Maybe he'd teach the young pups coming up through the ranks.

For his next and last sermon, then, maybe he'd just stick with what worked. "Amen" had gone over very well today.

In the last pew he found Daily Watts slumped over, his eyes closed. Sam put his hand on the man's shoulder and asked, "You need any help, Daily?"

The mechanic's bloodshot eyes popped open. "I see them following me, but they can't be real. I don't know if they're angels or devils." His words tumbled out in a drunkard's cry. "If I come in here and see them, I'll know they are angels 'cause devils wouldn't go in a church, I'm thinking. But they weren't here."

Sam remembered the three little kids following Daily the first night Sam was in town.

"All I can tell you, Daily, is that sometimes you have to face your fears."

"You may be right, Preacher. I used to get

drunk one night a week, but lately it's two. At the rate I'm going I won't keep my job and that's all I've got. Maybe my brother is right. I'm no good to anybody."

On a guess Sam asked, "Did you once have a kid?"

"Yeah, I was going to. I killed him. My wife was big pregnant. She wasn't wearing her seatbelt 'cause she said it rubbed on her tummy. I was going too fast and didn't have time to stop. They both died and I walked away."

"Were you drinking that night?"

"No, but have ever since. My wife always said we'd have three kids and now I've got three ghosts following me. I'd die if it'd bring my wife back, but it don't work that way." Daily stood. "I better be going. Good sermon this morning, Preacher."

"Thanks." He walked Daily to the door. "Do me a favor. The next time you see those kids, stop and talk to them."

"Why not," the drunk muttered. "I've already lost my sanity, nothing they can take from me."

Sam headed down to the basement where he thought he might find Anna Presley. If they were going to the Fair on the Square later today, they needed to get to know each other, or at least set some rules for not yelling.

He wasn't surprised to find her knee-deep in a project. "Want some help?"

"No, Stella said she'd help."

"Stella left with the organ player. They were discussing where they planned to eat lunch. Paul said he'd like to backtrack down the road about thirty miles. He said there was a little place that looked good and it had a sign that claimed they were always open. I didn't hear her answer, but she got in his car so unless the organ player is kidnapping her, I guess the answer was yes."

Anna tossed a box with *Easter* written on the side. "If she's gone, that leaves you as my helper. We're boxing up all the Valentine and Easter stuff in the marked boxes. Don't get them mixed up. Then we'll put those boxes in the back and pull forward all the fall decorating material."

He picked up a dozen coloring books with bunnies on the cover and put them in the box. When he tried to slip in paper hearts, she shook her head and tossed him another box, this time with Valentine's Day on the side.

Glue, scissors, markers, and putty had their own boxes, along with plastic eyeballs and paintbrushes. Used gum, broken toys, and chewed pencils had no box.

For a while they worked in silence; then she said with a smile, "You do know that you're being paid in donuts."

"I've already eaten four. I would have eaten another couple chocolate glazed, but Mr. Winston wrapped them in a paper towel and stuffed them in his coat pocket." Sam liked her smile.

"There will be food at the fair, Preacher. Since you're buying, we'll have a late lunch and dinner. I'm starving."

"You're sure?" He started working faster.

"Another hour and we'll be on our way. We can't stay long, though. I want to make sure I'm home before Stella gets back. She doesn't have a cell so we can't call her. If she comes here, you'll bring her to my place, right?"

"Right, but wouldn't it be simpler to call the organ player. Surely he's got a cell if he drives in and out every Sunday."

For some reason Anna hit him with another box. All he could think to say was, "His number's on the bulletin board in the office."

Sam considered that hitting him with boxes was her way of showing him affection. If he ever kissed her, she'd probably stab him with rounded tip scissors. If they made love, he had no doubt, given her violent nature, she'd run over him with that old Jeep she drove.

Sam went back to work, smiling. He was looking forward to defending himself.

While she called the organ player, Sam stepped out on the back porch. He noticed a tall woman leaning against a car he'd seen yesterday morning. She'd said it had been out of gas.

"Morning, Marcie. You find your secret love?"

She nodded as she dropped her cigarette and ground it into the gravel. "I did. When he heard I was looking for him in Honey Creek he came looking for me with a can of gas. I almost didn't recognize him in old fishing clothes and several days of beard."

"I'm happy for you."

He'd walked close enough to see her face. She was a tall, beautiful woman in her twenties who seemed to have a hundred years of sadness in her eyes.

"You all right, Marcie?"

She shook her head. "I'm glad he's back. He says he still loves me but we still can't tell anyone."

"Why?" Sam wasn't sure he wanted to know.

"Oh, he's not married or anything like

264

that, Preacher. He has plans, big plans. He's had some bad press lately. People digging up dirt on him, but that will be forgotten soon. He says he's going to inherit a lot of money and we can go to Mexico and live it up."

Sam was confused. She didn't seem very happy about her boyfriend's plan. "What bothers you about that?"

Marcie lowered her head. "Does that priest thing still apply? You can't tell anyone what I say."

"Sure, but I'm not a priest."

"I know, but you're as close to being one as I can find and I really need to tell someone."

Sam had the feeling he was on the last chapter of a terrible mystery novel. He hated the thought of what might come next, but he had to turn the page. "You can tell me. I may not be much help, but I'll listen."

Marcie pulled out a tissue, wiped her nose, and whispered, "He says there's a woman who played him along. Used him. Acted like she cared." She blew her nose. "He said this woman might have to die for everything to work out. It was all crazy talk. I know he won't really do it, but it scared me."

Sam heard the back door of the church

open. Anna was bumping her way out with a cart. He moved closer to Marcie. "You've got to go to the sheriff, Marcie."

"No," whispered. "I love him. He'll calm down. Now I know where he is, I'll stay with him. Maybe everything will work out as he plans. We'll be on the beach next week." She turned toward her car door.

"Come back tomorrow. Promise."

She didn't answer. She didn't even look his direction as she gunned the car and raced away as if she'd left her problem at his feet.

CHAPTER 22

Sunday afternoon

PECOS

Pecos drove slowly back to town. This might be the last time he made this back road, maybe for years. He'd write his brothers and tell them where he landed. He doubted they'd be surprised that he left home. Tucson had once mentioned that Pecos could come live with him while he was stateside. Pecos would figure something out. He wasn't going back; if he did, he knew his spirit, his drive, his dreams would all slowly dribble away.

It occurred to him that this was his parents' way of pushing their chicks out of the nest. If so, they needed some serious parenting classes.

Pecos parked a few houses down from the Lanes' place. Kerrie's dad probably wouldn't want an old pickup in his driveway.

As he approached, he saw that Kerrie was sitting on the front steps waiting for him. She jumped up and ran up to him, taking his hand. She seemed nervous.

"Let's just have fun tonight. Be happy. We can worry about tomorrow in the morning, and please don't tell my mother I cried."

"I wouldn't do that."

"I figured out that I want everything to stay the same as it's always been and you want it to change. Look at it this way. One of us is going to get what we want."

He sensed she was pretending to be the happy, popular, beautiful girl everyone loved to be around. He remembered watching her in middle school and wondering if Kerrie Lane ever got a mosquito bite or broke a sweat. She seemed so perfect. But at close range he saw the sadness in her eyes today.

Something was bothering her, but she didn't want to face it now.

"Okay." Pecos smiled down at her. "We have fun tonight. Tomorrow we'll talk about the world changing. If it's too much, we'll run away."

She shook her head. "I've already thought of running away. That wouldn't work. I've never been anywhere that didn't make me want to come back to Honey Creek."

He needed to see her real smile. "We

could join the circus. I could be a clown and you could walk the tightrope. We'd travel the world."

"You'd go with me?" she teased.

"I would, even though I'm pretty sure I'm allergic to the face paint."

They were laughing as they entered the house together.

Unlike last night, there were only a dozen people around. A few cousins on Kerrie's mother's side who drove in from Dallas for graduation — one with three noisy kids. The men mostly stood outside and smoked.

Everyone in Kerrie's family talked at once. Not one listener in the bunch. It was like trying to watch three or four TV shows at a time. Pecos was relieved when Kerrie grabbed his hand and pulled him to the door.

"Time to go. Mom's starting to tell family stories and believe me, you don't want to hear about my great uncles."

He thought he might, but she pulled him out. Pecos waved and yelled thanks, then they were off to walk the two blocks to the fair. There were rides for little kids and a water slide for anyone brave enough. A dozen games with all the money going to charities. Booths to sell local goods and three food trucks.

Pecos pulled a twenty from his pocket thinking he'd spend the whole bill on her.

The air was still hot on the square as they circled. Her grandfather had a green booth with bees painted on the fringe. All the bees were smiling.

Kerrie introduced Pecos to her grandfather, then went to get everyone lemonade.

Pecos was immediately comfortable with the old guy. He'd grown up talking to the senior citizens in town and one thing he'd learned was that they like to pass their knowledge along.

"Tell me about the bee business, sir. I'm fascinated."

Papa Lane laughed and slapped Pecos on the back. An hour later, Pecos had the yellow apron on and was selling honey as fast as he could count change, and Papa Lane was sipping lemonade with his granddaughter in the back of the tent.

The day aged and finally the strings of lights between the booths came on, forming a colorful square around what would soon be the dance floor.

Papa ate his second corn on the cob and announced that he was calling it a night.

Pecos offered his hand. "Thanks for the wisdom, sir. I had a great time."

As their palms touched, a hundred-dollar

bill passed. Pecos looked down. "No, sir. I didn't do it for money. I loved it."

"Always do what you love, son, and you'll never have to worry about money. You earned this today. You did all the work and I had so much fun. Sold twice what I could have and I got to sit in the shade with my granddaughter. If you ever need a job, there'll be one waiting at the farm."

"Thanks. I might take you up on that."

Kerrie walked her grandfather to his truck while Pecos loaded the last few boxes of honey. Then, as they watched the old man drive off, Pecos put his arm around her shoulder.

"You were great today." She linked her arm around his waist as they walked back toward the square. "He ships all over the state. My parents don't understand why he thinks he has to set up a booth on the square."

"He's proud of his work."

"I guess you're right. I think he loved teaching you the business. You might want to think about taking a job if you're not too busy on the farm this summer."

He didn't answer. Now wasn't the time to tell her he'd left home. That would be another day. Worry clouded his good mood. They were both pushing conversations they needed to have down the road.

Kerrie suddenly tugged on his arm. "Let's go see how long until the dance starts."

As if on command, the sound system blared through the loud speaker. The singer yelled, "It's almost dark thirty and time to do some boot scootin'. So, eat up, then join us."

Pecos pulled her back. "I don't know how." He was the worst date ever. "I've never danced."

She stopped just outside the circle of lights and smiled up at him. "I'll teach you here in the shadows."

And she did.

CHAPTER 23

Late afternoon

COLBY

Colby spent the afternoon investigating the woman he'd heard about named Marcie. Digger's advice had been on point, but Sam's casual comment had given him the clue he'd been waiting for since Friday. Several others backed up what the preacher told him about the dark-haired, long-legged woman looking for her secret boyfriend. She'd stopped several places in town before she ran out of gas.

He drove thirty miles over to the tiny town Digger said she lived in. A few people in Someday Valley thought they might have seen the guy with her a few times.

Colby asked if he looked anything like Boone Buchanan. None of the folks looked like the news-watching types.

No one remembered the man's name if

273

Marcie had mentioned it. Only that he drove a fancy car and was usually drinking.

One man at the gas station over in Someday Valley said he hadn't seen her around the past few days, but everyone knew she'd be at the fair in Honey Creek to sing backup with her brother. The guy added, "Those kids had a hard life growing up. Marcie pretty much raised him. But they were lucky; they had each other."

Carefully Colby pieced together all he knew. The stranger who always had money, who drove a nice car, who came in once or twice a month had to be Boone. Which would explain why he wanted to keep their relationship secret. Marcie wasn't the kind of woman a rich, powerful lawyer would date, especially one who worried about his image as much as Boone apparently had.

There were dozens of reasons men keep affairs private. But Marcie had told the preacher that he hadn't shown up for their date the same night as the BMW hit the river. The bartender in Honey Creek said he'd seen pictures of Boone Buchanan in the papers and swore he was the same guy who hit on one of his girls at the Pint and Pie a few months back. Apparently he'd even bragged about being engaged to Piper there as well.

But this theory had holes. Why didn't Boone show up after he drove into the water? What was the point of him staying out of sight? Unless he was dead at the bottom of the river. Another question. Sam had said Marcie disappeared in the time he walked to the back of the church and got his gas can. Where had she gone? Her car was out of gas and it vanished too. She hadn't clocked in to work Saturday night. Where had she been all day and night?

Colby had no idea if she was part of the problem or part of the solution.

If the guy was right about her making it to the fair to support her brother, Colby might have his answers tonight when the band took the stage. Something told him if he could find her, he'd find Boone. If he was alive.

From what he'd heard, the guy struck him as an awfully cold fish. No one around here liked him. No close friends. Even his family didn't seem all that worried about him. No members of the Buchanan family stepped forward to make a statement. Maybe disappearing was one of Boone's habits when things were not going his way.

Colby's brain was still trying to make the pieces fit together when he knocked on the Widows Park door. It was hours later than he'd said he'd be there to pick up Piper.

Two tiny women in flowery dresses a few sizes too big answered the door. They reminded him of the twins in Steven King's *The Shining,* only they'd aged about eighty years. One was a few inches taller and the other wore glasses.

"Afternoon, ladies, I'm here to pick up Mayor Piper and take her to the fair. I'm Colby McBride."

One pushed her glasses up on her nose and began to examine him, and the other leaned around him to get a long look at his Harley.

"I'm her aunt Nancy. She's not here," the one with glasses announced.

The other lady lifted her top chin. "I'm her aunt Geraldine, and I can tell you right now, young man, she won't ride on that." She pointed at his Harley. "Do you even have a seat belt for that thing?"

Both took a step back as Nancy began closing the door.

"Wait." Colby panicked. He'd told her he'd pick her up. Piper could have waited for him. "Do you ladies know where she is? I've got to find her."

Nancy, the one with glasses, made a face and her lips disappeared. "We've heard about you, Mr. McBride."

Geraldine nodded. "Some folks say you're crazy. Maybe you should stay away from our Piper."

Colby looked as sad as he could manage. "I'm crazy in love with her. She agreed to go with me to the fair, but I'm late and now she may never give me another chance."

Nancy frowned. "She's at the fair, of course. She's the mayor of this town. It's her duty. But don't you bother her if she says go away. The people of this town won't stand for it, you hear me?"

"Yes, ma'am. If she says go away, I'll be gone."

Her sister added, "She won't ride on that thing so you might as well leave it parked here."

Then the door closed, and Colby was staring at polished oak. He walked toward the town square, leaving his Harley parked in front of Widows Park like they told him. No one would bother it and he doubted any of the residents would go for a ride.

The late-afternoon temperature was cooling thanks to a few clouds floating above. Sunshine and shadows made a patchwork over the sidewalks. This was his third day in Honey Creek and he felt like he'd lived here forever. There was something about the people. The way they talked. The way they

277

told stories of the early days with a bit of a smile. The way they cared about each other and let people live the way they wanted. Crazy seemed a gypsy thread running through everyone's family quilt.

As he stepped into the square, people waved at him. One couple even rushed over to tell him that the mayor was on the shady side of city hall.

Colby took his time walking there. He liked hearing the sounds. A barker yelling for kids to pay for a chance to shoot a water gun at their teachers for charity. A mother calling her children by name and birth order. People talking and laughing. A few felt the need to yell hello to anyone they hadn't talked to in an hour.

He'd grown up in the cities. Dallas, Austin, even spent a year in Houston. Most of his memories were of being in the back seat of a car driving in traffic. His parents were focused on their careers. They loved him dearly but were disappointed when he turned down law school to be a trooper. Neither ever asked about his work.

He'd seen a great deal, but here it was like all his senses came alive. He wasn't just looking. He was feeling, hearing, smelling.

Speaking of smelling, he stopped by the cotton candy booth before finally finding

Piper sitting in the long shade from a dying sun.

One of the Jeffs he'd met in the bar the first day he'd arrived was sitting beside her as if keeping guard. As soon as he saw Colby, he stood and said his goodbyes.

"Evening, darlin'." Colby bowed slightly. "I see you're stepping out with another man even after our night —"

She stopped his rambling by grabbing his arm and pulling him down to the chair beside her. "Hello, cowboy. I see you haven't learned to tell time yet. You were supposed to pick me up at three for this, our first and last date."

Colby was aware there were people listening. "I drove all over the valley looking for a gift for you. A memento of our first date. But, what do I get a woman who has everything?"

Piper thought about saying his absence, but in truth the cowboy act was growing on her. "So what did you come up with?" She pinched off a bite of his cotton candy.

He grinned that irritating puppy-dog grin. "All I could think of was me. I'm yours, PJ. All yours." The band started setting up. Colby took a look at the small stage. Two men, no long-legged woman. "Promise you'll dance with me."

"You can dance?"

"I majored in it at college." He reached for her hand.

"I have no doubt." She pulled away as a man and a woman approached to say hello.

Colby was dying to tell her about what he'd found, but people kept interrupting. They'd say hello to the mayor, then cut their eyes to him. Piper was forced to introduce him.

"I'm her date," he'd say every time. She'd frown at him. The people would smile and leave. They'd found out what they came over to find. The mayor had a date.

After half an hour they were alone for a moment. She leaned close to his ear and whispered, "Stop telling people you're my date."

"But I am your date," he whispered back, his lips tickling her ear. His voice shifted slightly. All business now. "There are things I need to tell you. Information. Can we go somewhere to talk?"

"No, there are too many people watching. Later."

Another family came up to show Piper their newest grandchild. The chubby toddler grabbed Colby's finger and wouldn't let go. Colby felt like he was being attacked by a sticky jellyfish. Any minute he'd be stung.

Sure enough, while the grandparents were visiting with Piper, the little monster bit the tip of Colby's finger with his only two teeth.

Colby leaned down and said, "I'm not eatable."

As they went toward the kiddie rides, Colby moved close to Piper and whispered, "I'd be mad, too, if I was named Truman," which got a laugh out of her.

She shook her head. "That's not his problem, you were. You didn't taste good."

For once they both laughed.

When the music started Colby stood and offered Piper his hand. In her high heels and summer dress she looked ready to dance. She accepted his offer with a smile.

For a few dances he kept it simple, but the flare of her skirt made twirling her fun and she moved easier in heels to the western music than most women do in boots. Best of all he liked touching her and when he pulled her close, she came willingly. Her hand rested on his shoulder as her fingers played with his hair. The light touch drove him mad.

Colby tried to concentrate on watching the stage. He was waiting for Marcie to show up, but so far no one had joined the male band of three.

When a slow dance began, he pulled Piper into his arms and leaned close to her ear.

Piper managed to follow his steps as he told her all about what he'd learned.

He ended with, "If someone picked her up Saturday morning on the church steps, it was probably Boone. She'd been calling him. Likely she left word where she was and that she was out of gas."

"Well, that's if he's alive," Piper said. "She could have called her brother and he finally showed up before the preacher came back."

Colby took time to twirl her around. When she came back to him he murmured. "I love it when you whisper in my ear, darlin'."

She pulled away a bit and gave him a frustrated look. A few dancers around them smiled.

Colby looked around. "You live in a fishbowl, Mayor."

"I do. Remember that, cowboy."

As they danced, Colby got used to her in his arms. His great aunt, on the Mormon branch of the family, told Colby dancing was nothing but foreplay. Colby sure hoped she was right.

When the next slow song began, he pulled her close again and she did that whispering thing he loved. "I don't care what Boone's doing with some woman named Marcie. I just want him to be alive and out of my world."

Colby didn't answer right away. He realized if the case was solved, there would be no reason for him to stay. He closed his eyes and breathed in the smell of Piper, the feel of her so close made him feel high. How could he be falling hard for a woman in two days? It didn't make sense. He was a love-'em-and-leave-'em kind of guy.

Someone tapped him on the shoulder. Bringing Colby back to reality.

"May I dance with the mayor?"

Colby stepped aside as the lodge manager moved in. For a moment he watched them moving awkwardly like a clock wound backward. All the grace of Piper in his arms was lost on Digger, but the old guy was laughing. He kept one leg still like it was nailed to the ground and circled her round and round.

Colby's attention moved to the stage. There was a woman waiting in the shadows behind the band. Long hair tied back in a ponytail. A peasant blouse looking like it was held up by only her breasts. Her long skirt swayed to the music.

Then she was onstage and singing with the band.

One member of the band smiled at her. The brother, Colby guessed.

After three songs Colby saw that Digger had passed Piper off to another man. She looked like she was enjoying herself. He'd be lucky to get another dance. There was a line forming.

Which was fine. He needed to concentrate on the woman onstage. The one person who might know where Boone Buchanan was.

At the end of the next song, the pony-tailed singer in the long skirt kissed her brother and waved goodbye to the crowd. A moment later she was off the back of the stage and disappearing from view. She was moving fast.

Colby had no time to signal Piper. He was right behind the woman. Trying to keep up. Trying to be invisible as he followed her through a side street.

CHAPTER 24

Sunset

SAM

Sam Cassidy thought that he must have the worst tour guide ever born. Anna Presley was small and could dart between people, losing him in a second. What was worse, she blamed him for not paying attention when he finally found her. Along Main Street she spent more time telling him what used to be there than what was there now.

Someone must have wound her up too tight at birth and she hadn't slowed down since. Then there was her voice. Like an old record someone was playing on the wrong speed. To be honest, Anna sounded like one of the Chipmunks.

Of course, he was at a town square fair so he could see half the event from any one corner. Plus, her red hair was hard to miss. The only time she seemed to stay near was when they were in the food lines. In less than an hour she'd tried a fried Oreo, two hot dogs, and a plate of sweet potato fries covered in cheese. Sam felt like he was her walking TV tray.

Most of the people at the fair had been in the church that morning and several complimented him on his sermon.

Sam noticed Daily Watts wandering around and, for once, he didn't look drunk. There was a sadness about him that sank all the way to his bones. He mostly stayed on the edge of the crowd but when the music started, it drew him closer.

Sam guessed that at some time in his life Daily had loved music.

"You want to dance, Sam?" Anna asked as she circled him like a carnivore looking for her next meal.

Sam thought about it. He was over a foot taller than she was. It would never work. She'd have to stand on his shoes to keep up. "I was thinking about trying the taco truck."

Anna nodded. "We can split a dozen. You'll need to buy beer too." She led him to a few picnic tables between the food trucks. No one was eating there this late, and corners of the food trucks squared off the crowd almost like they were watching a big-screen TV of the fair.

The tables were too low and he had to turn his feet sideways to get in. It wasn't comfortable, but it was better than dancing.

While they ate, she told him about the people who passed by. "See that guy with a beard that must touch his belly button. He claims he is a direct descendent of Davy Crockett. His great-great-grandmother was delivering tamales to the Alamo and she had a fling with Davy."

Sam laughed. Who knows, Texas history wasn't his strong field, the guy could be right. Someone once told him the accounts of early Texas were written by outlaws, rebels, and saddlebag lawyers. Texas history was put together with lies, bragging, and tobacco spit.

Anna added, "If you look real close at the librarian, who is now selling balloons, you'll notice he has only four fingers on each hand. It's hereditary."

Sam kept grinning.

"And Digger over there." She pointed to an old man limping slightly. "He was once abducted by aliens. He claims he told such grand stories that they tried to keep him. He said they pulled his leg plum off when he escaped. He'll show you the stub if you want to see."

Sam stared at her. "Are you telling me that all the locals are loco?"

"I am." Anna shook her head as if sorry to have to enlighten him.

He leaned closer and asked, "And I'm talking to one of the locals?"

"You are."

He laughed. "Am I in any danger of catching this illness?"

She closed the distance between them and kissed him on the mouth.

He tasted hot sauce and paradise. Maybe it was because no one had kissed him in the three years since April died. Or maybe fire sparked when they touched like it does in old romantic movies. Or maybe that's how these locals drive the visitors crazy.

Sam didn't know or care. All he could think of was for the first time in a long time he felt alive.

As he leaned in for another taste of those lips, she stood. "I have to get home. Stella won't know what to do if she gets to my house and I'm not there. Fun's over, got to run."

Sam fought to get his legs out of the tiny picnic table. "I'll follow you home," he announced to air. Anna was already half a block away.

He realized that his words sounded a bit

288

creepy and was glad she hadn't heard him. When he ran to catch up, he said, "I'm worried about her too. Who knows what that organ player is really like? Maybe we should run a background check on him. I wonder if there is a file of organ players who murder people as a hobby. As soon as we get to your house, you make coffee and we'll start a round-the-clock stakeout until we know poor little thirty-two-year-old Stella is safe."

She shook her head as she marched two steps to his one. "I get the point. I may be overreacting. But I will make the coffee and wait. There is no need for you to come."

"I'm willing to be on guard all night. I'll stay over at your place until I know she's safe. It's the least I can do for the church bookkeeper."

"You don't fit in my house. You'll have to sleep on the porch, so you'd better hope Paul brings her back early."

Sam grinned. She hadn't said no.

Sam walked back to the church holding Anna's hand. She frowned, but she didn't pull away. When Paul's old van wasn't at the church, Sam followed her back to her tiny house.

She made coffee and they talked, but she didn't kiss him again. He realized that one kiss had changed his whole way of thinking.

289

Anna had probably forgotten it entirely.

After several minutes of silence, she asked, "Did you see Stella's brother, Benjamin, today?"

"Nope." Sam set down his coffee. "You know, maybe we're looking at this backward. Maybe he's glad she's finally jumped out of the nest?"

"Possible, but not likely. She took care of him. She keeps the church books and some say she's the one who does the taxes at his firm even though he's got the degree."

"Maybe he's planning how to get her to come back on her own?" Sam wanted to add that he didn't much care what the brother and sister did, as long as Benjamin wasn't forcing her to stay.

"That might be a good guess," she added. "It does seem strange that he didn't come looking for her. They both are always in church."

As the night aged and the stars came out in all their grandeur, Anna brought out a blanket and sat in the tall grass at the side of her house. When she leaned back to look at what she called her stars, he stood up from the chair on the porch.

"Mind if I share your blanket?"

"No, make yourself comfortable." She moved to one side.

He stood above her. "I wouldn't mind kissing you again, Anna. Any objections?"

She was silent for so long he thought she hadn't heard him, then she said, "No, I wouldn't mind. I guess it's only fair."

He lowered his body over hers and kissed her before she had time to comment. His kiss was deep and hungry with no hesitation and she tasted great.

When he lifted his weight just above her, she smiled. "When I said make yourself comfortable, I didn't mean on top of me."

He dropped to her side. "Are you filing a complaint? I did it in self-defense. If you took off like you did at the fair, I'd never find you in this dark."

To his surprise, she did that silent thing again. In the stillness he could hear her breathing. Finally, she said, "It's been a long time since I've been kissed like that."

"For me too," he answered. "What if neither one of us remembered how? We're both almost into our forties. Once there we're closer to death than birth probably. Not much hope of learning anything new."

She propped up on her elbow and was almost nose-to-nose with him. "Shut up and kiss me again, Sam. If you keep talking, you'll convince me never to speak to you again."

He closed the distance, almost touching his lips to hers. "I was in the army, Anna. I can follow orders."

Neither said another word. They had found other ways of communicating.

An hour later, when they saw Paul's car pull off the main road, Anna and Sam managed to make it to the two chairs on the porch before the couple pulled up.

If Stella noticed they both had grass in their hair, she didn't mention it.

Sam took a few gulps of cold coffee and said he'd better get back to town. The organ player said he'd stay for a cup so he'd stay awake long enough to make it home.

Anna walked Sam out to his car. When he bent to kiss her, she backed away. "What happened between us tonight, Sam — that was just something that happened, nothing more. You know? Physical attraction."

"I understand," he said, but he didn't understand at all. He'd felt her melting into him. He'd tasted the hunger in her.

"Don't go thinking that we're together, you know, like dating. I don't have time for that kind of thing. I figured out a long time ago that if I date at some point I'll have to break up with the guy. It's a merry-go-round I stepped off of years ago."

He wanted to kiss her again, if for no other

reason than to shut her up. She was ruining every fragile feeling beginning to grow in him. Anger boiled up from deep inside. He wasn't some kid on a first date, or a dreamer looking for love. He liked his life. He was surviving, even helping to make the world a better place. He didn't need to be told that this wasn't going to be anything to her.

"Good night, Anna. I wish you the best."

He was in his car and backing away before she could say another word.

"Forget doing this job for another week," he said out loud. "Tomorrow I'm going back where I belong. This was a crazy idea anyway." He pounded the steering wheel and almost ran off the two-lane road.

He pushed the window down and let the night air in. His heart slowed down and he realized he was feeling, really feeling, for the first time in a long time. A heart that had stopped three years ago and now it was pounding against his ribs. Deep down, he ached. The wall he'd built around his heart was crumbling.

Hell, it hurt. And it was all Anna's fault.

CHAPTER 25

Midnight

PECOS

After the lights went out in the town square, Pecos walked back to his pickup, trying to remember every detail about the fair. For a few moments under the tiny lights waving in the summer breeze with the band playing and everyone smiling at them, Pecos felt like a prince. But inside, he knew he was just the frog.

He glanced back in the direction of her house as he climbed in the back of his pickup. Pecos wished he'd spread hay in the back of the truck before he'd left the farm. At least he'd remembered an extra blanket. He pulled off his boots and used the suitcase as a pillow. Tomorrow he'd try to find a cheap place to rent, or even better, a room he could trade for free labor.

Leaning back, he closed his eyes and

thought he could still hear the band playing slow, going-home songs. She'd felt so good cuddled up next to him on the dance floor. He'd loved the way she'd whispered in his ear about little things she thought were funny. They were in the middle of a crowd and yet they were in their own private world.

A bump against the side of his truck rocked him out of his memories. Pecos frowned. Surely there weren't dogs big enough to jump into a pickup bed.

Another bump irritated him.

"You plan on sleeping out here?" a low voice asked.

Pecos sat up, preparing to argue. There was no law against sleeping in your own pickup. Plus, he had almost a thousand dollars tucked away on him and he wouldn't give it up without a fight if the shadow planned to rob him.

Then he saw the outline of the round, little man wearing a fedora hat. "Mr. Winston, I'm not bothering anyone."

"I didn't say you were, but before dawn it's going to rain. You'll get soaked. Go park under a bridge or something."

"No, I want to be close to Kerrie."

"You could go home and come back tomorrow. It's not that far."

Pecos pushed the blanket aside. "I left

295

home. I'm not going back. Come Monday I'm hoping to get a job and look for an apartment. I'm grown. I'm on my own."

Mr. Winston finally seemed to understand. "Sounds like a very logical plan. I just see a few problems. If it rains, you'll look pretty bad to go interview in the morning. Then there's the problem when lightning tags along with the downpour to come. It'll probably hit the pickup and then you'll be looking chicken-fried for weeks. They say if you're struck you don't die, you just go around jittering for months."

Pecos frowned. He'd had enough to worry about before the old man came along. "You got any ideas, Mr. Winston, 'cause I'm not going back home."

"Well, since you're parked at the end of my block, you might as well come home with me. I'll dust out one of the extra bedrooms. You could stay with me till you find a place."

"You wouldn't mind?"

"I wouldn't mind."

Pecos followed Mr. Winston into the old house that everyone thought was a bit frightening. A few of the older folks said that years ago, Winston used to come every summer. He'd hired a cleaning crew to polish the place until it shined; he'd even hired a gardener.

Then he waited. When asked, he'd say the family would be coming soon, but they never did. As the years passed he did less and less to prepare, and finally, he came one summer and never left. The garden died and Winston no longer hired cleaning crews. None of the family he talked about ever came.

By the time Pecos was old enough to know about Mr. Winston, twenty years had passed since he'd forgotten to leave in the fall. Some folks said he was rich but lonely. Others said he was broke and had nothing but the old house.

Just in case the second might be true, Pecos pulled out the jar of honey Papa Lane had given him. He handed it to Winston. "We can have this for breakfast."

"I'll make biscuits in the morning. We'll have a regular feast."

As they entered the once-grand home, Pecos followed close because Mr. Winston didn't bother to turn on any lights.

They moved through the shadowy street-lights that spilled into the hallways. They climbed a narrow stairway off the kitchen and Winston opened the first door he came to. The door creaked. The floor creaked. Even Mr. Winston creaked.

297

The old man pulled the drapes open to let in the streetlight glow. "You'll be comfortable here. I ran out of lightbulbs a while back and borrowed the ones in this room, but there is enough to see to move around."

Pecos dropped his suitcase and helped fold the plastic covering the bed.

"I keep the sheets clean. The bathroom is down the hall, but there may or may not be hot water. The plumbing seems to have a mind of its own these days. Breakfast will be at eight. That all right with you?"

"You're very kind, sir. I hope I can pay you back one day."

"Don't even think of it." The old man smiled. "I've been much blessed. I'm glad to have the company."

After Winston left, Pecos walked around the large room. Everything was covered in dust as fine as winter's first snow, but beneath looked to be delicately carved furniture.

Pecos stripped down, folded his clothes over a chair, and slipped into bed. The bed felt so much better than the pickup, he must be in heaven.

A lazy sliver of moon passed across his window like a lost smile among the stars, then disappeared behind clouds.

Pecos closed his eyes and grinned back.

What he'd been waiting for all his life had begun. He'd make his own way from now on. He'd carve out a career, a name for himself, a future.

Chapter 26

Midnight

Colby

By the time Colby made it back to the fair, the mayor was gone and the booths were all closed down. He walked the square, feeling terrible for abandoning Piper and worse for losing the trail of the dark-haired woman.

Marcie, the invisible barmaid the preacher told him about, had turned a corner and thirty seconds later when he reached the same corner, there was no one in sight. No girl. No car pulling away. Nothing. It was as if she simply vanished and along with her went his only clue to where Boone Buchanan would be.

Maybe the hotshot lawyer was at the bottom of the river. As far as Colby knew, he was chasing a ghost.

He thought about looking for Piper, but it was late. He didn't even bother to go back and pick up his Harley parked in front of Widows Park. He simply walked to the edge of town and turned in at the lodge.

Digger's office light was still on. Colby decided to drop in. The old guy was probably observing Colby's every move. This assignment had more layers than the Palo Duro Canyon.

The lodge keeper looked up from his desk when he heard the fish talking. Strange, no matter how many times Colby came into the office, it still made him laugh to hear the greeting.

"Evening, Digger."

"Evening, Colby. You lost your girl tonight. Mr. Winston walked away with the mayor on his arm."

Colby shrugged. "Just my luck. Women are always attracted to the sharp dressers."

Digger looked him up and down. "You could work on that a bit, son."

Colby considered the fact that the advice was coming from a man who was wearing overalls and a BEAM ME UP, SCOTTY T-shirt. He decided to change the subject. "I thought I saw that woman named Marcie up on the stage with her brother tonight. Then she disappeared."

"Why go after Marcie when you had the mayor in your arms? That's the first time

I've seen her dancing in a long time. Piper used to dance with her grandfather, but that was years ago. You two looked grand when you whirled her around. When you left her, every single man wanted to take her for a spin around the floor, but she said she had to call it a night."

Colby hated that he'd left her without a word. He'd been focused on the job. "I've got to try harder, Digger. I'm crazy about her." The words came easily. Colby realized he wasn't acting.

"That you do, son." The old man hesitated as if debating with himself. Finally, he added, "I've seen you walking the river's bank at night. You know there are fishermen who go out on the water only when it's dark. They stay pretty much to themselves, but they see things at night. You might want to talk to a few of them."

"How do I find them?"

"They got places close to the river. Mostly just fishing shacks. Turn off any dirt road and you might find one. There's a few two miles north on a road without a name. Try stopping to ask for help with getting the mayor's boat back to the Honey Creek Café. She stores it there as part of the ambiance. One of the fishermen told me you probably broke it. Said she's been riding that river for years and never had a problem with the motor until you came along."

"You know we were out there?"

"Sure. Several of them saw you floating by. You just didn't see them. They've lived out there so long they blend in with the night."

"Anything else?" Colby studied Digger.

The old guy smiled and pulled a box from behind the desk. "Yeah, this came for you yesterday, Trooper." He handed it over. "The box had been opened."

"I'll report it." Colby stared at Digger.

"No need to do that. I might have accidentally opened it thinking it was mine." He didn't meet Colby's eyes. "One service weapon, one badge, just in case you need them."

"Busted." Colby grinned. No use denying it now. Digger knew the truth. "I was sent to watch over Piper, and find Boone if I could."

"I knew something was up. I'm not sure what's between you and the mayor. You two were burning up the dance floor. But if you're protecting the mayor, I'm on your side. Call on me anytime."

"Thanks, Digger. I will. And keep this under your hat." Colby wouldn't be surprised if he'd already told half the town.

"I will. But you got to be careful with our mayor. I know you'll protect her, but don't you break her heart, cowboy. The act you're putting on is like playing with fire. You hurt her and half the town will line up to murder you. Then we'll dig you up every anniversary of your death and kill you again."

Colby nodded and left before he arrested Digger. Tampering with mail. Death threats on an officer of the law. Messing with a corpse.

Funny thing was, Digger was on his side. That was a frightening thought.

When he left the office, Colby took the back way to his cabin by walking along the water's edge. It was after midnight, but he realized he wouldn't sleep without apologizing to Piper.

He walked slowly, listening for any sound of the fishermen. He thought he saw one, but the shadow disappeared in a blink. Colby was halfway to Piper's room at the café when he saw a man sitting at the outcrop of a rock dangling his legs off almost in the water.

Colby stood in the pale moonlight five feet away. "How you doing, Daily? Thinking of jumping in?"

Daily raised his chin. "Ever' night. How about you?"

Colby moved over to Daily and sat almost touching him. For once he didn't smell alcohol on him. "You not drinking tonight?"

"No, I can't sleep, but if I drink I won't wake up in the morning. My brother, who turned into my boss, says if I'm late one more time he'll fire me." Daily's voice was low and deep, as if he were standing in a well. "I wouldn't blame him if he did. We used to own the place together, but I didn't hold up my end."

"You ever think of doing anything else?"

Daily shook his head. "I grew up in the shop. When my wife died I just stopped going to work. My brother took over. He pays my bills so I kept the house, and he gives me money for food and drinking. That's all I need."

Colby had heard a lot of stories in the years working as a state trooper, but this beat any of them. He thought of telling Daily Watts that he was alive and still young, but he doubted it would help.

"Any chance you saw a man climb out of the water almost a week ago."

"You mean the one who parked in the middle of the river?"

"Yeah."

"I don't think so. I did see something that night. Thought it was a beaver slithering up

305

on the mud. But this was way north of where folks claim the car went in. He would have had to be a strong swimmer to make it so far upstream. Anyway, the muddy critter rested on the river bank for a while, and then he stood on his hind legs and I realized he was a man. He disappeared back in the bush. It rained that night so there wouldn't have been any tracks."

"Have any idea who he was?"

Daily shook his head. "He was covered in mud."

"Did you tell anyone about this?"

"I told the sheriff that night. He was packing for his honeymoon, course I didn't know it at the time. He didn't seem to be interested in a mud creature who turned into a man. He said I needed to go sleep it off, but I wasn't drinking that night."

"You still seeing those angel kids at night?"

"Yeah, but only when I drink. The preacher says I should stop and talk to them."

"You want me to walk you home, Daily?"

"No, I'll stay awhile. It's quiet out here."

Colby took a step and turned back. "Do you ever see fishermen out here at night?"

"I do, but I leave them alone and they leave me alone."

Colby said goodbye and continued on his

journey. When he got to the Honey Creek Café it was almost two a.m. He'd learned several things tonight, even if he didn't get to talk to Marcie.

If he woke the mayor up to tell her, she'd yell at him. If he didn't, she'd yell at him. Hell, it was worth the argument just to see what nightgown she was wearing.

Yesterday at breakfast he'd left a window unlocked that was hidden behind a curtain. Much better way in than climbing the trellis.

He pushed on the glass window and it gave. Then Colby shoved his body through the opening, fell into a chair, and rolled across the dining room. He cussed as he dusted himself off and checked for broken bones.

He was heading to the front stairs when he heard an upstairs door open and then footsteps. Colby took a deep breath and looked up.

She was there. Green spaghetti straps holding up a forest-green silk gown that barely covered her bottom. It took a few heartbeats for him to see the old Colt .45 in her hand pointed right at him.

"PJ, do you have any idea how sexy you are like that? If we were in the Old West you could rob a bank in that outfit and no one would press charges."

"Do you know how close to death you are? You can't just break into my house." She waved the weapon at him. "And you stood me up tonight. Just disappeared. Left me at the fair."

"Sorry about that. I was chasing a lead."

"And did you find one?"

"No, the woman vanished. I crossed every major street in town looking for her. No luck. But I did find a man who said he saw a stranger covered in mud crawl out of the river the night Boone disappeared."

"Why didn't he come forward?"

"It was Daily Watts."

She lifted the Colt again as if using it as a pointer. "Daily Watts, the drunk who sees angels following him? There is no telling what he sees."

Colby knew he wasn't winning. He might as well start up the stairs and get shot.

"What do you think you're doing?"

"I thought I'd stay here and protect you."

She lowered the Colt and simply stared at him.

"I'll feel better if I know you're safe. Someone could break in here from any one of a dozen windows." He was on the same step. "I'll sleep here tonight on guard."

"You can't sleep in my room."

"Why not? I did last night." He opened her bedroom door wider and waited for her to enter.

"I'm too tired to argue." She set the Colt on the dresser. "But, I swear, Trooper, if you touch me, I will shoot you."

When he headed to the bed, she pushed him backward to the settee.

Colby didn't argue. He wrapped up in a quilt, put a pillow over the arm of the settee, and tried to get comfortable.

An hour later he was still wide awake and she was sleeping soundly. Almost sleepwalking he rose and moved to the empty side of her bed. He'd get up early and be back on the settee before she woke. She'd never know.

Just before he fell asleep, he felt her roll against him. Colby opened his arm and let her snuggle into his side. When he kissed her hair he whispered, "You're safe, honey. You're safe."

■ ■ ■ ■

MONDAY

■ ■ ■ ■

MONDAY

CHAPTER 27

Morning

PECOS

Pecos sat on the long couch in the Lanes' huge living room. He couldn't stop crossing and uncrossing his legs. This was his first day out in the world and he was feeling more and more like a man. He'd had breakfast with Winston at dawn. They'd talked about his plans as Pecos ate most of the biscuits with honey. Mr. Winston was a good listener but lean on advice.

Then Pecos went to the sheriff's office and asked for an application.

LeRoy Hayes frowned at him. "Well, I'll put you on the list, Pecos. But to tell the truth, I don't know when there'll be an opening. How do you feel about being sheriff? That will probably be the next posting."

Pecos thought for a moment and said,

313

"Why not. How hard could it be? You've been doing it for years."

To his surprise, LeRoy laughed so hard he almost fell out of his chair. "Tell you what. I've got an open spot for a dispatcher. You'd have to be trained, but that don't take long. And I should warn you, you'll have to work the ten to six a.m. shift with Daisy. I can't tell you why no one wants those hours. Could be they just don't want to work with her. She's mean as they come, but she knows the business."

"I'd love that time slot." He was already reasoning that he could get a day job, too, and still have eight hours to sleep, eat, and shower. "Do I get a uniform?"

"Nope, you can show up naked if you want to. Daisy probably won't notice. Pays eighteen dollars an hour with two rules. No visitors in the dispatch room, and no matter what, you show up sober and ready to work. You miss a night you're scheduled and you're gone. Understand me? No second chance."

"Yes, sir."

"Then you'll start training tonight. Come in a couple hours early to read the manual. We only got one and we don't pay for you reading. After a few weeks I'll have someone watching you to see if you're fast enough to do the job."

"You sure about no uniform?"

LeRoy mumbled a few cuss words like he was chewing them up before he spit them out. He opened the bottom drawer of his desk and tossed Pecos a handful of blue shirts with a sheriff's badge covering about heart level. "Wear these. All we got is mediums and all the deputies are too fat to wear anything but extra extra large." He looked Pecos up and down. "I'm hoping you wear out those shirts before you move into double Xs."

Pecos smoothed out the material bearing the embroidered badge. "I'll take good care of them and give them back if I leave."

LeRoy scratched his bushy sideburns. "You do that, boy."

Pecos wanted to run out and tell Kerrie, but he went around and applied for three more jobs first. None gave him much time or hope. Every kid in town wanted a summer job and most had relatives who were pressured into hiring them.

It was almost nine when he made it to Kerrie's house. He'd hoped she'd be on the porch waiting. He'd promised her last night that if he got a job, they'd celebrate with breakfast or lunch at the Honey Creek Café. After all, it was the best place in town.

Her father, Brad Lane, had answered the door without smiling and told Pecos to sit down. "She and her mother are talking, so who knows how long Kerrie will be."

Barbara, Kerrie's mom, yelled for Brad to come upstairs. Brad rolled his eyes. "This doesn't sound promising. The delay might be longer than I thought."

"I'll wait." Pecos had no place to go.

Ten minutes later he was still sitting in the empty room. The whole house reminded him of a showroom in some big furniture store. Everything matched and fit perfectly together. Creepy, he thought. None of the tables had anything useful on them.

There was shouting from upstairs. Pecos couldn't make out the words. So much for thinking Kerrie had the perfect family.

This couldn't have anything to do with him, could it? He knew he was just the "almost boyfriend" until someone better came along. He wasn't important enough to warrant all that shouting.

Another ten minutes passed. Now he heard crying. The need to go up and comfort Kerrie was strong, but he didn't move. This was none of his business. He felt like he was trespassing just sitting on the couch.

Finally, Kerrie came down the stairs in a full run.

He stood and caught her as she slammed into him as if he were her only safe place in the world. He held her tight, unable to think of anything to say. His clean shirt Mr. Winston had insisted on ironing this morning was getting wet with her tears and Pecos felt helpless. All he could do was hold her.

Her heart finally stopped pounding against his and her breathing slowed. "They . . . hate . . . me. I thought they'd love me no matter what, but my parents hate me."

He rocked her from side to side. "I don't know what's wrong, but I can pretty much swear to you that your parents don't hate you." He kissed the top of her head. Maybe he should tell her about his parents. Then she'd know what having parents who hate you is really like. Only Pecos had to admit to himself that Mom and Dad didn't hate him either. More accurately they simply forgot about him.

Pecos looked up and saw Kerrie's parents frozen halfway down the staircase. Both looked furious.

"I'll kill him," Brad said through gritted teeth. "I swear, I'll kill him. I can't believe he just walked into our house as cool as you please."

Pecos wanted to point out that Brad had been the one to open the door, and invite him in, but the man didn't look like he was interested in logic. He looked more like Mel Gibson in *Braveheart* with a club in his hand as he waited to run into battle.

Pecos stepped in front of Kerrie. For a few seconds he wondered who the man was talking about. No "him" was in the room, just Kerrie and her mom.

Then her father stormed close, his stare never leaving Pecos's face, and Pecos realized he was the HIM.

Instinct took over. Pecos widened his stance in front of Kerrie. As he turned to face her obviously crazy father, the nutcase swung and caught Pecos in the nose. The fist continued into his eye. Pecos was so shocked he hadn't even tried to block the hit.

He raised his arms when the second fist flew toward him, but he couldn't fight back. This was Kerrie's father.

Brad shifted his weight and prepared to attack again. Pecos wanted to run, but he was all that stood between Kerrie and her father. He'd taken a lot of blows in his life. He could take more, but he wasn't sure he could take her getting hurt.

Just as Brad swung, Pecos bent low and rammed her father in the stomach. Both men fell, shattering the glass coffee table and cutting themselves in several spots as they landed.

Pecos rolled on top of Brad just as Kerrie's mother screamed for them to stop. Her scream was so loud it seemed to shake the house. "NO. NO. NO. This is not happening! Stop!"

Right now both of the parents seemed to be cracking up. He almost wished for his own house, where his parents simply ignored each other and cold silence reigned. Pecos might not be able to do anything about the screamer, but he was strong enough to hold the father pinned.

To his surprise, Brad's muscles began to still. Barbara's screams had broken the madness somehow.

Barbara knelt beside her husband and tried with a Kleenex to wipe off blood throbbing out of her husband's arm. "This can't be happening. It just can't. This is not us, Brad. I can't stand this. I can't."

Brad looked at Pecos. The fire was gone from his eyes now. "Get off me. I'm not going to hurt you. I can't. It's tearing my wife apart. The desire to kill you wouldn't be worth shattering her. She's already dealing with enough right now."

Pecos slowly moved away but stayed at the ready. "I don't know what this is all about, Mr. Lane, but I suggest we worry about that cut on your arm, then figure out why you want me dead later."

They moved to the kitchen. Somehow the insane father had settled back down. Both his daughter and his wife were fussing over him while Pecos sat at the other end of the bar dripping blood.

After a few minutes of trying to stop the blood, Barbara said, "I'm taking him to the hospital. Do you need to see a doctor, Pecos? Your eye's almost swollen shut."

"No, I've been hit much harder by my old man."

Kerrie brought the medicine kit over to him. "I'll patch him up."

Barbara helped Brad to his feet. "Call me if he faints or starts throwing up. I'll be right back to get him if you call. Dad's going to need stitches."

Pecos felt like he was on a bizarre merry-go-round. Nice dad, killer dad, nice dad, killer dad. Good mom, screaming mom, then back to good mom.

Kerrie talked to him softly as she cleaned each scrape, doctored it, and bandaged it. When she was finished, his nose was still bleeding a bit, but the cuts on his palm and on his elbow would heal fine. She put a cute little ice pack that looked like a penguin on his eye and told him to lie down on the couch.

As he closed his good eye, he tried to make sense of what had just happened. He had come in, sat down, and heard voices. Kerrie had run to him, and then her dad had tried to kill him. Man, he hoped this wasn't an average Monday morning at the Lane house.

As his heart slowed and his body relaxed, he drifted to sleep vaguely aware that she was cleaning up the glass. Kerrie was safe. She hadn't been hurt and that was all that really mattered.

Sometime later the front door opened and Brad and Barbara were back. Kerrie's dad's arm was wrapped in a sling and he had more bandages in other places than Pecos did. Barbara was crying now as she bossed her husband around.

Brad walked past the couch and dropped into the armchair facing Pecos. "I'm sorry," he said without much meaning in the words. "I was so angry for what you two did. My wife said that it's both your faults, but I don't see it that way."

Pecos felt like a fog had settled in his brain and with only one eye the whole room didn't look right. Somehow her parents must have figured out they went swimming yesterday after graduation. He would expect them to get mad, but they were carrying it way too far.

"Dad, Pecos had nothing to do with my problem."

Pecos raised up on his elbows. "Yes, I did. I was all in when she suggested it."

All three of the Lanes stared at him and Pecos saw a bit of the fire crawling back into Brad's eyes. He didn't know if he should run, fight, or play dead.

"Once I had my clothes off there was no going back. I jumped."

Yep, the fire was back, Pecos decided. At least they had the coffee table out of the way.

"Stop, Pecos," Kerrie cried. "You're making it worse. You don't know what we are talking about. I told my parents I'm pregnant and they assumed it was you."

Brad leaned forward like a lion posed to pounce. "Kerrie, are you saying he's not the father? Then who is? Damn it, tell me. I don't want to kill the wrong sperm donor."

"No one is." Kerrie cried as if no one was listening to her. "This is my baby. Just mine."

Barbara was so calm now they could have been having tea. "No, honey, you know that's not true. But you have to tell us. Were you raped or drunk? Oh dear, were you drugged? We need to know what happened."

"No, I wasn't drunk or drugged. I wasn't raped."

"Then tell us. Stop trying to protect Pecos or whoever it was."

Brad sneered at Pecos. Since he still felt bad about the swimming, he probably looked guilty. But Kerrie was taking all the blame. She wasn't trying to involve him. That might have been the easy way out. He was no one. A "weekend boyfriend" still hanging around on Monday.

"You're going to tell us, Kerrie, or I swear I'll beat up every boy in this town."

She shook her head and began to cry.

Pecos put his hand over hers. Now he understood. He'd been an idiot for not noticing the signs. He'd had sex education in school. Crying all the time, bigger boobs, rounded stomach. She had all the signs he could remember.

"Who is the father of the child you are carrying?" her father demanded.

Kerrie lifted her chin but didn't answer.

The house was so silent, Pecos's voice echoed, "I am, sir. I came here this morning to make it right. I know girls don't get married these days, but I want to be a father to this baby and I think we need to marry to do that."

The whole Lane family seemed incapable of speech.

Pecos tried again. "I love Kerrie and I'll love the baby."

Still no reaction. The Lanes looked like they had turned to porcelain. If they didn't move soon, he'd have to set them on the shelf.

In his mind, Pecos saw his dreams tumbling down. But he had to do this. Deep down he knew he was nothing but a dumb farm boy who barely got out of high school. And Kerrie was a shining star.

He'd give up his goals and do all he could to allow her dreams to come true. He'd stand beside her for as long as she needed him, and then he'd walk away so she could get on with her life.

Brad came out of his shock first. "I still want to kill you."

"Fair enough. It was my fault, but I'll do my best to make it right."

"No," Kerrie cried. "No, it is mine, all mine."

Barbara stood as if she were the guest lecturer at a sorority party. "It doesn't matter who is to blame. It's done and it can't be undone. Now we have to make the best of it. You two can go somewhere for a few

324

weeks and come back married. Everyone will know when the baby is born that it's early, but Kerrie is right. Folks don't care about those things these days. Your friends will still be your friends and no one will even talk about it after a while."

"I can't go away," Pecos said. "I have a job at the sheriff's office. I report for duty tonight to be trained as a dispatcher." He had to keep his job. He was about to be a husband and a father now. If Brad didn't kill him.

"He's got a job, Brad." Barbara almost clapped her hands as if Pecos had finally done something right.

Brad frowned. "Great. He'll be leaving our daughter alone every night. Could this mess get any worse?"

"She won't be alone. Mr. Winston will be there. I'm staying with him."

Brad glowered. "You're staying with us and that's final."

Kerrie, Barbara, and Pecos all spoke at the same time: "No."

When her parents left to go have a discussion, Kerrie leaned close. "Pecos, you don't have to do this. It's too much."

"I'm doing this, Kerrie. If you'll have me."

There were tears in her eyes and a smile on her lips. Kerrie leaned over and kissed his cheek. "Who would have thought a knight in shining armor would show up in a tie?"

"I'm no knight. But I'll help out for as long as you need me. Now how about we walk down to Mr. Winston's house and ask if we can rent from him for a few months?"

She stood and took his hand. "How are you going to explain that black eye when you show up for work tonight?"

"I'll just say my new wife is very passionate."

Kerrie stepped aside and Pecos saw her parents staring at them. Barbara smiled slightly as if she thought they were cute together. Brad still had that future killer look in his eyes.

Barbara took over. "We've figured it out. We'll call that new preacher and get him to marry you two this afternoon. Just a small ceremony in his office. Then we can work on fixing up your room for two. Your father insists."

"There won't be any celebrating." Brad glared at Pecos. "There is nothing happy about this wedding."

Kerrie pulled him toward the door. "Pecos and I have got a lot to talk about, Mom. See you later."

Barbara opened her mouth to say something, then stopped.

Pecos and Kerrie ran to his old pickup. He'd been on his own for two days and everything was about to change again. He had a feeling life might not go the way he planned, but it was certainly going to be interesting.

CHAPTER 28

Morning

SAM

Sam took his time dressing. He wanted to
look proper for his last day as a pastor in
honor of his father. He now understood his
dad better than he ever had. It's hard not to
get mixed up in people's lives, their problems, their dreams, when they look to you
for help. He really felt a duty to lead them,
not just yell at them on Sunday.

He had learned something else, too. He'd
discovered that he wasn't dead yet. He'd
lived in a desert so long he barely recognized
the rain of emotions until Anna Presley
wrapped her arms around him and pressed
her warm body against his. He came alive.

He refused to dwell on the way she hurt
him when she made light of what happened.
She had given him so much, he could deal
with the sting of rejection at the end.

For that one hour they'd held each other, he'd felt newly born and he was thankful for that. He'd learned he could still feel. But he wished she hadn't started something she had no intention of finishing. Last night when they were rolled up in the blanket and his arms were around her, he thought there was something between them. The start of something that might grow.

But she'd made it plain when they said good night at his car that she was just playing around. Passing time. She wasn't looking for more than an hour under the stars. Meanwhile, Sam had no idea what he wanted. Not love — he'd given up on that. Not a relationship, considering that if they were talking they were arguing. What, then?

Now that he thought about it, Sam figured Anna had been smart to stop something that had no chance of going anywhere.

Sam strolled around the bachelor parsonage. The place had grown on him. He was starting to give the plaster angels names.

At ten he headed to the church, and found the back door locked. Maybe Monday was a day off and no one had bothered to tell him. He used his key and went in.

Sure enough, in his office he saw that church hours were posted. *No office hours on Monday.*

Stella wasn't at her desk, of course. She probably stayed up all night talking to Anna.

Without its usual activity, the church felt strangely empty. Sam heard no janitor bumping his way down the hallways. The lights were all off, giving the place a melancholy feel, as if yesterday's joy and peace had slipped away.

Sam sat down in his plain, little office and wrote out a short note saying he that he had to leave. An emergency. He was sorry.

It wasn't a lie. He did have to leave. The emergency was a fire up north of Denver. He'd had a text saying that if it kept growing, they'd need him tomorrow, if he could make it. Since Sam could either fly the plane or jump in if fighters were needed more than pilots, he was always in demand.

A part of him regretted having to leave. Sam realized he'd always think of this as his hometown. If anyone asked, he'd simply say, "I'm from Honey Creek, Texas." If they wanted to know where the town was, he'd add the slogan on the town sign, Where the Heart of Texas Beats.

Sam stared at his note. He'd planned to give it to Stella, not just leave it on her desk. If her brother showed up, Sam could give it to him, but who knew where Benjamin was. People in this town seemed to appear and disappear at will. Like that sheriff who'd caused such a happy uproar during the Sunday service when he showed up with his new bride. Or Boone Buchanan, who didn't even live in town, but was said by some to be the mayor's fiancé. The way the mayor was dancing with that cowboy, she didn't seem to be too brokenhearted about her missing boyfriend.

Sam shook his head. He was turning into a local. He was even starting to worry about poor Daily Watts.

He heard a thump coming from the hallway. Then another and another. Anna, he guessed. All the staff might be off today, but no surprise if Anna came in anyway.

He leaned his head out of his doorway. It was Anna, but for some reason she was all dressed up, almost like a lawyer. Almost. If only she had bothered to comb her hair, or — his gaze reached her feet — wear something other than ten-year-old ECCO sandals with her suit.

"Looking very professional, Miss Presley."

She turned around and now he could see the tie-dye shirt she was wearing under the suit jacket.

"I'm only dropping off a few things. I'm on my way to examine the wills of Stella and Benjamin's parents. They went through

331

probate, so it should be on record. They were not rich, but if the house went to both kids, Stella will have enough to go to college. You got time to open the door for me, Preacher?"

"Sure." He closed the distance between them and took the biggest package from her. "How about I carry it down for you?"

When he took the weight of the box, he was surprised she'd carried it as far as she had.

They were both silent as they walked downstairs to the after-school playrooms.

It seemed they were strangers again, not two people who had spent the night rolling around under a blanket together.

He set the box down and felt his heart closing as she simply stared at him. No smile. No need to say more than thanks.

Then he saw the tear on her face. One tear. It traveled over a freckled cheek and dripped past a perfect mouth.

"You all right, Anna?"

"No, Preacher. I lied to you, and I'm not a person who allows myself that luxury."

He smiled. "I'm not a priest. You don't have to confess."

"Yes, I do." She took one step toward him. "Last night I was scared. What I said just before you left was meant to push you away.

Before you could reject me, I guess."

Sam held perfectly still. He didn't want to open up again, not one inch. She would just hurt him again. He was a firefighter and he knew what happened when you walked straight into the flames. "As I said last night, you like to strike before someone gets close to you. I shouldn't have been surprised. But I don't think I could take much of that."

"It doesn't matter, I guess. It would never work between us, Sam. You're all good and sunshine, and I walk the gutters looking for my clients. I'm short-tempered, say what I think even when no one cares to hear it. I take on too much and get frustrated that everyone in the world doesn't care as much as I do about every injustice." She put her fists on her hips and added, "Feel free to stop me at any time."

Sam shook his head. "So far I'm agreeing with you. Besides, it's dangerous to disagree with you."

"Thanks a lot. You just proved my point." Another tear worked its way down her cheek. Her confession was costing her dearly.

He held out his arms. "Come here." He might not want to get involved with her, but she was hurting. Inside she was looking in a mirror and didn't like what she saw.

He'd stood in the same place many times.

Holding her close, he whispered, "You're not so bad, Anna. You've got a fire in your blood to make the world better and you run as fast as you can, even when you're running the wrong direction. If I was going to stay around we'd probably be best friends after a dozen or so fights."

"You're leaving soon, I know that. You were only hired for two weeks, but they'd extend it. Everyone loves you, Sam. There's no time for us to be polite friends."

"You're right. I'm quitting today, or at least, I have written the letter. Can't find anyone around here to take it. I may have to leave it on the bulletin board in the office when I walk out."

"You're leaving because of me?" She stilled in his arms.

"No, I just came to do what I had to do. I learned a great deal. It's time to move on."

She pressed closer. "Are you really quitting being a preacher, or just giving up on this town?"

"I'm giving up being a preacher. I never really was one, you should know. It once was my goal, but not any longer. I thought I'd find peace pretending to be like my father. I'm going back to being what I was trained for, a firefighter. I'm good at that. I love the work, the danger. I thought I'd find the happiness I had as a kid when my dad traveled around preaching. But a man can't go back. I'll be leaving for a fire in Denver as soon as I get the call."

Anna's beautiful blue eyes were wide as she stared at him as if she'd never seen him before.

"I don't want to lie to you, Anna. I'm just a firefighter, not a preacher. I have been for years. I have an apartment that's barer than a hotel room and I keep a bag packed in the trunk." Finally, his words were sinking in. She'd stopped crying. "Coming here was about me taking a look at another kind of life, a memory."

She moved to the door and turned the lock.

"Anna, you can't keep me here by locking me in. The church will survive without a preacher for one week."

"I'm not locking you in. I'm locking the others out. I couldn't sleep last night thinking, *If he just wasn't a preacher.* Men like him need someone with them who can help them. I could never fill that role and I'd feel like the devil tempting the preacher away from his pure thoughts."

As he sat on the little table, she pushed his knees apart and moved closer to him.

They were now at eye level. "Now you tell me you're not a preacher. You were playing around trying to relive the past. That changes things."

Sam felt her breasts touching his chest, her breath brushing his ear, and her hands on his shoulders as if she could hold him in place. "Are you telling me that now I'm not a minister, you're attracted to me?" She was so close. The body he'd held last night seemed so familiar now.

"You got it. Can I kiss you again? You may be leaving but I'd like to kiss the man, not the preacher. It was so hard holding back last night."

"You were holding back?" If she'd been holding back he wasn't sure he could take full out.

Sam felt like he was going the wrong way on the turnpike. No matter what he said, no matter what he did, he was about to take a hit.

But if she'd been asking for a tender goodbye kiss from a man who was almost her friend, that's not what Sam had in mind.

He pulled her against him and kissed her like this was the last time he'd kiss a woman in this lifetime.

To his surprise, she returned the fire. In what seemed like a few minutes he broke

336

the kiss to try to catch his breath. His head was spinning and he felt like he had a fever.

She pressed her forehead against his and tried to slow her breathing as well.

Sam noticed he had his hand over her breast. He couldn't feel much between the suit jacket and her T-shirt and bra but what surprised him was she didn't seem to notice or mind.

So he left it there a moment longer.

When she grinned, he moved his hand beneath the jacket and got to know the feel of one very nice breast.

As she breathed, he shoved her jacket off so he could kiss his way down her neck. She leaned her head back and sighed.

"I want you, Anna. I'm starving for you."

"Me too." She rested her head on his shoulder. "There's been this need to be near you from the moment I saw you. But we can't. Not here."

Sam looked around. The after-school art classroom didn't seem the right place. Plus, they were in the church.

"My house out back would work."

"No, I couldn't."

He remembered all the angels staring at him every morning and decided he couldn't either. He'd have to blindfold them all, and the forest creatures, and the figurines of caroling Precious Moments characters.

"How about your house? I might fit in there sideways."

"No, Stella's hiding out there."

"We could get a room in town or at the fishing lodge?"

"No, I know too many people. Before we turned the key in the door, it would be all over town."

"Damn, I feel like I'm back in high school." He pushed her curly hair back from her face and kissed her still-damp cheek. "As much as I want to make love to you, I'm not doing it in the back of my car."

She laughed. "How do normal people do this? They must have found a way. Kids are popping up like weeds all over the place."

Sam moved his hand lightly over her hip. "We could drive a hundred miles and find a hotel."

She shook her head. "I have things I have to do. Can you stay another day?"

"I got a text to be ready to move as soon as the call comes. If the fire grows, they'll need a pilot. I'll have to go."

"How long will you be gone?"

"Until it's under control. A few days. A week. No one knows."

"I don't think that's so long. I'll have time

to read up on how to do it. It's been so long."

He slipped his hand beneath her shirt so he could feel her skin. "We'll just feel our way through it. Are you sure you want to wait?" He grinned. Anna probably never waited on anything in her life. She undoubtedly opened her Christmas presents early every year. He went back to kissing her ear while she figured it out.

She tasted so good.

"I have an office directly below the mayor. At five the place shuts down. Meet me there. If you don't get called, at least we'll have tonight."

"Is there a couch?" He started kissing her neck again.

"Yes, but it squeaks."

"If I'm in Honey Creek at five, let's make it squeak." He pulled her so close against him neither could breathe. "I promise, Anna, this is not going to be a one-night stand. If I have to leave, I'll be back."

She tried to pull away, but he held her tight for a moment more. Part of him knew she'd hurt him again. Maybe not today or tomorrow, but soon. But it felt so good to be holding her. To feel alive. To want another person near. He'd take the pain when it came. Right now he wanted joy.

"You have to let me go. I have things I have to do."

"One more kiss. One more minute."

"All right, but don't get in the habit of making demands. I'm not a woman who follows orders. I like —"

He covered her mouth with his and she didn't protest. Half an hour later, when their minute was over, they walked out of the basement looking like they'd just faced tornado-level winds.

He couldn't stop smiling. Tonight he had no doubt that the whole tornado would hit. Ground zero, the third floor of city hall.

As they reached the top of the stairs, Benjamin was just coming through the back door. He was carrying mail stacked to his chin and barely noticed them as he turned into the main office.

"I'm not talking to him," Anna whispered. "I'm out of here."

"Coward," he said softly as she ran toward the front door.

Sam decided to go check on Stella's brother. After all, Sam hadn't handed in his letter yet, so he was still the pastor, and Benjamin looked lost.

Benjamin was sorting mail in his office when Sam walked in. "Morning, Mr. Blake. Can I get you a cup of coffee? I was just

340

about to make a pot."

To his surprise, Benjamin accepted the offer, "I usually don't drop in on Mondays," he explained, "But — well, who knows how behind on the books Stella is."

When Sam returned with the coffee, he decided to play dumb. "Miss Stella not coming in this morning?"

"I don't think so. I'm the official bookkeeper, you know. She just helps me out. She likes to work on Monday when everyone is gone. She doesn't like talking to people, dreadfully shy, you know."

Sam thought about the organ player. Stella had no problem talking to him.

Benjamin opened the ledger book. "I got my degree online, but Stella only took a few courses. But, make no mistake, she does them as well as I would."

"Do you tell her that?" Sam sat down in the chair across from him.

"I don't have to, she knows it." Benjamin looked so sad. "She's smart, but the poor girl has no common sense. She left the house without doing the dishes."

Sam studied the man. "Do you know where she is?"

Benjamin shook his head. "I have no idea. She's probably lost without me. I have to tell her what to do all the time. If we go

341

beyond the city limits, I do the driving. Highways frighten her. Someone called and said she was in church yesterday, but she didn't come home to make lunch. Now and then she does something strange like this — goes off and forgets to mention her plans to me."

"That's not very comforting."

"Oh, it's nothing improper or dangerous. For instance, she likes to walk through the cemetery on rainy days or hide out in the library and read a whole book. Once she was so lost in reading she got locked in the library from Saturday to Monday. I wasted my time worrying. Come Monday the librarian found her. She'd eaten all the peanut butter crackers in the vending machine."

Sam smiled. "She must have been one frightened kid."

"No, she was twenty-eight at the time," Benjamin huffed. "This time maybe she went to see our cousin in Fredericksburg. I know she was thinking about it. I was in a pre-council meeting yesterday and the cell phone reception is spotty in there. Maybe she tried to call and couldn't get through. I'm sure she meant to call me last night, but just forgot. We'll have to set some rules down when she gets back."

"You're not her parent, Benjamin. You're her brother and she's old enough to go her own way."

"She's too shy to do that. I knew by the time she was twelve that I'd need to take care of her all her life. She's always wanted to go to college and study music, but she'd never make it away from home and I don't think she can get that kind of degree online."

Sam saw the worry in his eyes. Benjamin wasn't a bully, he was trying to protect Stella. He wished he could tell the brother that his sister was safe, but that wasn't his place.

The phone rang and Benjamin jumped to answer.

It was Stella. Sam could hear the voice on the other end and recognized the cadence, although he couldn't hear what she was saying.

Benjamin's voice was rough. "You all right? Where are you? When are you coming home? . . . No, I don't like it one bit that you won't tell me where you are, but if that's what you want, I guess I'll have to deal with it. I'm here at the church right now doing your work for you. . . ." Then, in a lower tone: "All right, I won't raise my

343

voice. Just come home soon. I worry about you."

Sam left the room, satisfied that shy Stella was beginning to stand up for herself.

Back in his office, he put his letter in an empty desk drawer.

He'd resign later. Right now he had to spend his day waiting for five o'clock. He had a fire to put out here before he caught a flight to Denver.

CHAPTER 29

Mid-morning

COLBY

The trooper rolled over and found Piper
sound asleep beside him. She had a lock of
her hair across her face, but he thought she
looked adorable. One strap of her nightgown
had fallen off her shoulder and the top of
her breast was almost free of the lace. The
lady had no tan lines; she must not spend
much time outdoors.

She said she gardened. He could almost
see her in long sleeves and a hat wide as her
shoulders. The mayor was proper, modest, a
bit old-fashioned. Seeing her like this must
be a rare pleasure for any man. Colby had
seen her covered in mud and sound asleep.
He considered himself lucky.

The thought occurred to him that he
wouldn't mind waking up to this view every
day for the rest of his life. Too bad she didn't

even like him, so the chances of that happening were pretty dim.

When the bright sun slid through the French doors, he knew he must be in trouble. Big trouble. Sleeping with the mayor was not part of his assignment. The muffled sounds of workers moving around below confirmed his theory.

"PJ." He touched her bare shoulder. "PJ. Wake up."

She opened one eye and stared at him. "Who are you and what are you doing in my bed?"

"I'm your bodyguard. I've been watching you all night." He couldn't resist drawing out his next words Texas style: "And I gotta say, ma'am, you got one great body to guard." He hooked a finger around that thin strap and pulled it back in place.

She pushed her hair away and tried to focus on the clock. Apparently, having a man in her bed wasn't as interesting as what time it was.

He looked at his watch. "It's almost eleven, Monday."

Piper looked back at him. "You wear a watch to bed?"

He thought he'd pad his excuse for being in her room. "I do when I'm on duty."

"Well, you might want to be on full alert,

Trooper. I think I just heard footsteps in the hallway."

"No ghosts, remember." Colby turned as her bedroom door creaked open.

Piper's cousin Jessica backed into Piper's room with a tray.

"About time you woke up, Piper."

When she faced them she didn't look at all surprised to see the cowboy in Piper's bed, again.

"I figured you'd be here, Colby. You left the window downstairs open last night. If this is going to be a habit, I'll have to get you a key. I hate to leave the café unlocked. No telling who might wander in." Jessica glanced at the two weapons on the dresser. "Apparently my house ghosts come armed. The place might be safer than I thought."

"I was just checking on Piper." His reason for being here sounded lame even to him. "How did you know she was here this morning?"

"Family knows where she is, of course. Two of our aunts phoned and told me to inform her that she'd better not miss the city council meeting at one. They also told me to tell that Hells Angel to get out of bed and come over and remove his bike from the front of their house." Jessica laughed. "I told them I had no idea where either of you were." She looked at Piper. "I said you probably crashed in your office like you sometimes do the night before the council meeting and that I don't talk to Hells Angels or any bikers."

"But your first husband was a biker," Piper said.

"That's the reason for my rule. I start talking to a man who rides a Harley and the next thing I know my clothes start falling off. I lost half my wardrobe one summer in Sturgis." Jessica frowned at Colby. "I don't want to hear a word from you now that I know you ride."

Colby stood. He hadn't bothered to undress last night so he figured he was presentable even though wrinkled. "I'm not a Hells Angel. I do own an old Harley. That's all." He stared at Jessica. "I also didn't sleep with Piper." He couldn't say more without having to reveal too much.

"Sure." Jessica set the tray down. "And I'm your fairy godmother delivering breakfast to two people who are not here."

Piper sat up, her strap falling almost to her elbow. She smiled and said in a sexy voice, "Did we sleep at all, cowboy?"

Jessica backed out of the room, laughing.

"You — you —" Colby couldn't get words out. "You just ruined my reputation."

Piper had the nerve to laugh before she darted for the bathroom door.

When he heard the door lock and the shower start, Colby put on his boots and left a note that said simply: *5:00 at your office.* He slipped down the back staircase. If anyone in the kitchen noticed him, they didn't comment.

An hour later he'd collected his Harley from in front of Widows Park and was driving the back roads near the river. He planned to talk to as many of the fishermen as he could.

Chapter 30

Pecos

Kerrie and Pecos helped Mr. Winston rearrange furniture for what seemed like hours. He showed them two rooms that were connected and said if they helped, it could be theirs until they found a place. The old guy was so happy to have company that he couldn't stop smiling.

Pecos tried to get his head around what had happened this morning. He ate breakfast, got a job, and went over to Kerrie's place to pick her up. Then the world shifted on its axis and everything changed. He wouldn't be surprised if the world news reported Australia had fallen off the earth and was now floating free toward the moon.

Lost in thought, he carried furniture to the basement. Kerrie was pregnant. How could that have happened? Hell, he knew

350

how, he was raised on a farm, but it made no sense. The smartest girl in school, the one with the spotless reputation had gotten knocked up.

Halfway down the basement stairs Pecos missed a step and tumbled down holding on to a chest that looked old enough to have come over on the *Mayflower.*

He hit the concrete floor, then the chest landed on top of him.

"You all right down there?" Mr. Winston yelled.

"No," he mumbled as he lay spread eagle on the dirty floor.

"Pecos?"

"Yeah, I'm fine." He yelled back without bothering to remove the chest. Somehow the weight seemed to be pressing only on his heart. The girl he'd watched every day he was in school wasn't perfect. Apparently she was just human like the rest of the world.

As he'd done ten times before, he started back at the night he picked Kerrie up from the dance and tried to remember everything they'd said and done. He'd been counting the times she kissed him on the cheek.

She'd been sad Friday night, like she wanted to run away from life for a while. She'd already been pregnant.

When she'd given her speech at graduation about aiming for the stars and being the best you can be, she'd already been pregnant.

Every minute they'd laughed together or swam together or talked . . . she'd already been pregnant.

He felt like he was the rough wooden frame that boxed in her life but she was the picture. Everything was happening with her and he was simply the borders of her drama.

"You going to lay there all day?"

Pecos opened his good eye and saw her standing above him. He swore she was so beautiful that sometimes it hurt to look at her. "I'm smashed," he said without emotion.

"Want some help?"

"Sure."

Kerrie lifted the trunk off his chest. "Why is it, Pecos, that I keep going around saving you? If not for me, your life span would have been measured in minutes, and you never would have learned to dance, either."

Pecos sat up and looped his arm around one knee. "Would you answer me one question about the past if I promise never to ask again?"

She sat down on the chest. "One question. I owe you that much." Her smile melted away, but she straightened her back as if knowing exactly what was coming.

He was silent for a moment, then said, "How did the pregnancy happen?"

Kerrie stared at him. "I'll tell you, and only you. When I'm finished you can leave and I will not try to stop you, but you can never, ever tell anyone else. Agreed?"

"Agreed."

She took a deep breath. "As soon as it began to get warm I wanted to go with some friends to a beach house down at Galveston, but my parents said partying on beaches is for college kids. They did let me go see my cousin in Dallas for a weekend. She's three years older than me and lives at an apartment complex that has a pool and tennis courts. Mom claimed it would be cleaner than the beach.

"The first night we were there my cousin and I met these boys. We went swimming and walked around the huge complex. The boys said they were in college and I felt older somehow. They didn't know anything about me, so I could be whoever I wanted to be. My cousin had fun telling them all about my wild adventures that she made up."

Kerrie smiled at Pecos. "Did you ever want to be someone else for a while?"

353

"Most of my life," he answered.

"For me it was just one night. I flirted with one of them and told him I was twenty. We drank wine, but I wasn't drunk. I just thought I'd just step over the line a bit. But . . . I went too far. I made a mistake. When I started crying he must have figured out I wasn't as old as I told him. He got mad and said he never wanted to see me again and walked away. He called me terrible names.

"As I walked back to my cousin's apartment, I realized I didn't even know his last name or where he lived. Nothing. For all I knew he'd lied to me as much as I'd lied to him."

She covered her face with her hands. "I wouldn't blame you if you left. This is my mess, not yours."

Pecos rose to his knees and pulled her hands away so he could look straight at her. "I'm not walking away. The baby is mine, Kerrie. From right now on, it's mine. Don't ever think about that creep again."

"You don't know what you're getting into, Pecos. We're too young to take all this on. It's my mistake, my choice, my problem. I don't want to mess your life up too."

"I don't have much of a life to mess up. That's the truth. But if you're willing, I'd

354

like to stand next to you through this. All the way. For as long as you need me. I've been thinking. We can work all summer and this fall take a few classes over at the community college."

"Why, Pecos? Why would you give up your dreams for me?"

He didn't know what to say. Could he say she was the one bright light in his world most days? That living through any storms with her was better than facing the world alone.

Finally, he answered, "Because I want to always be the one you run to when you need help. The one you go through wild times with. I want to hold you when you cry, and laugh with you. I know I'm not good enough — not the kind of man you'd want to marry. But I'll work hard."

She slid off the chest into his arms. "You are the kind of man I want to marry. You're kind. You're perfect." She touched the dark bruise under his eye. "A bit beat-up, but still perfect. You're my knight."

"Well, that settles it, then. We'll get married because we want to, not because a baby is on the way. The baby will just be an extra blessing. I've delivered enough calves to handle anything you drop."

She frowned. "That's comforting, but I

don't think women drop babies." She stood and pulled him to his feet. "We'll talk about it later. I'll get dressed at home and meet you later. Mom told me we all should be in the church office at three."

CHAPTER 31

Afternoon

COLBY

Colby drove the dirt roads near the Brazos River looking for information about Boone Buchanan from the local fishermen.

Finding a fishing cabin was like looking for gray Easter eggs in gravel. Half the cabins looked like they were made of downed trees. The bark was still on the lumber and the wood had aged to ground-cover brown.

Several times he'd left his Harley and walked in only to find that no one was home. Or maybe they didn't bother to answer his knock. None had a doorbell.

After an hour he found a man near the water working on his boat. Colby tried to talk to him. He said he'd seen a BMW floating in the river but didn't see anyone climb out. The fisherman wasn't interested in the

357

car or in talking. The only complete sentence he offered was about how grand he thought the mayor was.

The second man he came across was fishing in the shade of a live oak that looked older than the state. He seemed friendly enough. Colby decided to come at the interview from a different direction.

"You haven't seen my cousin Daily Watts out here lately?"

"I might have," the fisherman admitted. "What side of his family you on?"

"I was on his mother's side. He's my second cousin."

The man who smelled like bait shook his head. "Don't remember her. She left old Watts with two boys to raise. They grew up in the garage, but Daily was the only one interested in working. His brother left for the big city when he got grown, but he came back to take over when Daily started drinking. The brother runs the place now and bosses Daily around like he's just a hired hand."

More information than Colby needed to know so he shifted direction. "Was Daily out here the night the BMW hit the water?"

"Probably. He is most nights. When he's drunk he goes home, but if he's trying to stay sober so he can work the next morning, he comes out here."

Colby digested the information. Daily had described a man crawling out of the car. If he wasn't drunk, his account might be accurate.

"Did you see the driver of the BMW?"

"No, but I came across a man's jacket floating in the water that night. I gave it to the police, but they didn't seem too interested. Less than a week later I found two graduation robes snagged on a branch. Didn't bother to turn them in."

Colby ignored the information about the graduation robes. Some of the other boys found other pieces of clothing. It's like whoever the driver was, he stripped on his way to shore.

Colby kept hunting, but he learned little. One question kept nagging at the back of his mind. Why would a man strip off his clothes in the river? Easier to swim? He was hot? He feared he was wearing a tracker?

For Boone to completely disappear, he had to know there was nothing on him that could be traced. To take the risk of the crash, swimming in dangerous waters, and having to walk out after midnight nude, Boone would have to be in deep trouble. Life and death kind of trouble.

And somehow Piper was mixed up in this.

The tennis shoe print. One detail that didn't make sense. Boone was a city boy. He might swim without clothes, but he wouldn't walk away barefooted. Somewhere in his journey he'd picked up a pair of shoes and he hadn't bothered to hide all of his tracks — literally. Maybe Boone was dumb enough to think he'd never be tracked. Or maybe Boone was smart enough to leave that footprint on purpose just to lead them on a wild goose chase. Colby decided to place his bets on dumb.

Colby asked the last fisherman, who only nodded, if he might know someone who'd help him tow the mayor's boat back home. To his credit the guy nodded and said he'd take care of it.

"I'll be happy to pay you." Colby pushed his hand in his pocket.

"No need. Ain't doing it for you."

The fisherman walked away without another word.

Colby checked his watch. He needed to get home to clean up for his five o'clock date in the mayor's office. The pieces were starting to fit together.

CHAPTER 32

Monday

PECOS

Pecos walked Kerrie home but didn't go in. Her dad's car was gone, but he didn't want to push his luck. He'd been engaged for only a few hours and he was already dreading every Thanksgiving and Christmas for the rest of his life. He had a feeling that with Brad around, trips to the ER might be their way of bonding.

Pecos went back into Mr. Winston's house and took a shower, then stared at his clothes. He had black slacks he'd bought for graduation, a white shirt, and a black tie. It didn't seem good enough.

Mr. Winston watched him from the hallway. "They'll do fine for a wedding, Pecos. It's only in the church office."

Pecos frowned. "I know, but it's not an 'only in the office' kind of wedding. It's my wedding. It's Kerri's wedding. I don't know about her, but I'm sure this is my only wedding. How much do you think it would cost to buy a suit? I've never had anything but a few hand-me-down ones."

"A few hundred dollars, I guess." Mr. Winston grinned. "But I know where you can find a fine, hand-me-down one for twenty. She might even throw in the tie."

"Two hundred is a lot to spend." He had the hundred-dollar bills his brothers gave him. It might be worth it. "Maybe we should check out the secondhand one first."

"It'll be between you and me. I'll never tell that it's not brand-new."

Pecos helped Mr. Winston into his pickup and they drove across town to a place he'd never gone. The flea market. It looked like a long row of carports lined up three feet apart. Homemade signs hung above each space, and the sides and back were closed in with blue tarps that flapped in the breeze, making the tent stores look like they were breathing.

After strolling past the first three vendors, Pecos realized he'd finally found an outdoor mall full of things he didn't want or need. One was all garden gnomes. Another had a dozen mailboxes made from tree trunks carved to look like bears. One had a hundred stuffed unicorns that must have been left in the rain. When he saw the booth full of everything knitted, Pecos got a little worried. Hats, dresses, towels, baby toys. He sure hoped Mr. Winston wasn't thinking of a knitted suit.

"Can you believe this place is only open on Mondays?"

"Yeah." Pecos looked around. No one looked under the age of eighty. He felt like he was aging just looking around.

"I used to walk here, but the road got too long." The old man laughed at his own joke. "Now I usually walk over to the coffee shop where most of the vendors stop in for coffee before they head here. One of them always offers me a lift."

They reached the last carport on the row. Mr. Winston pulled a small plant out of the bag he carried. "If you'll allow me a few minutes."

Pecos watched as the old man went into the booth lined with vintage clothing. A tiny woman stood up from her chair to greet him. They smiled at each other, and he gave her the plant. Pecos wondered what they were saying to each other that made them look so happy.

It occurred to him that maybe they loved each other. They might be what he and

Kerrie would have always been if he hadn't picked her up after the dance. They'd be living in the same town, polite to each other, maybe even loving each other but never saying the words. They'd be endearing strangers like Mr. Winston and the lady.

A dark cloud seemed to cover the sun right where he was standing. When he tried to picture the future, nothing came into focus. Kerrie didn't love him. She'd called him her friend. So what would happen tonight? Would they sleep together? Would they have sex? Would he be brave enough to tell her he loved her? He did, he knew. But why would she ever love him? No one else ever had.

He'd just play it by ear. Whatever she wanted to do, he'd try to figure out how.

"Pecos," Mr. Winston interrupted his thoughts. "Come meet my Claire. I told her what you need."

Pecos shook her hand, feeling as if he needed to fold himself in half to talk to her.

While Mr. Winston told him that they'd been friends for forty years, Miss Claire walked around Pecos.

"He's a thin one. How many hours we got?"

"Two," Mr. Winston answered.

She shook her head. "It'll take a miracle."

Before he could object Claire pulled a plastic box out from under a display table of sweaters and started pulling out jackets. "If he's got black slacks we're going to find a jacket and a tie of course. There is no time to tailor fit pants."

"I thought a bow tie might be nice," Winston said as he began stripping Pecos like he was the carport mannequin. Some of the other vendors gathered around to offer their opinion as shirt and jackets flew through the air. The bear carver, the knitter, and the gnome painter didn't look like they had a lick of fashion sense.

Finally, everyone was staring at him and smiling.

Pecos looked down. A light brown jacket with threads of chocolate running through, a dusty green shirt, and a tie that pulled everything together. He would never have put the colors together, but with his dark skin and brown eyes, it worked.

The bear carver offered to give him a haircut, and Claire offered to shorten the sleeves. Without much discussion, they all put out their signs, Closed for Nap, and headed over to Winston's house.

While Pecos brought in Miss Claire's sewing machine and the boxes, he overheard them talking about him, remarking how handsome he was and how lucky his bride would be.

Pecos laughed to himself. He now had an idea how Cinderella must have felt when she found the mice.

An hour later, he stood in front of the mirror and didn't recognize himself. Winston had shaved him, and the bear carver gave him a cut that made him feel like he could walk down Wall Street and belong. Claire had found a vest that fit just right, and Winston pulled out an old gold watch chain for the pocket.

Like proud parents they watched him walk out the door.

Pecos drove the few blocks to the church. Kerrie was waiting on the steps. When she saw him, she turned away, then turned back. "Pecos?"

He was smiling as he walked toward her. "I know this is a hurry-up wedding, but for me it's our wedding and it's special."

She smiled back, looking beautiful as always in a white sundress with flowers along the hem. "I can't believe you're doing this for me."

"Not just for you. For me."

Inside the church, the expression on Kerrie's dad's face was more of a puzzled look than an I'll-kill-you-later-look.

Pecos felt like he was floating through a dream. Any sign of the high school kid he had been just hours before was gone. He looked like a man about to be married.

The county judge married them because no one could find the preacher. The bride and groom hugged but didn't kiss. Since Kerrie's father had said there would be no celebration, the wedding was over in ten minutes. Brad shook Pecos's hand and said simply, "Give us an hour and we'll have her clothes packed up and on the porch. No sense sending her winter things — she'll be too big to wear them."

"Thank you, sir. I'll be by before dark to pick them up."

"Barbara said we gave her the car. She can keep it or sell it. It's hers. She's got a college fund, but — well, it's a college fund . . . for college. I guess that's out the window now."

Pecos felt his hopes and dreams rising. She'd be able to go to college no matter how poor they were. Brad looked like all his dreams for his only child were falling.

Pecos straightened his shoulders. "I'll make sure she goes to college, sir. I'll take care of her."

A touch of murder flashed across Brad's face. "You'd better, kid."

Pecos raised his chin. "I'm not a kid, Mr. Lane, and you'd best remember that."

Kerrie pulled him away then, and they were practically running out of the church.

They drove around for a while and ended up stopping for cherry-limes at the Sonic. Then they went out to their rock and talked.

Pecos loved sharing his plans and dreams with Kerrie. She said she'd take a few classes this fall if he'd drive with her and start on his degree too. They'd take her car just in case she went into labor. She might have to take incompletes on her classes if the baby came before she made her finals, but she'd manage.

"I don't know. If I have to deliver a baby, I think the pickup would work better than that little car."

She held his bruised face in her hands. "Let's get one thing straight. I'm not a cow and you are not going to have to deliver this baby. My car will drive faster and get me to the hospital."

"I wouldn't mind." He tried to look disappointed. "I've got time to read up on it. I could probably Google whatever I need to know."

They held hands and planned a future, a future that had seemed so dark just hours before, but now was full of hope. They'd

368

starve their way through diapers and college, then together they'd build their dreams.

When they made it back to Mr. Winston's house, all the flea market helpers were waiting. Claire had made lemonade and Mr. Winston bought cupcakes for all.

There was laughter and hugs all around.

While Pecos was helping Mr. Winston refill everyone's glasses, he glanced out the window, and saw that Kerrie's parents were standing on the sidewalk looking uncertain.

"I'll talk to them," Mr. Winston said.

Pecos nodded and slowly opened the window a few inches so he could listen.

"Evening," the old man said. "You're welcome to come in and join the party."

Kerrie's father shook his head, but her mother looked willing.

Mr. Winston nodded politely. "She'll always be your daughter. The baby will be your grandchild. And I have a feeling Pecos will always be your son-in-law. He loves her, you know."

Winston turned and came back inside, but Pecos noticed he left the door open a few inches. Pecos closed the window and went back to Kerrie. He put his arm around her knowing she must be mourning the loss of her parents at the party. Her father had said there would be no celebration.

"You sorry?" he whispered.

"Never. I married the best friend I'll ever have."

There was that *friend* word again, but he wouldn't complain. Friends seemed to be a good place to build from.

Ten minutes later, her parents came through the back door. Brad never said a word except to claim he had an accident when Claire asked about his arm. Barbara was polite and seemed interested in all the people around the table. She even laughed as they each took credit for turning Pecos from a frog to a prince.

Kerrie cuddled next to him.

"Sorry about all the drama today and the quick wedding," he whispered.

"I thought it was grand." She kissed his cheek . . . again. "We'll tell our grandchildren about it one day."

Pecos smiled but considered grandchildren might not be in the picture if she didn't work on getting her kisses a bit closer to his lips.

Chapter 33

Late afternoon

SAM

Sam packed up and decided to drive around the valley, memorizing every view. He had no idea what would happen in Anna's office at five, but no matter what, he wanted this town to be his base. He'd been living in his new apartment in Denver for six months and hadn't bothered to unpack the boxes. Honey Creek would be a longer commute, but there was a small airport in Clifton Valley. He could store his plane there and be anywhere in the Rockies within three or four hours. There would be several weeks a year when he'd be gone training, but he'd always have this quiet place to come to.

With or without Anna in his life, this would be his home.

Eventually, Sam found himself heading deep into the valley looking for the cemetery in the woods where his parents had been buried. It took him a bit of time, but he finally found it. He hadn't returned since the funeral, but he remembered there was a peace in the place. Huge oak and tall pines bent by the winds cradled the cemetery. Thick grass spotted with wildflowers blanketed the uneven ground. The graves weren't in rows, but clusters. A wooden gate swung open and closed with the wind as if invisible visitors were passing in and out.

As Sam walked toward their plots he didn't feel closer to death, but closer to Heaven.

He placed the thin white clerical collar on his father's headstone. "Well, Dad, I gave it a try, but it wasn't for me. I'll have to find another way to save the world."

After a moment, he went on. "And, Mom, I haven't found the perfect woman. I did a good job of finding a woman who has just about everything I don't want in a woman. She's shorter than me by a foot, talks all the time, bosses me around, but she's got a fire for life that rubs off on everyone around her."

Sam lowered himself to the grass beside the headstone and started talking as if his parents were on the other side of the stone listening. He told them about London and the horror of seeing innocent people dying. He described how the army settled him and gave him direction. He talked about April Raine, who loved nature and him. He described how he felt dead inside most days. He told them how it felt to be part of a community if only for a few days.

When he was done, he rose, and stood before the two headstones a moment longer. "I'll come back and visit again soon."

Sam walked away smiling. It was almost time to meet Anna and his phone hadn't rung. There was a good chance he'd have time to make that couch in her office squeak before he had to leave.

He laughed. That would be one thing he wouldn't talk to his parents about.

CHAPTER 34

4:30 p.m.

PIPER

Piper rolled her shoulders. She'd just lived through the longest city council meeting in her career. Every person in the room had a complaint or wanted something changed immediately. Twice she'd had to call for a fifteen-minute break so people could calm down, have a cup of coffee, and think.

Neither break seemed to help, but the three dozen cookies she'd had delivered at three o'clock had at least turned the volume down while everyone chewed.

Now she had a stack of papers and requests to go over before she could call it a night. At least most of the reporters were gone. It seemed Boone Buchanan was about to become yesterday's news. He wasn't dead or found. Maybe he'd just fade into one of Honey Creek's legends. She'd rather have him found. Boone Buchanan wasn't worth legend status.

A new rumor had surfaced that he'd lost his car in a poker game that night. Rather than hand over the keys, he'd driven the BMW into the river.

Piper thought that sounded like something he'd do. Boone hated to lose.

She climbed the wooden stairs from the third floor to her office on the fourth. As always, the meeting hadn't made it to a budget vote. The elevator would have to wait a few more weeks to be fixed, along with half a dozen other repairs on the building.

She paused in front of her grandfather's picture just outside her office. "Maybe you were right. Sometimes it's not a matter of winning or losing. Sometimes it's just a matter of outlasting your enemies."

A small square envelope fell out of the pile of papers in her arms. Piper bent down and picked it up, then walked through Autumn's open office door.

She got a stack of papers every meeting, but she'd never received a letter from someone at the council meeting. It was addressed to her but had no return address, no stamp.

A chill passed through her. She'd seen a

note like this before. Same letter size. Same handwriting on the address. No stamp. Just like the one she'd found shoved under her door shortly after Boone disappeared.

She set the papers down and collapsed into one of the waiting chairs across from the secretary's desk.

"You need something, Piper?" Autumn, for once, looked too busy to talk.

"I'm fine. Just tired." She opened the envelope and pulled out the one piece of paper.

Autumn almost sounded like she cared. "I don't blame you. I could hear the yelling in the meeting when I had to go downstairs to get to the restroom. I wish someone would fix the ladies' room on this floor or that dumb elevator. I hate walking down those creaky, old wooden stairs every hour. Nothing ever gets fixed around here."

Autumn grimaced and continued. "The shouting from the boardroom gave me a headache. But, as usual, I had to spend some time in there, what with my peeing problems, so I eavesdropped. Didn't sound like anything new. Just the same old problems."

Piper quit listening to her secretary. She unfolded the note from the square envelope.

One line. *WATCH OUT. YOU DIDN'T CRY*

FOR ME. I WON'T CRY FOR YOU.

"Oh, you got another one of those strange notes." Autumn opened her left top drawer and pulled out three more square envelopes. "I've been finding them all around, but they don't make any sense. I was planning to toss them in the bottom file drawer with all the other weird mail."

Piper held her temper in check. "Why didn't you give them to me? After all, they are addressed to me."

"I didn't want to bother you. You've got enough to be worried about. And, you know, I open all the office mail. It's my job. If I passed you every nut's letter or threat, you'd be afraid to come to work. I'm used to them. Besides, after three kids nothing frightens me. Gotta say, you get less than your granddad did."

Piper returned to her office with the letters, and hurriedly read them. One said: *REACT.* The next said: *SOMETIMES TRAGEDY BRINGS CHANGE.* The last note issued a warning: *LOCK YOUR DOORS AND STAY INSIDE IF YOU WORK LATE.*

The clock chimed five times. Autumn began her routine of locking up. "I'm calling it a night. My bottom's tired from sitting and my back hurts. If I'm pregnant again I swear I'll kill my husband."

The office door closed just as Autumn said good night to the office. As always she didn't wait for Piper to say anything.

Piper realized she was alone. In five minutes the whole building would be empty. Hugging herself, she moved to the window. For the first time in her life, she didn't feel safe in this office. Her grandfather's office. Her office. The mayor's office.

As if to mirror her mood, the sky was darkening with a summer storm. Murky, rain-filled clouds shoved away the white ones as rain seemed to spit against her window, driven by the wind.

Lightning blinked in the trees at the edge of town as if sending a warning of trouble yet to come. She couldn't see the river but she knew it would be raging.

For a while she just stood by the windows letting the storm blend with her mood.

Finally, she turned back and spread the five notes out on her desk. Someone was threatening her. Somebody wanted her to be afraid.

Could it be Boone? He'd joked once that they should marry so that in case she died in office, the town would automatically elect him as mayor. She remembered how envious he'd been of her title and position.

Another thing he did when they were

alone: He often talked about money. Her money. The Mackenzies' money. "With your family's political power and deep pockets, you could run Texas."

She'd never really liked him, but they'd grown up together, and Piper remained loyal to her friends. Plus, he was a handy escort, and a great excuse to turn down invitations from other men, the better to avoid awkwardness and hurt feelings. She supposed you could say she'd used him. And he'd used her. To get the attention he craved.

His family had influence and the legal power, but they didn't have a presence in politics. Boone wanted to be that presence and for a short time she'd let him use her to climb. But men like him tend to slip up. Shady deals, backing the wrong cause. Cutting corners and stepping on people.

Pretending they were engaged was his latest attempt to draw attention — at least, until he'd disappeared. Maybe it was a mistake to let him get away with that. She'd always been very clear with him. Even when he became more pressing recently. She'd come right out and told him that if he was going to continue to pester her and claim he loved her, she would go public about their fake engagement. She'd told him she was tired of the whole thing, and was soon going to want to put an end to it anyway.

The north wind rattled the windows as day darkened to night and the office moved into shadow.

What if Boone hadn't been totally exaggerating when he professed love for her? . . . whatever his version of love was, which she knew bordered on obsession.

He'd seemed to take the news well that she didn't want to pretend much longer, but what if he'd secretly been enraged? She knew better than to think he'd gone off and killed himself over her, but maybe it was his weird way of getting back at her. . . . That would line up with the creepy notes she'd been receiving.

Piper moved closer to the window until she faced the outline of her own reflection. Maybe she'd underestimated Boone. Maybe she'd been wrong to write off all his craziness as — well, just being Boone. Maybe his psyche was darker than she'd ever imagined.

Or . . . maybe she was just guessing. Maybe she was "barking up the wrong tree," like her granddad always said when she invented answers to questions that had never been asked. Maybe Autumn was right about the notes. Just some nut.

A stern voice came fast and angry from behind her. "How long have you been getting these threats?"

She might have fired back, but when she turned she saw the worry mixed with anger in Colby's eyes.

"You're late."

"Forget that," he replied. "How long?" He held up one note.

"I got one the day Boone's BMW went in the water. The last note came today. And my secretary hadn't bothered to show me the others until a half hour ago. I thought it might be Boone sending them to rattle me, but maybe the person responsible for Boone's car ending up in the river is now coming after me. What if Boone was in some kind of trouble, and they think I know something, or have something that can't go public? Maybe they think the lawyer and the mayor discovered a secret and now we both have to die."

To her surprise, Colby didn't tell her she was spouting nonsense. "Do you have something like that?" he asked, still studying the notes. "Something that could ruin someone, or get him arrested? Some deadly secret? Could someone have something on you? Could Boone?"

"No, no skeletons in my closet."

381

She began to pace the length of the windows and back.

"What if this person writing notes thinks I know something on him and plans to kill me, or worse, end my career? Or maybe there is another nut out there who wants us both gone and he's halfway to his goal. Boone could have been murdered and I'm next."

Piper's hands began to shake. The stress of all this was finally getting to her. Wild guesses. Fear. She didn't even know if she was making any sense.

The trooper rounded her desk and held her tight as he pulled her away from the window so no one would see them. "It's all right, PJ. I'm here. If someone wanted to kill you, they probably wouldn't send you warnings. Maybe they just want to scare you so that when some kind of demand comes, you'll be so afraid you'll do whatever they want. Or maybe it's just a game a wacko thinks he's playing with the mayor. He's daring you to find him while believing he'll always be able to outsmart you."

Colby shifted her so he could look at the notes, while still holding her close.

"Something's bothering you about the notes, isn't it?" She pressed her cheek against his shoulder, feeling safer with him near.

He looked down at her. "Don't you think it's odd that your pen pal put your full name and address on the envelope when he planned to shove them under the door? He even has the zip code."

"Oh great, now we have another suspect. First, my almost boyfriend/make-believe fiancé, then there's a guy who thinks he's playing a game with me, and now an unknown postman because that is the only person I know who would care about putting the full address on."

"We'll talk it out, PJ, even if it takes us all night." He slid his hand along her side, more a comforting gesture than a caress.

As the wind pounded the windows, Colby flicked on the desk lamp, pulled paper off the printer, and began making lists. All they know about Boone. A lineup of people who were either hostile to her or the office.

Piper even added Autumn. She was either hostile or pregnant again. Piper wasn't sure which would be worse.

Colby also insisted she make a list of every person she saw on the floor today. Everyone who routinely walked her hallway. Anyone who never came up four floors but had in the past week.

Like a master he tried to link a clue to a person as she talked, telling Colby every detail about her life. Colby stared at the notes, the lists, the clues as if he might find a list within a list, or a clue that stood out among the clutter.

Piper tiptoed out of her private door and returned with two Cokes. "Let's take a break. We've been working an hour." She handed him one can. "In ten minutes we'll be looking at it with fresh eyes."

He pulled her granddad's huge chair around the desk and sat beside her, his elbows on his knees as he leaned closer. "How come you have such a tiny office? Your secretary's office is twice this size."

Piper took a drink and relaxed. "My grandfather had it made this way. He believed if the mayor's office was small he'd never be stormed by a crowd bigger than three."

"Makes sense."

She turned in her chair until her knees almost bumped the side of his chair. "Lift your leg up an inch."

Colby looked at her as if he suspected a trap. When he lifted his leg, she slid her toes under him. "Cold toes?" he asked.

"You guessed it. I need to relax and talk about something besides my problems."

"Like what?"

"How about your problems, Colby? What's on your mind?"

"Nothing. Just keeping you safe." For once he sounded serious.

"Come on, Trooper, talk to me for a change."

He grinned. "All right, since you asked." He shifted and covered her foot with his fingers. "This is a matter that might not be the right time to bring up, but it's been bugging me for two days."

She leaned closer. "What is it?"

"You promised me a kiss if I let you patch me up. And you did bandage me up more than once. I stayed still and never complained, but no kiss."

"You can't be serious. I'm about to be killed and you're worried about a kiss."

Colby frowned. "I knew this wasn't the right time to mention it. But around you, when is? Besides, you don't want to die without paying your debt."

"You're crazy."

"One long kiss and we call it paid and then we can go back to work. I promise. It'll clear my head. Think about it. When is a guy like me ever going to kiss a mayor?"

"Oh, all right. I've kissed babies and puppies. I even kissed a donkey one time. I

385

might as well kiss you."

He took her hand and pulled her into her grandfather's office chair with him.

She wiggled, settling in for the duty. "First, I want you to know . . ."

"The kiss comes with a speech?" Colby groaned. "You're not breaking ground on a new building. All you have to do is kiss me."

"Right."

He frowned. "I want you to know that this is me kissing you. Not the trooper kissing the mayor. It's me, Colby, kissing you, Piper, for no reason other than I want to kiss you and think I have since we met."

"I understand."

He kissed her so softly, as his arm held her gently, that she felt herself melting into him. Then the kiss deepened and neither showed any sign of stopping.

As the storm grew beyond the window and the room drew darker, Piper found herself lost in Colby's tender ways.

CHAPTER 35

SAM

Sam had slipped into Anna Presley's office at exactly five o'clock. They were both adults. They both knew what was about to happen and he hoped she was as excited about it as he was.

For Sam, though, it wasn't only about the sex. It was the connection with another person. There had been times when all he wanted from a woman was a warm body to hold on to. He'd been too lost to want more than the physical comfort.

But tonight it wouldn't be just any woman. He wanted Anna. Even though they had nothing in common. Even though she wasn't his type, and he figured she didn't even have a type.

He looked around her cluttered office. Degrees on the walls, law books mixed in with toys, and a desk stacked high. It reminded him of a garage sale for careers. Someone had told him Anna didn't have any family. She's been a foster kid who'd ended up with foster parents who were good to her. They even helped her get scholarships before they moved away and retired to South Carolina. Anna went away to college, but she came back to Honey Creek in the summers. After three degrees she settled here and began fighting every dragon she could find.

He admired her, even if he didn't understand her.

Sam had changed into his firefighter clothes knowing he might have to leave soon. His gear was packed and ready. He knew the call would come. He'd be ready as long as he got just a little time with Anna before he had to leave.

He looked at his watch for the tenth time. She was late. Wasting the short time they had.

He watched the clouds move in and hoped this rain would move north. People were running from building to building or to their cars. Trying to outrun the rain. Something Sam never did. Rain had saved him more than once when he'd been jumping into a burning forest fire.

He moved a few boxes off the couch and spread out. He could see the storm outside and it was putting on quite a show.

As the room darkened, he closed his eyes and dreamed of how he planned to make love to Anna.

The sound of her opening her office door, bumping bags as she moved, woke Sam.

In the hallway light he saw her outline.

"I'm sorry." She sounded like she might cry. "I wanted to get my hair done. I thought it would take minutes and it took hours. It's a real mess."

Sam smiled. Her red tumbleweed had been darkened to almost brown and curled in a Shirley Temple style. Or maybe more like Medusa. He had thought any style would be an improvement over the tumbleweed. He was wrong.

Sam slowly sat up. "I'm not in love with your hair, Anna."

She met his gaze. "You can't be in love with me, period. We haven't made love yet. I'm probably more of a failure there than I am in picking a hairdresser."

He extended his hand. "Then come here. Maybe all you need is a little practice. Let's get this over with so I can tell you I love you." For a blink he thought of all that was wrong with her. Too short. Too bossy. Too

389

driven. Didn't know how to dress. "You're perfect, Anna." Sam was surprised how much he meant the words. "I wouldn't want you to change a thing."

She lifted her chin. "No one has ever said that to me."

"What, that you're perfect?"

"No one has ever said that they loved me." She took a step toward him. "Or that I'm perfect either. I'm thinking you need glasses."

"Well, I'm about to prove it to you. We're going to make love, then we'll talk, then I plan to make the old couch squeak again. And again, until you believe me."

She took one more step and took his hand. He gently pulled her beside him.

"How do you like to be held?"

"Tight," she answered. "Like you're never going to let me go."

He wrapped his arms around her and gently leaned her back as his body rested against her.

"How do you like to be touched?"

"I don't know."

Sam moved his hand along her side. "Then we'll experiment."

As he unbuttoned her blouse and slipped his hand over her breast she stopped breathing.

He tightened his grip. She let out a tiny sound of pleasure. "Take a breath, Anna. It may take a while, but I plan to learn the feel of you, the taste of you. All of you. Any objections?"

"No, but can you say it again?"

He didn't pretend to not know what she wanted. He kissed his way to her ear and whispered, "I love you, Anna Presley. If you want to stop this right now, I will not change my mind. I'll go on loving you."

He wanted to tell her he loved her because she needed love and she deserved love, but it wasn't that unselfish. He wanted her, needed her too. He was starving for all the complications that came with loving her.

She wrapped her arms around his neck and kissed him with a need that surprised him and he knew he'd always hold her tight.

An hour later, he smelled smoke, and for a moment he thought their lovemaking had actually started a fire.

CHAPTER 36

Twilight

PECOS

Pecos walked between the trees lining the city hall lawn. It was still raining, but he didn't care. He wanted to get to his new job early. In truth, the day had been so packed with emotion he needed the rest.

He was married. Really married as soon as all the paperwork was filed. He was out of school, had a wife and a job. Man, life moves fast once you graduate.

Kerrie had kissed him on the cheek, as always, and said she'd make him breakfast when he got home.

When he'd asked if she could cook she'd said no, but that it couldn't be that hard.

Pecos smiled. He didn't care. They could eat fried pies and cereal for the rest of their lives.

He looked at the lightning clashing to the north.

When he looked at the city hall, for a moment he thought the windows were reflecting the lightning back.

Then, he realized the blinks of light were only on the second floor.

It wasn't lightning. It was fire.

He grabbed his phone and dialed 911. No answer. Whoever was manning the phone must have stepped away. He heard a click and realized the call was being relayed. There would be a backup plan. Someone would answer.

As he waited he started running toward the fire station half a block away. When he barreled into the open bay door he heard the phone ringing but all the volunteers were eating dinner. Their laughter was blocking out the ring.

"Fire!" Pecos yelled. "The city hall."

Plates crashed, chairs toppled, and men ran to their posts. The town's one fire engine and one pickup were pulling out as men were still climbing on.

Pecos ran back toward the square. For a moment before the sirens started, he could hear his phone still ringing.

Pecos ran to the place he'd seen the flames as the three volunteers and three teenagers

393

in training backed the trucks across the grass.

When he took time to breathe Pecos saw flames spreading to the third floor. Then, as he looked above the fire, he saw something that made his heart stop.

The desk lamp in the mayor's office was on. Everyone in town knew that meant that she was working late.

Pecos ran to join the firemen. He didn't know what to do, but Pecos knew he had to do something fast.

CHAPTER 37

Evening

SAM

Sirens blasted outside the window as Sam jumped off the couch. "Get dressed!" he shouted as if Anna wasn't a foot away. "I think there is fire in the building."

For once Anna didn't argue.

He grabbed his jeans and moved to the window. Lightning flashed and rain still dribbled. When he looked down, he saw fire reflecting off the fire truck's windshield. One floor below!

"The truck is too close," he wanted to yell. "Turn the sirens off so you can hear each other." He needed to be out there helping. He needed to stay here with Anna.

Anna was instantly beside him, buttoning her blouse. "What's happening?"

"From the size of the flames and the smell, the first two floors are on fire. But

395

buildings made of concrete, marble, and bricks don't burn like this. It seems to be burning like a smokestack. The fire's not spreading, it's climbing."

"It's the wooden stairs below us." Anna's voice was almost calm. "They were put in when the building was built. Everyone uses them when the elevator breaks. The plan was to replace them, but the city never got around to it."

She looked up at him, their lovemaking still shining in her eyes. For a moment he thought she was the most beautiful woman he'd ever seen, but there was no time to tell her.

Sam stepped to the left and felt the wall and pulled his hand away. "We got to get out of here fast. We'll go to the other end of the hall and drop out a window if we have to. I'll lower you as far as I can. One of us might break a leg, but we'll take the fall."

"No! We can't. I saw the mayor climbing the stairs ahead of me. She's above us. Four stories up might kill her if she had to jump."

Neither said a word as they finished dressing.

Sam took her hand and opened the door. Smoke already filled the hallway and the temperature was rising. "Stay close, Anna.

396

I'll get all of us out. Is there another way up?"

"The elevator stopped working. No other stairs." She started shaking her head, then tugged him down the hall. "Off the boardroom is a balcony. We could climb up to the smaller balcony on four, but the windows will be locked from the inside on the fourth floor."

Sam grabbed the emergency hatchet off the wall.

A moment later he swung at the first boardroom door and it shattered.

They were running for the windows when she held back and watched Sam swing again. The gentle preacher had turned into a warrior.

Thanks to the brickwork on the fourth-floor balcony Sam had no problem swinging up. He lowered the ax. She grabbed on and he pulled her straight up. When he grabbed her, for one moment he held her tightly.

He was aware of people yelling below. They must have thought he was confused to be climbing.

She followed as he fought his way into a small meeting room, and then they were running toward Piper's office. Huge boxes had been piled against her office doors.

Whoever set the fire wanted to make sure Piper couldn't get out. Even the secretary's office door was blocked.

Anna worked frantically by his side as they shoved one box at a time away from the door.

Sam heard Colby yelling on the other side. As soon as the door opened a few inches he was fighting hard.

A long minute later Colby carried Piper out of her office. She was wrapped in what looked like a curtain.

"We've got to get them out and fast. Follow me." Sam marched back the way they'd come.

Glass and splintered wood marked the way as they stepped on the fourth-floor balcony. Without hesitation, Sam hooked the ax on the bottom molding and swung down to the third balcony built six feet wider. The wedding cake design of the building was helping them now.

Colby unwrapped Piper. She slid down the curtain into Sam's arms, then stepped back for him to catch Anna.

"You next."

"No." Colby stood above them. "I think whoever set the fire is still in the building. I'm going to go after this coward."

There was no time to argue. The windows

along the stairs were shattering.

"Preacher! Preacher!" someone below screamed.

As Colby disappeared back into the smoke, Sam kept hearing someone yelling.

Anna leaned over the third-floor balcony. "It's that kid who thinks he's an Uber driver. He's got a ladder and he's lifting it up, but it's about four feet short."

"Preacher, want a lift?" Pecos smiled. "I saw what you were doing. I thought you might come out this way."

"Will do." Sam lowered Anna the first four feet until her feet could touch the first rung. He stretched as far as he could until she touched the second rung on the ladder. Sam's fingers slipped away. She pressed against the brick like Spider-Man as she lowered on the next rung, then another, until finally her hands were gripping the ladder.

When Anna was halfway down, Sam lowered Piper. The kid caught both when they reached him.

Sam hesitated, about to swing over. Then he stood. "I love you, Anna Presley," he yelled and backed away. "But I have to go back to help Colby."

"No!" Anna screamed. "Don't."

The echo of three words floated down.
"It's my job."

CHAPTER 38

Fire in the night

COLBY

Colby stood at the broken elevator. The door was wide open and the yellow strip of tape was gone. The trooper could hear Sam storming toward him. He wasn't surprised Sam came back.

"Are Piper and Anna safe?" he yelled.

"Yes." Smoke was thickening, but the fire hadn't reached them yet. The old stairway would go up fast, but the rest of the building would burn slowly.

Colby knelt to look down the open shaft. "This is how he got out. Somehow he slid down the shaft. I'll bet the first floor is on a concrete slab. The stairs didn't go down into the basement. I saw gardeners pushing their mowers down a ramp Saturday. They probably just dug it out to allow for the elevator."

401

Sam leaned in. The air was less smoky. "With all the people around, he may be waiting until it either gets too hot below or he's able to blend in with the crowd. You want to go down?"

"I'm in."

Sam stepped back a few feet to where he'd seen the hose on the fourth floor. No water came when he turned the wheel, but he pulled the hose out and tied a knot in the nozzle end. "All we have to do is grab hold and slide down." He tied another knot ten feet farther down. "The knots will slow us down. The last thing you want to do is hit the bottom hard."

Colby leaned in. "I'll go first."

"I'll back you up, Trooper."

Colby grinned. "How'd you know?"

He didn't wait for the answer. He was flying down the wide, flat hose hoping he had the grip to stop before he hit bottom. He hit the first knot and wrapped his legs around to help slow the pace.

The next knot helped slow him more.

When Colby hit bottom he pulled his weapon and stepped away from the make-shift rope. It was cooler here, but still smoky. Whoever had set the fire could be standing three feet away. In the smoke and the dark, he couldn't see anything.

He heard Sam hit the floor.

Colby figured if the guy had a gun they'd both be shot by now, so he shoved his weapon back in place and then spread his hands, feeling his way. Colby could hear Sam breathing beside him. The idea of finding anyone seemed impossible.

Colby bumped into a pole and swore under his breath. As he paused to see if he was bleeding, he heard someone far into the darkness calling, "Help me. Somebody help me."

Following the cry, they moved closer until Colby's boot tapped what felt like a leg, and a man cried out in pain. He pulled the weapon again and stood his ground.

Sam knelt. It sounded like he was patting his way along a body. "Where are you hurt? Blood's everywhere."

"I think I've broken both legs. You got to help me. I can't take this pain."

The man whined as Sam felt his way down the man's body. "I feel where a broken bone has pierced the skin."

All was silent.

"I think he's passed out," Sam finally said. "Let's get him out."

Colby's eyes had adjusted enough for him to see the outline of Sam. He pulled his T-shirt off and ripped it, then wrapped the

403

man's legs together.

As he worked, Sam said, "It's going to hurt like hell, but we'll have to take him out. Parts of this cellar could cave in at any minute."

They lifted the man and slowly moved toward where Colby thought the ramp might be. It took several tries, but they finally saw water dripping beneath what had to be the cellar door.

"Who do you think we have?" Colby asked.

"I don't know, but whoever he is I'm betting he set the fire and barred the mayor's door." Sam kept moving. "The way he's bleeding, he won't last long if we don't get him out of here."

They moved one step at a time until Colby shoved open the unlocked door with a shove of his shoulder.

The banging of the doors falling away must have attracted attention. A cheer went up as the two men stepped into the night air.

Colby breathed, really breathed, for the first time since he'd smelled smoke.

Suddenly everything seemed to happen at once. Pecos was there to help carry the man. The sheriff took over bossing everyone around. The ambulance driver and his one

EMT rushed over with the stretcher.

The man was loaded and strapped in when he came to enough to start moaning.

Sam and Colby looked at him, dirty, dressed like a homeless person. A week-old beard on a face twisted with pain was hard to see.

"Who do you think he is?" Colby saw mostly blood and dirt.

Sam shrugged.

The sheriff moved between them. "That's Boone Buchanan. Though he don't look so good right now. I've got a few arrest warrants on him today. Seems he robbed an illegal poker game. Thought no one would file charges." LeRoy laughed. "He don't know ranchers. They'll pay the fine for gambling before they'll allow someone to steal a dollar from them. If you fellows don't mind, I think I'll ride with him to the hospital. I've got a list of questions when he wakes up. I don't think he's going to like the next picture that hits the papers."

They all walked behind the stretcher. Colby and Sam didn't say a word.

"Pecos," the sheriff yelled at the kid ten feet in front of him. "You're late to work. I told you that's one rule you can never break."

"Am I fired?"

"Yep, but I think I can find you another job. I'm thinking this town needs more deputies."

Pecos was almost jumping up and down.

The sheriff didn't seem to notice. "Did your father give you that black eye?"

"Nope, my father-in-law."

"Should I look into this, son?" LeRoy yelled, with half the town listening.

"No, it was kind of a welcome-to-the-family slug. He's calmed down since then."

Boone was enraged as they shoved him into the ambulance. He told everyone that he was a lawyer and planned to sue the whole town.

LeRoy squeezed between the stretcher and the bench. He accidentally bumped Boone's leg. Boone shrieked, and the sheriff said he was so sorry.

When Sam and Colby walked away, Colby said, "I'll take Piper and Anna to Widows Park. It's close and they'll be safe. You coming?"

"No, I need to stay until the fire is out. These volunteers look like they could use some help. They used enough water to put out the fire and with luck most of the damage will be smoke damage except where the wooden stairs were. If the volunteers hadn't got here so fast it could have been a lot worse."

Sam offered his hand. "You're still standing guard, aren't you, Trooper?"

"That's what we do. Right?"

"Damned straight."

Sam remained in the shadows as Colby went to join Anna and Piper. When Colby looked back, Sam had disappeared among the other firemen.

CHAPTER 39

PECOS

Mr. Winston's house was dark, but Pecos knew his way from the kitchen door to his new bedroom.

Mr. Winston had set them up in separate bedrooms with a connecting door between them. Pecos paused outside his door. There was no light under Kerrie's door so she must be asleep. He'd have to wait until morning to tell her everything that had happened. The fire, the rescue, the arresting of Boone Buchanan. Pecos had heard the ambulance driver say that Boone would have bled to death if Colby and Sam hadn't found him.

The sheriff heard it, too, but just shrugged like he didn't really care which way tonight ended.

When he opened his door a low bedside

lamp was on. He walked in slowly, his wet shoes in his hand.

He shrugged out of his clothes.

"Pecos?"

Kerrie's voice made him jump. He turned, and there she was — in his bed.

"What are you doing here?" Maybe she got mixed up. Or maybe he had.

"My bed was such a mess with all the clothes piled on it. I thought you wouldn't mind if I slept in with you tonight."

"Sure," Pecos said. He took a deep breath.

She rubbed her eyes with her fists like a kid would and sat up. "How was your first night at work?"

"I didn't make it in." He thought it best to give the abridged version of his night. "I saw a fire starting at city hall. I couldn't get 911 to pick up so I ran for help. The preacher saved Anna and the mayor. The sheriff saw me at the fire and not at work. He fired me, then gave me another job as a deputy." He slid into bed next to Kerrie. "Is it just me or has this day seemed like we've been living ten years? Marriage ages a fellow. At the rate I'm living I'm guessing I'll be ready for retirement by the end of next week."

"Tell me all about it." She giggled. "Isn't this fun? We can stay up talking as long as we want to. It's like a sleepover."

He had no idea what a sleepover was like, but this was great. He told her all that had happened — how he'd felt, how he'd been able to help . . . and that the sheriff had called him son.

When he got to the part about seeing what a broken leg looked like with a bone poking out, he looked down at Kerrie. She was cuddled under his arm and sound asleep.

He covered her shoulder up with the sheet, then leaned down very slowly and kissed her on the lips.

He didn't feel like a husband and he doubted she felt much like a wife. It didn't bother him that she thought of him as a friend. He could handle that. As long as he was helping her, being with her, having a sleepover in his bed, Pecos felt he was a lucky man.

And he was a man. Any boy that had been in him at dawn had melted away by nightfall.

CHAPTER 40

PIPER

Piper's grandmother and aunts at Widows Park all came down in their robes and hairnets to take care of Piper and Anna. They fussed over them and ignored Colby. Which was fine with him, but now it was Piper's turn to worry about her trooper.

Finally, Piper convinced them to feed him something. She said she felt like she'd calmed down from all the excitement, but Colby was still on guard, still pacing.

"He looks as if Boone might steal a wheelchair, beat up the sheriff, break out of the hospital, and come looking for me," she told her grandmother.

They brought him hummus and crackers, and he prayed it was the appetizer. He passed the plate to PJ and waited for the meal.

411

Fortunately, Piper's grandmother brought him a sandwich and beer.

Two of the aunts took Anna up to the guest room so she could shower while they found her a nightgown. They seemed to have one in every size.

At one point, they saw Aunt Nancy and Aunt Geraldine sneaking out of the house wearing matching purple jogging suits. Nancy had on a blue crocheted hat, and the taller Aunt Geraldine wore a red one.

"Are they making a ten o'clock ice cream run?" Colby asked Piper. "Maybe we should put in our orders."

Finally, it was just the two of them. Piper said, "That was the longest kiss in the world. If a fire hadn't started downstairs, we'd still be curled up in my office chair kissing."

"I would never have thought that the kiss was the first thing we'd talk about after we both almost died tonight." He laughed. "But it's as good a place to start as any."

"So" — she leaned closer — "tell me about the kiss."

"It has never happened to me like that. I always thought a kiss was just the beginning of foreplay, but, PJ, I could be happy just kissing you forever. It was like an addiction." He watched her closely. "You probably know I'm falling for you hard. I'm not playing a part now. No one is listening. This is me talking just to you."

"I know." She ate one of his chips. "You did your job when trouble came. You kept me safe and you found Boone."

"More like he found us. But there is more to us than the job."

Piper didn't want to talk about that. She'd never been good at expressing her feelings in words or actions. If she wasn't careful, she'd make a fool of herself by telling him how much she wished he'd be near all the time. That wasn't her way. No emotions in public. No scandal. Give people nothing to gossip about.

Somehow she'd carried the rule over to her private life. Maybe that explained why she didn't have a private life. Maybe that explained the shocking fiasco with Boone.

She had to change the subject.

"What I don't understand is why Boone hated me so much."

After a moment, Colby said, "Some people are just twisted up in their souls. You always had what he couldn't have. The pretend engagement satisfied him for a while, but that couldn't go on much longer. And then he got mixed up with some bad people, and he got desperate."

"Or maybe he just hated me. Because of me, the media started digging into his life. The dirt on him ran back to his college days. If his family hadn't had money, a few of his pranks might have landed him in jail."

Colby offered her a bite of his sandwich. As she shared his meal she pushed her toes under his leg. "You can sleep down here in the parlor if you like."

"I plan to. I'm still on guard." His hand rested on her leg, warming her all over.

The sneaky purple getaway drivers appeared at the study door. They still had their red and blue hats on, but now they had Walmart bags in their hands.

Colby smiled, and whispered, "Those two could get away with murder." Raising his voice, he spoke to the aunts: "What's up tonight, ladies?"

"We made a run to the store and bought you some clothes," Nancy said.

She pulled out a Hawaiian shirt and a black T-shirt that said, BORN TO RIDE. Geraldine pulled out sweat pants and a pair of jeans, and said, "You'll have to try them on. If they don't fit, we'll make a run back. The store's open till midnight."

"What — right here, right now?"

Nancy scoffed at him. "We're both in our eighties and we've both had a couple of

414

husbands and raised sons. You haven't got anything we haven't seen."

Piper fought down a giggle as both of her aunts sat down.

Colby was too tired to argue. He peeled off his shirt and dropped his jeans. In truth it was probably a relief to get out of his dirty, smelly clothes.

When he reached for the shirt, Colby looked up at the night riders and found them looking as if they were staring at a crime scene.

"You're hurt," Nancy said. "Look, Piper Jane, he's got more patches than a quilt."

"No, it's someone else's blood." But when Piper looked again, she saw the patches she had put on, and the bruises and a few scrapes he'd gotten when climbing over the balcony. Hell, he looked like one of those voodoo dolls women name after their ex-husband and torture.

The room was silent. Finally, Piper said calmly, "He's got a beautiful body, but this assignment seems to have been a bit hard on him."

Nancy stepped closer for a better look. "Your grandmother called your brother, Piper, and demanded the facts tonight. He told her Colby McBride is a trooper assigned to protect you. Now we all know that, but we didn't know he was taking a few blows protecting you."

"And probably dragged." Aunt Nancy pointed to a scrape on his arm. "And poked. Oh, my dear, dear boy."

Colby just stared, as the two aunts went into action. One said she'd wake up the night nurse, and the other grabbed a throw and covered his shoulders as she ordered him not to drip blood.

"I've been telling him that for days," Piper said as she followed Colby and her diminutive aunts to the stairs.

Men, Nancy informed him, were not usually allowed on the second floor, but an injured hero would just have to be the exception.

A brawny bulldog of a nurse appeared at the top of the stairs. Before Colby could object, the nurse and the two army aunts hustled him to bed.

"If he needs oxygen I'll pull it off of Frances. She don't really need it, she just likes the sound," Nancy said.

Colby closed his eyes. After a long day, the real nightmare seemed to be just starting.

"I think he just passed out," Piper said.

"What if he's dead?" Geraldine asked.

The nurse pinched him hard. Colby

opened his eyes. He stared at Piper with one of those "help me" looks like she'd given him at the café when she thought he was leading her into making a scene.

"He's alive," the nurse announced. "Help me strip off these bandages. We'll clean him up, then do the doctoring."

Piper crawled onto the bed, her back against the headboard, Colby's head on her lap. As the ladies circled around, she whispered, "There will be more than a kiss waiting for you if you live through this."

He managed a smile just before the nurse and her helpers attacked.

Ten minutes later, Colby whispered, "Now I know what being abducted by aliens must feel like. I can compare stories with Digger."

She kissed his head.

"You missed, PJ, and your laughter didn't make it better."

Just before the door closed, the bulldog said to Piper, "Only stay a few moments. He'll need his sleep."

Piper covered her mouth until the door was closed.

"What's so funny?"

"They brought you some pajamas."

"I don't wear pajamas."

"You might want to. I think the nurse

417

makes hourly rounds."

He sat up and put them on, not even bothering to ask why a widows' commune had men's sleepwear.

"I'm sorry."

"For what?" he asked as he crawled back in bed and sat beside her.

"For everything. For giving you such a hard time when you first got here. For not believing that I might actually need someone to watch over me. For causing a few of those wounds on your body. I can't take the blame for all of them."

"My beautiful body," he corrected. "The mayor said it, so it must be true."

She leaned over and pressed her cheek against his shoulder. "I have to go. The aunts are probably standing in the hallway with a stopwatch."

He leaned back and she covered him up.

She kissed him lightly. "One last thing, Trooper. I think I'm falling hard for you too."

Colby drifted off wondering if those were the last words she'd said or the beginning of a dream. He'd remind her of the kiss she owed him when he woke.

CHAPTER 41

Almost midnight

SAM

Sam wasn't surprised that he bonded with the firemen within minutes. They'd seen his bravery and realized he knew his business. As they cleaned up and headed back to the station he was already talking to them about what needed to be done. Better equipment, routine checks of every building, regular testing of alarms.

By the time they sat down at the station, the men were kidding him about yelling that he loved Anna Presley.

"You're braver than any man I know," one man said. "And I'm not talking about the fire. Now don't get me wrong. She's a great lady. Not a person in town doesn't admire her, but I've seen her skin a man alive for making an improper comment. Once, she heard a guy tell his wife that he should slap

419

her for voting against his candidate. It took two men to pull little Anna off him."

Sam smiled. "That's my love."

The firemen burst out laughing.

By the time he started home it was after midnight. He took the long way back to the parsonage he'd been trying to move out of for two days. He wanted to think, to remember loving Anna in her office, then how brave she was fighting alongside him. She never once screamed or panicked.

He wasn't going to just follow her around. If she wanted them to work, she'd have to meet him halfway. Funny, he was looking forward to clashing with her, getting angry, making up.

As Sam passed the bar, he felt no pull to go in. He'd need every brain cell he had to keep up with Anna.

The bartender was closing up. When he saw Sam, he called out through the open door, "You seen Daily Watts?"

"Nope, it's Monday. I thought he just came in on the weekends."

"Always does, but I heard his brother fired him today. Said he was tired of having him come in late." The bartender shook his head. "You ask me, Daily is the only one who works around that garage. When I take my truck in, all I see the brother do is lift his coffee cup. Daily's the one who works late so I can pick up supplies before I open."

"He's a good man fallen on hard times," Sam added.

"Watch for him, Preacher. I fear the Devil's got ahold of him."

"I will." As Sam walked away, he looked in every dark corner and alley. If Daily was fired this morning he could have been drinking all day long.

As he rounded the church, he was happy to see it dark inside. No Stella crying. She was probably happily wrapped up in the organ player's arms.

His guesthouse was still there, but tonight the little statues and forest animals lining the walls made him smile. He'd had so much excitement tonight he'd have to fight a forest fire to calm down.

He took a long shower and planned to sleep, except now and then in the night he found himself reaching for Anna. It was as if when they made love she had become a part of him. He wondered if he'd ever again feel complete without her around.

Just before sunrise he was half awake and wondering where Anna was. Storming the Widows Park house didn't seem like a good idea. When his cell rang, he wasn't surprised to see her number.

"Morning. You miss me?"

"Say it again, Sam." He swore he could hear sunshine in her voice.

"I love you, Anna Presley."

"Can you sleep?" she asked like it was the emergency question of the day.

"No, I'm getting used to sleeping on top of you. Nowhere else feels right." He laughed, imagining her still in bed.

"I got to get out of this house. Everyone in the place snores except Colby, and the nurse walks the hallway every hour to check on him."

"Colby's there?"

"Yes, Piper told me the aunts stripped him down and doctored every bruise, scratch, and bullet wound he had."

Sam sat up straight. "Colby had a bullet wound?"

"Oh, don't worry. It was last week's problem."

"Then back to why is Colby there with you?"

"He's not with me. He's across the hallway. The old ladies are killing him with kindness. I expect him to be dead by morning."

Sam swore. "I should have gone with you. They could have finished without me, but it sounds like I'm needed there." He grinned.

"The guys at the station kidded me about yelling that I loved you."

Her voice was little more than a whisper. "You sorry you did that? The whole town could hear you yelling."

"No, I'll do it every night if you like. I'll be like a chime."

"Don't kid me."

"I'm not, but I want to do this right. We don't have that many years left. I don't want to waste any of it without you." He scratched his stubble. "I'll ask later, all formal, but right now I have to know if you're willing . . ."

"Willing to do what?" she snapped.

He couldn't tell if she was excited or confused.

"Would you, Anna Presley, consider being my next of kin?"

She laughed and answered as soon as she could catch her breath. "If I hadn't been a foster kid I might not understand. I'd love to be."

He tried to think. "I know we've only known each other a few days, but it feels so right."

"Sam, look at the bright side. Like you said, we're almost forty. If we find out it was a mistake, we won't have long to live to regret it."

"That cheers me up. How fast can you get dressed? I'll pick you up in ten minutes and we'll go eat at the Honey Creek Café. We'll make plans. I'll call Stella and see if she knows the name of that judge who married Pecos yesterday."

"We could ask Stella to sing," Anna added.

"Sorry, you're cutting out on me. Get dressed. I'll be outside Widows Park in ten."

As he clicked off he thought she said something about the café not being open this early. Sam didn't care; they'd think of something to do.

CHAPTER 42

7:00 a.m.

PIPER

Colby's room was still in shadows when Piper slipped under the covers next to him. He looked so handsome in sleep. The hard line of his jaw was relaxed and she couldn't see worry in his eyes.

"You're my hero, you know," she whispered.

One eye opened. "Who are you and what are you doing in my bed?"

"I broke in while everyone else is downstairs having breakfast."

Colby closed his eye. "I'm not going down to breakfast with old women who have seen me naked. I'll starve first."

She sat up. "No, you won't. I brought your clothes. We're running away and having breakfast at the Honey Creek Café. Just me and you, out in the morning light, in front

425

of the town. It's about time the folks knew that you won your fight to win my heart, or at least a real date."

He slowly rolled out of bed. "I'd like to stay here and have pillow talk, but I haven't had a real meal in twenty hours. You ate most of my sandwich and all my crackers and mud."

"It's not mud, it's hummus."

He wasn't listening as he dressed. "If you agree, we can come back here after breakfast and I'll talk you into going back to bed. You can talk and I'll sleep."

"I don't agree." She watched him slowly pull on his new clothes. "We can skip the talk."

He stopped and looked at her. "We could skip the breakfast."

"No, I don't want you passing out on me from hunger."

Fifteen minutes later they pulled up next to the only other car at the Honey Creek parking lot.

Piper thought about trying to ignore Anna and Sam when she walked in, but since they were the only other guests in the place it would have been impossible. Anna had the same look as Piper when she invited them to join Sam and her for breakfast.

Jessica brought both couples' meals at

426

once. She flashed a quick smile at Colby. "Good to see you dressed, Trooper Mc-Bride. You could have told me you were guarding her. I had fun guessing what you two were doing upstairs. Now I know the truth, I'm back to PG daydreams."

Colby had no answer to that. He changed the subject. "I don't remember even ordering yet."

"Oh, I know what you like." Jessica set his plate down. "Anything that doesn't crawl off the plate. And Piper, she always orders the same thing every morning."

As they ate their breakfast, they all knew a storm of reporters would come soon. Tons of questions. But no one wanted to talk about it. For a few minutes they just wanted to be two couples having breakfast together.

Piper couldn't stop smiling at Colby. There were things she needed to tell him. Things they needed to talk about. Plans to make. But she'd have to know him a great deal before she opened up. Before she let him, or anyone, know. There was a proper way of doing things.

As if they were lifetime residents of Honey Creek, Colby and Sam talked about the people in town and other town matters — like Pecos's marriage and what the firehouse needed to be up to standard.

When Sam mentioned that Daily Watts was missing, Colby's face darkened.

"He told me once that the job at the garage was all he had." Colby stood. "I think I'll go walk the river."

Sam nodded. "He was hanging to life by a thread before his brother fired him. You think we might find a body?"

Colby nodded slightly, then turned to Piper. "I'd feel better if I knew you were safe, PJ."

"I can't go to the office so that leaves Widows Park or the church."

Anna patted her hand. "I'll go home with you. We've both got calls to make and we won't be bothered at Widows Park. After we finish, I plan to play poker with your aunts for their crocheted hat collection."

When they all walked over to Piper's SUV, Colby and Sam each kissed his lady right out in front of the café.

Colby and Sam turned off toward the river as Piper backed out of her parking spot and drove away. In her mind she was already organizing. In a few months they'd start dating. Colby might even go meet her father. He'd like the trooper; after all, both his sons had been troopers before they became Rangers. By Christmas Colby could come stay a few days at Widows Park.

She smiled. Who knows what would happen from there.

Within five minutes of walking through mud, Colby turned back and borrowed Piper's boat.

As he and Sam drifted down the river, every fisherman who hadn't talked to him earlier suddenly waded out to shake his hand. They all promised to watch for a body even though Colby didn't mention a name.

One old fisherman said he noticed a couple staying in a cabin back in the pines. A woman and a man.

Colby asked if the woman was long legged with long brown hair.

The fisherman nodded. "Real pretty."

"If her name is Marcie, you might want to tell her that her fellow is in the hospital. Broke his leg in a fall."

The fisherman saluted as if taking on a mission. "I didn't see the guy's car this morning so I'll offer to drive her in."

Colby and Sam floated on down to the bend, then pulled the boat to shore and walked out on the road toward town.

A few hours later when they returned to Widows Park, both women had lots of news. There was going to be a ceremony on

Wednesday, the governor was coming, and Piper's father and a dozen Texas Rangers would attend.

All four of them were to show up at the sheriff's office to give statements of what had happened at city hall; then the facts would be released to the press.

"Not everything," both women said at once, and both men laughed.

Colby listened to all the plans, but he didn't really care. The assignment was over. He'd be going back to work and Piper would go back to being mayor. They'd probably promise to keep in touch, but he knew that would be impossible. It might work for a month or two, but then they'd each start making excuses. The visits would stretch from two weeks, to four, to someday.

When the sheriff called to say Boone would live, LeRoy also said he'd personally come by to pick up Piper. There was an emergency meeting of the city council.

Anna and Sam excused themselves, claiming they had plans to make at the church.

Colby suddenly found himself alone with the aunts and he did not plan to play poker for crocheted hats.

He walked out of the house and checked an address his buddy had texted him. First the garage, then Daily's home. One last loose end he wouldn't let drop.

Daily Watts's brother wasn't very friendly. Said he was busy even though he was just sitting at a desk talking to one of the customers. He claimed he didn't know or care where his brother was. He'd been a pain in the neck for years.

Colby left the shop and walked the few blocks to the address he'd gotten as Daily's home residence. The house was a good size but in sad shape.

He knocked, then banged on the door loud enough to bring the neighbors out. No one had seen Daily lately. After he was fired he hadn't come home.

Colby went back to the bar, hoping the bartender might know a friend who could give information.

No luck. Daily sat alone and rarely spoke to anyone. Colby figured maybe the three little angels got him.

About dark, Colby tried to call Piper, but she didn't answer. Probably deep into running the town.

He got on his Harley and rode the back roads for a while, then went back to the lodge.

Digger was on the porch of the office. "Heard about your day yesterday. The whole town thinks you're a hero, Trooper. Saved

431

the mayor and caught the bad guy."

"I was just doing my job." Colby didn't want to talk about Boone, or the fire, or how they almost died. "You see any more of that big guy who smoked on your porch?"

"Yeah, turns out he was just a trucker. A nosy one, nothing more. You know there are always folks who think they should get into other people's business."

"I've heard of them." Colby grinned.

"Guess you're staying in your cabin tonight. No need to guard the mayor." Digger laughed. "You almost had me believing that cover story. Guess it was just a job."

"Just a job."

Colby then headed over to his cabin. Who was he kidding? One long kiss didn't mean anything. She was a mayor. A few months from now she wouldn't remember his name. Probably wouldn't even take his calls.

Part of him wanted it to be so much more. He'd spent ten years walking away from every relationship before it got serious. This time she'd be the one to walk away.

When he opened the door, the low porch line sliced a pie-shaped beam across his bed.

There was a big bump in the middle. Apparently while he was gone the raccoon moved in. Colby thought of pulling his weapon, but he didn't want to hurt the poor thing. Leaving the door wide open, he slowly walked to the bed ready to yell and hoped the raccoon would dart for the door.

Just before he roared, an arm moved out from under the blanket. Then a bare shoulder. Correction, a bare shoulder except for a spaghetti strap.

"Mayor," he tried to keep his voice calm. "Want to tell me why you're here?"

"I can't sleep without you in my bed. Do you think you could guard my body for one more night?"

He pulled his clothes off so fast he ripped one sleeve and popped two buttons. This might be goodbye. It might be a thank you for all he'd done. She might just simply want to be close to him. Colby didn't care. He just wanted PJ.

They made love with the moon shining on them and a raccoon watching from the porch. When she slept in his arms, he whispered, "Don't go, PJ. Don't ever leave."

CHAPTER 43

Evening

PECOS

Pecos had been busy all day. He'd shadowed the sheriff, copying everything he did.

When he finally made it back to Mr. Winston's home, he found that Barbara and Brad had been invited to supper. Great . . . his new wife came with bookends. Kerrie had cooked supper with Mr. Winston's help. He served the meal. Pecos didn't say much. Brad didn't say anything, but at least he wasn't growling.

Dessert was Barbara's famous key lime pie. Mr. Winston was polite enough to ask for the recipe. After they each had a slice, the Lanes left with Barbara chatting all the way out and Brad nodding his head once or twice.

Mr. Winston was tired, so Pecos offered to do the dishes. The old guy didn't argue.

Finally, he was alone with Kerrie. As had become their pattern, they talked and laughed together, catching up on all the little things, full of ideas for the future. Getting to know each other a day at a time. "We're just kids," she admitted.

"I know. We'll make a lot of mistakes." He handed her the last plate. "Just you and me, kid, through the good and the bad."

"Agreed." She kissed his cheek.

When they went up to bed, Kerrie changed into her cotton pajamas with a pattern of sandals and beach balls on them. He'd just climbed into bed when she came into his room.

"Mind if I sleep with you again?"

"I'll never mind. You don't have to ask."

As she cuddled in beside him, she said, "I remembered the last line of my graduation speech."

"Tell me."

She rose to her elbow. "It's from Eleanor Roosevelt. 'You must do the thing you think you cannot do.' I didn't think I could have this baby and take care of it and still go to school. You made me believe. We can do it, can't we?"

"We can."

She kissed him on the cheek. "Good night, Pecos."

He was silent for a minute, then said something he thought he'd never be brave enough to say. "Kiss me on the mouth, not the cheek, when you kiss me good night."

"All right." She kissed him gently on the lips.

Pecos smiled in the darkness. That was enough, he thought.

■ ■ ■ ■

WEDNESDAY

■ ■ ■ ■

CHAPTER 44

Morning

PIPER

The mayor stood at the podium and gave her speech; then she awarded Sam and Colby medals. She proudly gave Pecos the key to the city. He'd find out later it didn't really open any door, but the kid didn't seem to need much luck. He had all he wanted.

Pecos stood tall in his wedding suit. He whispered to Piper that it was all the people from the flea market who were yelling his name. And then a few kids in his senior class who had never talked to him before came up and hugged him.

The sheriff extolled the bravery shown during the fire, and the head of the council talked about the changes that would be made because of the fire.

No one mentioned Boone Buchanan.

Piper gazed out over the crowd. She could call almost every person by name. This was her town. She belonged here. The memory of one night with a loving man would have to be enough to last her for years to come. After all, neither of them had talked about tomorrow. She knew she belonged here, and he had his goals that no doubt pulled him elsewhere.

But he'd always be the face in her dreams.

The governor greeted the crowd. Her father thanked the heroes. Her two brothers in their white Stetsons stood beside him.

Sam wore his fireman's suit, and Colby wore the state trooper uniform. She was very proud of them both. They'd saved her and Anna's life. They'd also saved Boone's life, not that he deserved it.

Pecos brought Mr. Winston and Kerrie to stand as his family. He did not invite his parents. Winston couldn't have looked prouder if he'd raised Pecos himself.

Anna had the same look. Pride. She'd asked Piper to be her maid of honor tonight at a private wedding. "We don't know what the future holds, but we want to step into it together. It'll take some work, but we'll fit each other in our lives."

Finally, the speeches were over. People circled around talking and shaking hands. It

440

seemed Piper blinked and Colby was gone. Maybe it was for the best. Neither had the nerve to start the conversation they needed to have.

She searched the crowd and finally spotted him talking to a family near the back almost against the trees. Piper touched Sam's arm and whispered, "Who is that Colby's talking to?"

"That's Daily Watts. Anna was telling me about him. It seems Monday he did pass out on his way home and those three kids took him to their house. That's why he was late Tuesday and got fired. Their mother had known him years ago when he ran the garage. He was always fair and nice to her, so she let him sleep it off on her couch. The next afternoon when the kids got home he'd cleaned up her house. So, she let him stay for supper since he'd cooked it. When he started to leave the kids started crying and begged for her to let him stay.

"We found him. We get to keep him," one said.

After a million tears she agreed they could keep him if he was willing to stay until he got on his feet.

He said he had nowhere to go, so he'd stay but only if he could help out around the place. Her car needed work. Plumbing

441

needed fixing. The roof could use some patching.

Piper shook her head in disbelief. "Things like that don't happen anywhere but here."

"That's not the best part. Anna checked. Daily owns his house outright and he also owns the garage. Their father had not left it to both boys, only to Daily."

"Does the brother know?"

Sam grinned. "I'm sure he knew, but now the whole town will know."

Piper smiled as she was pulled away to talk to people. Half an hour later she entered the firehouse bay area to join a party thrown for the heroes.

Sam was there standing behind Anna while she told the governor what needed to be done at the state level.

Piper had a feeling the governor would be leaving soon.

She saw Colby standing over by a group of troopers and Rangers. She made up her mind that she didn't want to spend her life remembering him. Wishing she'd said one thing to let him know how she felt. Wishing he'd said one word that she needed to hear.

She'd always done the right thing for the town. Always been honest. Always been proper. This time she had to take a risk. Even if she lost, Colby was worth a try.

Fighting back tears, she knew that she'd found the one thing she couldn't give up for her career. The one thing she couldn't live without.

The men parted as she slowly walked right up to Colby, pulled off his hat, and kissed him. Not a polite kiss, but a take-me-home-cowboy kind of kiss.

Colby's arms circled her as if they were the only two in the room. Her heels dropped off as he lifted her off the ground.

The troopers were laughing and yelling before she finally pulled away.

Colby looked only at her. As he always had, he saw deep inside her. "Mayor, you're starting something that will be hard to stop."

"I don't want to stop. Not ever." There was so much more she wanted to say. She didn't want to stop seeing him or loving him or sleeping with him. "Are you okay with that plan, Trooper?"

He pulled her against his chest and whispered, "I'm in. I'll be your bodyguard for as long as you'll have me."

He slid his hand down her arm and laced their fingers together. "Boys," he shouted loud enough for her brothers to hear. "I think it is about time you met my lady, Piper Jane Mackenzie."

Everyone in the firehouse except her two

brothers began hooting and cheering, and eventually even Max and Alex couldn't hold back a smile.

ABOUT THE AUTHOR

With millions of books in print, **Jodi Thomas** is both a *New York Times* and *USA Today* bestselling author of more than 50 novels and a dozen novellas. Her stories travel through the past and present days of Texas and draw readers from around the world. Jodi has been inducted into the Romance Writers of America Hall of Fame. With five RITAs to her credit, along with National Readers' Choice Awards and Booksellers' Best Awards, Thomas has proven her skill as a master storyteller. When not working on a novel, Thomas enjoys traveling with her husband, renovating a historic home, and "checking up" on their grown sons and four grandchildren.

The employees of Thorndike Press hope you have enjoyed this Large Print book. All our Thorndike, Wheeler, and Kennebec Large Print titles are designed for easy reading, and all our books are made to last. Other Thorndike Press Large Print books are available at your library, through selected bookstores, or directly from us.

For information about titles, please call:
(800) 223-1244

or visit our website at:
gale.com/thorndike

To share your comments, please write:

Publisher
Thorndike Press
10 Water St., Suite 310
Waterville, ME 04901